SUSPENDED ANIMATION

by Sylvie Grayson

GREAT WESTERN PUBLISHING
Copyright © 2014 by Great West Publishing
Excerpt from *Earthquake* copyright ©2014 by Great West Publishing
All rights reserved.
For information write to
Great Western Publishing
c/o sylviegraysonauthor@gmail.com

ISBN: 978-0-9938288-1-2
First Great Western Publishing paperback printing September 2014
10 9 8 7 6 5 4 3 2 1

Great Western Publishing is a registered trademark of Sylvie Grayson.
For information regarding special discounts for bulk purchases, please contact Great Western Publishing

Cover art by Steven Novak novakillustration@gmail.com
Printed in USA

Other books by Sylvie Grayson

contemporary romantic suspense

Legal Obstruction

The Lies He Told Me

My Best Mistake

sci-fi/fantasy

Khandarken Rising,
The Last War: Book One

Son of the Emperor,
The Last War: Book Two

Truth and Treachery,
The Last War: Book Three

Praise for Sylvie Grayson's books

I've been reading Sylvie Grayson - can't seem to put them down. How do you come up with these exciting mysteries? Very fun reading!!

Suspended Animation

Wow! This book is amazing, its very well written and the characters are very well developed. This is my first book by Sylvie Grayson and it won't be my last. I was hooked from the first page and this book was very hard to put down.

Interesting characters, family conflicts and divided loyalties make this a book that kept me up half the night

Legal Obstruction

I loved this book! I've found my new favorite author. Emily is a fiercely professional woman who is on her own and determined to protect her little family. Joe is a solitary guy who often doesn't deal with problems until they are front and center. But boy does Emily wake him up and does he take notice. Add in a wildcard assistant and a few unsavory characters and I was up all night finishing the book to find out what happens.

The Lies He Told Me

If you are a fan of the heartwarming craftiness and domesticity of a Debbie McComber romance, and the intense intrigues of Danielle Steele, you'll enjoy the writing style of Sylvie Grayson; where the bad guys are not heartless, and the good guys are virtually flawless.

Just a quick note to let you know how much I enjoyed your book. You drew on your vast experience as a result of being a female, a wife, lover, mother, business woman, lawyer, friend, gardener, homeowner, compassionate and caring individual. It was an intriguing read which kept me guessing and very interested. Well done, Sylvie.

The Last War: Book One, Khandarken Rising

The General of Khandarken sends his son, Dante, to investigate the situation. When Dante meets the lovely Beth she eyes him with suspicion. But he won't stop until he solves the tangle of motives, fueled by greed, which threaten Beth and her family. I enjoyed this book very much. The well-developed characters and sensuous love scenes make this a page turner. I look forward to reading Book Two and Book Three

… this story is one of a kind in its own and couldn't be truly compared to anything but itself. It has so many unique characteristics to it. The personal relationships are intriguing and different from many other fictional relationships. The names are cool, the plot gets thicker with each page, and I loved the author's style. It became evident that I was addicted to reading the book once I was sad to be finished. I'm going to give this a strong recommendation. It's my kind of book.

The Last War: Book Two, Son of the Emperor

I am a big fan of The Last War series. I loved Book One, the story of Major Dante Regiment and Beth Farmer. The dystopian world Grayson has created, where women are scarce and Clones are used to replace them, where the Emperor has finally been defeated but his son takes up the fight, just gets better in this second book. …Thrills abound on the race to freedom and home. I really enjoyed this book and can't wait for Book Three. Grayson has great imagination, the fantasy series is awesome.

DEDICATION

I am blessed with wonderful support that has enabled me to write. To my husband, who leaves me alone when I need to work but is always ready to listen, read and lend a hand with difficult passages. To my children who had faith in me and helped with their support and practical suggestions.

To my critique group: Anna Markland, author of *Hearts and Crowns* and many other medieval romances, Helena Korin, Jacquie Biggar who supported me to polish the words for publication, my many thanks. Any errors or omissions are mine alone.

Sylvie Grayson

www.sylviegrayson.com

SUSPENDED ANIMATION

.

CHAPTER ONE

Brett Rome stood in the dressing room of the Victoria hockey team and pulled the jersey over his head. He sat down to lace his skates as the coach gave them the talk. He listened carefully. This was a new team, the guys had only been playing together for a couple of years. And he was the newest member.

He hadn't expected to play hockey here. He'd come to town because his father was ill. He thought he'd be in Victoria for a few weeks, do what he could to help out till Paddy got back on his feet. Two months later, angry and frustrated, Brett felt tied to this place and to his father's company, Rome Trucking.

Tonight he was determined to get out on the ice and show some substance. Excited as always before a game, he was wired, tight and ready to play. Glancing at his friend beside him, they exchanged a grin. The fact that Jerome had been taken on to the team just made it that much better.

They filed down the tunnel and out onto the ice. The crowd looked big and they were loud, the stands full. The shouting started the minute they emerged from the dressing room and escalated with bullhorns, clappers and screaming enough to deafen them. But once play started he barely heard it.

Coach sent him out in the middle of the first period when one of their defence was winded. He climbed out of the box and skated onto the ice to take his place. It felt terrific.

Here, he knew exactly what was expected of him, for the first time since his last game with the Vancouver team which seemed like eons ago. There was no guessing, no trying to figure it out on the fly, no catching up from behind. Just get into position, always move into position and be ready when the break came. Because sooner or later the break always came. What he did with it showed what kind of hockey player he was today.

The end of the hard fought second period showed them up three goals to two over Seattle. Brett trundled back into the dressing room with the rest of the players and sat on a bench, breathing heavily, wiping sweat and listening to the pep talk.

Now Coach focussed on maintaining the lead. "Be protective," he said. "Be proactive. Don't let the other guys in for another goal and do your best to score once more, because a lead of two is so much better than a lead of one." A burst of laughter erupted among the players.

"It's early in the season, fellas, but we don't want to give anything away. Hang onto your lead, that's what I want you to do."

In the third period play was faster. Seattle poured on the coals trying to tie up the game. Brett seemed to be in line to take most of the blows from one of their power forwards. When he stepped out onto the ice again, the enforcer came straight for him. Brett saw him come in low and to his side and realized he was about to get laced straight into his injured knee. He stopped short and managed to deke out of the way, going down in a controlled slide and holding his stick steady as the Seattle player's skates came closer. He took a header straight into the boards but brought his opponent down with him. Before he could get up, the enforcer attacked.

Suddenly Brett was swamped with an overwhelming tidal wave of anger. Scrambling madly to his feet, he threw his full force into the fight. His helmet was gone, fists and bodies were flying as his team mates dove into the action. He launched himself at his opponent, the jersey clutched in a death grip, his other fist pounding.

The first hit landed to the side of his face and instantly he felt a wild rage wash over him out of all proportion to the fight he was in. That wave nearly felled him, almost knocked him to his knees. He staggered back to his feet before it swallowed him whole.

He hit back and then again, his arms and fists lashing out wildly, pumping like pistons. The feelings swelled and boiled. *His girlfriend Marilyn had finished off their two-year relationship by simply bringing her new lover into their bedroom.* It had knocked him flat on his face with humiliation. He seethed with resentment, he roiled with fury, he exploded with vicious power.

Wildly he hit out again, one fist then the other and exulted when one struck home with a jarring blow that he felt all the way to his shoulder.

That was for Paddy. His father had suckered him into running his company when Brett had other plans. He was running the crew and the trucks with no authority, just a lackey to pull the old man out of a tight spot. Paddy hadn't bothered to explain why the company was operating in the red, apparently ignoring it in the hope that Brett would deal with it.

He took one to the mouth and his head snapped back. His mouth guard popped out and went flying. Roaring like an elephant, he charged back into the fray, dealing another blow that knocked his opponent reeling backward.

That was for Dancy. Paddy's girlfriend had treated him like a piece of meat, a man without morals in his own father's house, a man with no self-respect.

He pounded, he bellowed, something tore loose inside him and rattled around roaring to be set free, demanding to take on the whole team, needing to prove himself worthy.

Hands hauled on his uniform but the adrenaline surged. Someone grabbed his left arm and his right lashed out, until he was caught round the neck from behind. By the time it was over he was flat on his face on the ice with a referee and two of his own team members on top of him.

The ref ordered him off the ice, suspended for the rest of the game. He slogged back to the change room to shower. But not before Coach sent the medic in. He was swabbed with alcohol, stitched up here and there, then ice packs applied. By the time he was out of his uniform the adrenaline rush was over and he was shaking. Grateful to be showered and changed, he fumbled to button his shirt with unsteady fingers as the rest of the team filed in.

They'd won the game, hanging onto their one goal lead. As the noise level rose to a dull roar in the dressing room, Jerome leaned down to speak urgently in his ear. "What the hell, Brett. That isn't your usual game."

Brett gritted his teeth.

Then Coach sat down beside him and gave him a tight look. "So, what happened out there?"

"Uh, it was stupid." He took a deep breath, rubbing a shaky hand down his still sweating face. "I just saw him coming and knew that he was going to hurt my bad knee. I overreacted."

Coach nodded abruptly. "Come and see me tomorrow, call me in the morning."

"Okay, Coach." Some of the team eyed him guardedly as they changed but most grinned and gave him the thumbs up. He waited for Jerome and they went off with a couple of the other players to unwind over a beer.

But Brett didn't stay long. He could feel the rage still sloshing in his gut, weaving back and forth like a sea dragon seeking to escape. It made him queasy. He was back at his father's house by midnight, uncertain how he felt, uncertain if he could even sleep.

Ten minutes later he was out like a light. But not before he'd locked his bedroom door against Dancy."

CHAPTER TWO

Two months earlier….

Brett tugged his ringing cell phone from his pocket as the waitress dropped a tray of beers on the table in a noisy downtown Vancouver pub. "I'll get it," Jerome said, taking out a bundle of cash.

Brett nodded and put the phone to his ear. "Rome." It was his father's number on the screen but a feminine voice spoke in his ear. "Sorry, Fancy", he interrupted, "I can't hear you. Can I call you back later?" The noise level in the bar was stratospheric and her voice kept fading into the background.

"It's not Fancy, it's Dancy", she snapped. "And I'm trying to tell you, your father…." Here the din in the pub escalated again, surging around him and drowning her out completely.

Brett rolled his eyes. His father's girlfriends were interchangeable as far as he was concerned. They came and went so rapidly he didn't bother trying to remember their names. So it was Dancy, okay. And the old man was always doing something to get himself in a fix. "Hold on, hold on," he said. "I'll just step outside for a minute."

Moving through the crush of bodies, he threaded his way between the crowded tables toward the open doorway at the far end of the dim room. He fielded comments from his

Vancouver teammates for a good game well played, shrugged good-naturedly at congratulations called by fans of their hockey team.

At the door he gave a grin, then hunched his shoulders against a group wanting to draw him into conversation, and put the phone back to his ear. "Okay, Dancy. I'm outside. So what has Dad done now?"

He heard her huff into the phone. "Brett, Paddy's had a heart attack. He's in the hospital and he asked me to call you. He needs you to come home."

"Hold it, hold it. Wait a minute. He's had a heart attack? When? How bad?"

"Brett, if you would just listen." Dancy sounded totally impatient. "He had it early this evening. We were out with some friends and he collapsed right there in the lounge."

Brett grimaced. Here he was ordering beers in a bar, same modus operandi as his father. The apple didn't fall far from the tree. "So, the ambulance took him from there," he said. "Was it the Moonlighter?"

The Moonlighter Pub was his father's favourite hangout, had been for years. He knew all the staff by first name, nearly every patron knew him. Old home week, over and over again.

"Yes, and they came real quick, did some kind of intervention. He's stable, they say."

"Oh, okay. Well, that's good. What does stable mean? Is he able to talk?"

"Of course he's able to talk! I just told you, he asked me to call you! He wants you to come home."

"I can't get over there tonight, Dancy. It's too late for a ferry to Vancouver Island and the flights have stopped by now. I'll be there first thing tomorrow."

"I'll tell him. Bye."

"Wait, hold on a minute…"

But Dancy was gone, the phone signal went dead.

Brett stood for a moment, immobilised, the phone gripped tight in his fingers. A heart attack. The old man had a heart attack. He looked around trying to get his bearings. The landscape had shifted without warning. He'd never thought of something like this happening.

Dad went on and on, he was an institution all on his own. Rome Trucking plugged along and Paddy ran it part time while he drank full time. It had been that way for years. And the old man wasn't that old.

He tapped the phone against his chest. His heart. Who would have guessed? Dad was still strong. Brett should know. It wasn't that long ago they'd had their last wrestling match, a tussle where Brett had been hard pressed to hold his own.

Quickly he dialled information and asked the number for Victoria General Hospital. Yes, Patrick Rome was a patient. What was his relationship to Mr Rome? Ah, a son. Well, Mr. Rome was in intensive care, but stabilized. It meant the damage had been contained. They gave him the doctor's name and he hung up.

Did his sister Liz know? He called her but disconnected when it went to voice mail. Maybe she was already at the hospital.

Back at the table where most of the guys were still hanging, Jerome pushed a beer across at him and raised his eyebrows. "Trouble?" he mouthed.

Brett nodded and downed half the glass, taking in the noisy room for a minute. Mentally gathering himself, he downed the other half. "I've got to go," he shouted. "Problems back home."

Jerome pushed over to his friend's side. "What's going on?"

Brett put his hand on Jerome's shoulder, pulling him close to speak directly into his ear. "Dad's had a heart attack. He's asked me to come home."

Jerome nodded. "Hey, I'm sorry, Brett. Is he going to be alright?"

Brett shrugged. "Can't tell. He's stable, that's all they said. But he can talk, got his girlfriend to give me a call, so that's something."

Jerome nodded again. "Okay. Well, the season's finished.

We're done here, aren't we?" The game tonight had been a fundraiser, the season itself had ended two weeks ago with the Vancouver team in second place in the league. Jerome and Brett wouldn't be playing with this university team next year, they'd both graduated.

Brett peered around the dim room, spotting Coach Vance standing at the bar, one foot braced on the brass foot rail. "I have to talk to Coach. I'm going over to Vancouver Island first thing in the morning."

Jerome gave him a thump on the back and said, "Good luck, man. Keep me posted, eh? I'll feed your dog for you and see you when you get back."

Brett tapped Vance on the shoulder and waited while he finished his conversation with the bartender. "I have to be on my way, Coach. I've got a problem back home in Victoria."

George Vance dropped his foot and turned fully around. "What's going on, Brett? We were going to talk about coaching for the team. You'd be my right hand man if you're interested."

Brett turned his head, heaved out a sigh. "Yeah, I know." He eyed Coach carefully. "My father's had a heart attack and he's asked me to come home. Dad has his own business and I don't know how sick he is. Thanks for the interest in me, I'm very excited about the opportunity. I'm just not sure about the short term, you know?"

Vance scrutinized his face. "You're a good hockey player, Brett, maybe a great one. You'd be long gone by now into the NHL if it weren't for that injury. And even with it, you're damned good. Don't turn your back on a great career."

"No, sir, I won't. I'll be in touch."

"Well, this takes priority. And remember, skills don't disappear just because you don't use them for a while. You're still the best candidate for the job."

Vance frowned and leaned forward. "What about this? The Victoria team is new. Why don't you play with them while you're over there? It's a way to keep your hand in. I can give them a call."

"Thanks, Coach. I don't think I'll be over there that long. Just a few weeks till Dad's back on his feet."

~~~

The next day Brett stood at his father's bedside and tried to reconcile the man laying there with the father he knew. Paddy Rome was a tall, lean, well-muscled man who'd been an athlete in his youth. He still carried vestiges of that legacy, his arms and shoulders roped with muscle, his neck thick and corded.

Paddy had a pallor to him now that was startling, dark marks gouged beneath his eyes, his facial muscles slack. The number of machines hooked up to him was alarming, the beeping and whirring an unsettling muted background symphony to the hospital sights and smells.

His girlfriend Dancy stood from her chair by the bed when Brett arrived and without a word left the room. Paddy dozed and when he roused for a minute, he frowned at Brett in seeming confusion.

"Dad it's me, Brett."

"I know it's you," he said, his voice slurred. "It's all these damn chemicals they're pumping into me. I can hardly think. Sit down."

He sat. Paddy dozed again.

Soon he paced the corridor, then found a newspaper in the visitor's lounge and took it back to his father's room. Paddy woke again when the nurse came to check him. Finally, the possibility of some information.

But the nurse didn't have much to say. His father's vital signs were stable. The drugs would make him drowsy and a bit confused. Brett could see Dr Wilde if he had questions.

Brett took his father's hand in his, gave it a squeeze. "The doc will be in later tonight, Dad. We can get some answers then."

Paddy gave a weak answering press with his fingers. "We already know, son. This is temporary. Just need a few weeks to get over it. Then we'll be right as rain." His slurred voice dropped off as he slumbered. Brett watched and wondered.

There was still no answer at Liz's house, so he left a message. When he came back from a soggy sandwich and lukewarm coffee in the cafeteria, the doctor was there. Brett introduced himself and watched him check the chart, Paddy's vital signs and appearance.

When he finished he motioned Brett into the hall. "So, you're his son."

Brett nodded.

"Yeah, I can see some resemblance."

Brett looked at the doctor in surprise.

Dr. Wilde smiled. "Your Dad and I played baseball together. I've known Paddy for years. Now, tell me what you know about his lifestyle."

Brett narrowed his eyes. "In what way?"

Dr. Wilde made an encouraging motion with his hand. "Everything. Spill it."

"Well, I haven't really lived with him since I was fourteen."

Dr. Wilde appeared surprised.

"I've been playing hockey. I left to play with the Prince George team and moved on from there. I was only home for visits."

Wilde pursed his lips and considered him thoughtfully. "So you're not aware of what your father's lifestyle was like."

Brett gazed down the hallway and narrowed his eyes, considering. "I'm only guessing, okay? Heavy drinking, heavy smoking, womanizing." He knew there was a bitter twist to his mouth. "Exercise? I'd estimate next to none."

Wilde nodded. "That's what I figured. I'm surprised you haven't been around. Your father talks about you a lot. Kept saying it's a shame you never made it to the NHL. Something about an injury."

Brett felt the heat climb his neck. "A knee injury," he muttered.

"I see." Wilde was still studying him. "Well, here's the info on your Dad. He's got major damage to his heart. We were able to do some very good early intervention, put in a couple of stents within the hour. He'll take a few days to stabilize.

"The medications are heavy, and he'll have to keep taking them to prevent another event. It probably means he can't work, certainly in the short term."

Brett shrugged. "I don't think he's worked for a long time anyway. I mean, he stopped driving truck years ago. Frank handles the trucks and drivers and Dad quotes the jobs. That shouldn't be a problem."

"I don't think you understand. The stress is bad for him. As a result of medication, there may be some mental confusion. He won't be running his trucking company. He can't do the day to day, can't take the stress."

Brett stared as the light slowly dawned. Now he got it. That's why he was here. They'd already told Dad all this. He couldn't keep the company going himself and Brett was going to be stuck with it. For a moment he stared down at the toes of his leather dress shoes.

He had a life and it wasn't here. Vancouver was where he lived, where his friends were, where there was a job waiting for him. Yes, his girlfriend Marilyn had moved on. The ugly memory hovered at the back of his mind and he did his best to push it away. But he still had a life in Vancouver.

This wasn't quite what he'd had in mind when he left home as a kid, lived in billets for years sharing a room with other young players, school part time and hockey full time. When he stepped up to the university team, older than the other students because of his commitment to the game, he'd had a plan.

Again, courses part time because the focus was hockey. Hockey practices, hockey games, hockey workouts. He'd played his team position, took his degree in economics, graduated and was ready for the next step in his career.

To end up running his father's trucking company in Victoria? Not gonna happen!

CHAPTER THREE

Katherine Dalton perched on the spindly chair at her little desk under the narrow bedroom window. Organizing papers into piles, she reviewed her conclusion, the only conclusion possible. She was broke.

The bank statement was a litany of her life - rent, utilities, her car loan payment. Her credit card showed the cost of a month's worth of gas, groceries, a pair of shoes she'd bought. And the statement from the National Student Loans office detailed the amount her student loan payment was and when it would begin. That day was today.

Katy still had her part-time job in a downtown restaurant on weekends. She'd worked there since the beginning of college. In the summer she'd also been a lifeguard at one of the public pools, but this year a new head lifeguard had taken over and set a deadline for applications. Katy hadn't known anything about it. So when she went in to find out what day she'd start work, she'd been blindsided by the fact that she hadn't been hired. Someone else had her job.

This whole thing was dumb. She shouldn't be in this position. A few months ago she hadn't even been worried because she'd actually saved money.

She critically surveyed her room. She used to think of it as the broom closet. Her rent was less than her roommates because her room was so much tinier, which suited her just fine.

Eating at the restaurant where she worked on weekends helped her save money, as well. No, it wasn't that she spent too carelessly. It was that she'd lost her savings.

Her hands shook as she shuffled the papers again. Damn Bruno. He'd been around, phoning, dropping by. He'd taken her on dates, a dinner or a movie. And he'd sounded so knowledgeable, so confident when he talked about investing her money. He thought she should get a return on her investment rather than leave it sitting in the bank, and he knew the best place to put it. He described a company called Rome Trucking with their big jobs and brand new trucks, and she'd been convinced to put her money in with his.

Now she couldn't even get him to answer his phone.

Katy grabbed her laptop from her desk. She knew Bruno's cell number, but didn't have an actual address for him. A search of the internet didn't bring up any information about him either. More alarmed than ever, she realized she'd gone into this with her eyes tightly closed.

But she did know where to find Rome Trucking.

The next afternoon as she left another hopeless job interview feeling particularly dejected, she made up her mind. She'd go and see Mr. Rome. If he was the businessman that Bruno portrayed him to be, he'd know not only how to reach Bruno Morelli, but also where her sixteen thousand dollars was. At least if she told him the story, he'd have the opportunity to make it right. It was her last hope but she felt confident it would work.

She laid out her best suit. The skirt stopped just short of the knee and paired with a pale pink shell that seemed to glow under the navy jacket, it was a feminine yet businesslike outfit.

Her portfolio contained a clean copy of her resume and diploma as well as reference letters from previous employment. The change at the bottom of her tip jar would cover the gas.

~ ~ ~

Next morning Katy drove cautiously through huge metal gates hung on heavy iron hinges, a large 'Rome Trucking' sign wired into the right hand gate. Dusty gravel spread across the wide yard where several buildings dotted the barren landscape. Tall weeds sprouted in clumps along the fence line. An old grey stucco-clad bungalow stood to one side on what appeared to be its original foundation with eight or ten pickups parked in a staggered line near the door.

It was surprising how many vehicles were on site already. Katy checked her watch. They must start work early. Carefully parking a safe distance from the last truck, she unsnapped the seatbelt, gathered her folder and purse and stepped gingerly out onto the gravel yard. All she had to do was explain why she was there, tell Mr. Rome that the money Bruno had invested with him was partly hers, and everything would be fine.

Drawing a deep breath, she straightened her shoulders and glanced around. Bruno had talked about this marshalling yard, how enormous it was, how dusty and busy, how vital, what a great investment it would be.

It must have once been three or four city lots. Several older dump trucks were parked farther back against the fence on the other side, their behemoth shapes hulking, casting low early morning shadows across the ground. A steel-clad workshop ranged at the back of the property and the sound of hammer ringing on metal rose from its dim interior.

Katy glanced toward the house where the front door stood open to the crisp morning air, a lone fir tree, ancient and gnarled, leaning protectively over it. That must be the office. Standing straighter she took a firm grip on her folder, mentally braced herself and started forward. This shouldn't be too difficult. She could ask for her money back, the money Bruno had loaned them.

As she climbed the wooden steps, standing out sharply new against the exterior of the old chipped and faded stucco, she heard strident masculine voices from within. She paused, her hand clutching the banister tightly as the shouting escalated in volume.

Goodness, maybe this was bad timing on her part. Should she have phoned first, made an appointment with the owner? She hovered uncertainly, one foot on the top step, her fingers seizing the hand rail in a nervous grip.

But Bruno had assured her it was a very informal place. People dropped in to talk to the owner, no one made an appointment. Surely it would be the same for her.

She moved cautiously forward across the wooden landing and peered around the cracked door frame. Gazing straight into what must have been the living room of a modest family home, the remains of a timeworn kitchen stood against one wall, the old fashioned cupboards still clinging to the walls. Dated furniture marked off that end of the large room.

The rest of the space held a couple of desks, one with a curious set of speakers on it, the other with a mishmash of papers strewn across its surface. And beyond that, a door led into what was obviously a separate office. Two figures stood in the doorway to the inner room.

That must be Mr. Rome. He was a shorter man dressed in khaki pants and shirt neatly tucked in, heavy shouldered and thick with muscle, maybe in his late fifties. He looked business-like in a rough sort of way, standing squarely in his bulky steel-toed boots. His head was thrust forward, salt and pepper hair clipped short and brushed straight back from his strong featured face.

He was speaking to a taller man in the doorway who had his back to Katy. Rome held a stub of cigar in his hand, and as he spoke he jabbed it forward for emphasis.

"We're going to keep calm," he said in a gravel voice. "This will work out, these things always do." He gazed keen-eyed up at his companion. "You have to hold onto your temper or we won't be able to pull it together. You know that."

The second man stood even straighter if possible, his shoulders blocking the interior of the room from Katy's gaze, his head nearly grazing the top of the door frame. He was dressed in a black tee shirt, ripped at the neck, and sagging cargo shorts. His feet were thrust into a pair of heavy leather boots, scuffed and marked, the laces dragging on the floor.

His head jerked back as if he'd been slapped and his voice started at a growl, rising steadily. "I'm going to kill him! Broke his leg, you say? I'll break his other fucking leg. I told him, I told them all!"

Just then, Mr. Rome caught sight of Katy and turned his head toward her with a look of surprise. "What can I do for you?" His manner was deceptively mild given the tone of the conversation she'd just heard. Katy was amazed. She wouldn't have thought he'd let one of his employees talk to him like that.

"I don't mean to interrupt, Mr. Rome", she said. "I've come to see you about a matter of business, but I can wait until you're free". She cast a disparaging look at his companion's back and folded her arms to indicate she was willing to be patient.

Mr. Rome regarded her for a moment, a slight smile marking his face. "Mr. Rome?" he asked. He gestured with his cold cigar, pointing at the younger man. "This is Mr. Rome."

The second man turned impatiently to stare at her. His face was heavily flushed, jaw tight and muscles bulged in his neck. His arms flexed as he braced his hands low on his hips and glared in her direction.

Glared with his good eye, that is. The other eye was black with a gash above it running up across his eyebrow, stitches crawling along it like a caterpillar, the plastic ends bristling. The eye itself was blood red and badly bruised. His mouth was swollen on one side, the lip split.

Katy stared. Her mouth fell open and she took an involuntary horrified step backward, steadying herself against the battered metal desk behind her. This was Mr. Rome? This was the man Bruno the rainmaker, Bruno the deal arranger had loaned all her money to?

~~~

"Mr. Rome," a woman's soft voice said, "I don't mean to interrupt. I can wait."

Brett turned his head to stare at the girl standing in the open doorway. He didn't think he'd ever seen a woman in this office in all his years of coming and going at Rome Trucking.

But to have one more thing thrown at him when he was already off his stride was almost more than he could handle. He slowly realized from the expression on her face that he had redirected a ferocious glare from Frank to this young lady. He tried to dial it down a little.

"What can I do for you?" It came out as a growl. His eye ached, his mouth was tender, the stitches pulled and his head hurt. He stood straighter, took a deep breath and held it for a second, cleared his throat.

He needed to get himself under control. The fight last night was one thing, a bit over the top but still acceptable in the rough and tumble world of hockey. But he couldn't afford to lose it here in the office. Not if he wanted to keep his head up. Not in front of a stranger.

He took another look. She wasn't very big, but impressive none the less with her short skirt and shapely legs. She wore a business suit and heels, clutched a purse and folder against her side as if her life depended on it. Her hair was pinned up in a roll of some kind. It was dark brown, maybe wavy. Small curls had escaped at her temple. Her face was expressive with wide grey eyes and a full mouth currently set in a determined line. She looked like she was trying to appear confident but her nervous gaze betrayed her.

"I can be with you in a minute." Grabbing Frank's arm, Brett dragged him into the office and slammed the door. It probably didn't make a good impression but he had things to take care of.

"Tell me again."

"Okay. Russell called the office as soon as I got in here this morning. You weren't here."

"No, forgot to set my alarm."

Frank examined his eye carefully. "How'd you get that?"

"Hockey. There was a fight."

"Yeah, I can see. Must be something in the air. Anyway, Russ says he can't drive for a while. He got in a fight at a nightclub last night, something to do with that girlfriend of his, and fractured his leg. It's in a cast."

"That stupid idiot."

"I think we've covered that."

Brett gave him a hard look. "I told them all! We have to be ready to work for the next few months. We've absolutely got to keep these trucks rolling. The bank is breathing down our necks. And what does he do? Gets his stupid leg broken!"

Frank nodded but didn't reply.

Brett pivoted to glare out the window. The last truck and pup was just rolling out the gate, Pete driving. He wasn't as proficient at handling the new trucks with the hydraulic pups as Russ had been, but he was competent.

Brett huffed out another breath and swung back to face Frank. "Well, I can't drive this morning. I've got to get some decent clothes on and go see the banker. Then I have a meeting with Coach. But I'll be back this afternoon and we'll come up with some kind of plan. Keep them rolling, Frank."

"What about the woman?"

"What woman? Oh, that woman." Brett frowned. "Maybe she's gone."

Nope. When he opened the door, she was standing in the same spot just inside the open doorway.

"Sorry about that, just had to take care of a few things." Brett moved forward. "I'm Brett Rome. What can I do for you?"

She shook his hand with a firm grip and quickly let go, the colour high in her cheeks. "My name is Katherine Dalton and I've come to see you about a couple of things. Um….." She dithered for a moment under his steady gaze. "First I wanted to ask about Bruno Morelli. He's been talking to you about investing in your company." She searched his face for a reaction, taking in his blank expression.

"Do you know Bruno? Do you know anything about an investment in Rome Trucking?"

Brett gave his head an impatient shake, a frown taking form on his forehead.

She hesitated, then continued a little desperately. "Also I wondered if you have a job available. I'm looking for work." Opening her portfolio on the cluttered desk, she busied herself tugging out a packet of papers stapled together at the corner and handed it to him.

Brett stared at the pages in his hand as if he'd forgotten how to read. He glanced back at her with his eyebrows raised. "I don't think….."

Frank cleared his throat and Brett half turned his head. The girl's cheeks flushed darker. Leaning forward, she pointed at the bottom of the resume.

"I have my diploma in Business Administration," she said. "I can do anything in an office. I handle the phone and arrange meetings, of course, but more importantly I can do a set of books, do payroll. I balance the monthly accounts, bill customers, apply payments on account." She paused, as if not sure she should go on.

"Anything else?" Brett turned a surprised look on Frank, but Frank was focussed on the girl.

Her expression perked up. "Oh, yes," she said, turning to talk to Frank. "I can develop a marketing plan for the business, make efficiency studies of your equipment…"

Her mouth was still moving when Frank waved her to a chair. "Have a seat," he said. "We'll be a minute, if you don't mind." He grabbed a dispatch call.

Brett felt like he might have his mouth open, so he closed it. His eye ran down the resume. There wasn't much there in the way of business experience. She'd been a lifeguard. He stole a glance at her. He'd bet she looked pretty spectacular in a bathing suit, getting warm at the thought. She'd been a waitress. He knew that hotel, liked the food in their dining room, at least the last time he ate there a year ago.

Flipping the page, he waited for Frank to enlighten him as to what he was thinking. The diploma was brand new. She'd attached her transcripts. Darned good marks, he had to give her credit there. But no experience.

He snapped the page closed and rolled the sheaf of papers, tapping the desk with it as he watched her. She was pretty, very feminine with a heart shaped face and curly dark hair. Her cheeks went even pinker under his gaze.

"Okay," said Frank, flipping a switch. "We'll be a minute, like I said." Grabbing Brett's arm, he dragged him back into the office and closed the door.

"What's going on, Frank?"

"I've just had a thought."

"Yeah, I can see that. I can't figure out what it is. Just the one thought?"

Frank chuckled. "You don't look too good, fella. Your eye's getting redder as we speak."

Brett gingerly rubbed his eyelid. "Doesn't feel great either."

"Well, here's the thought. We're both going to have to drive truck as much as we can to get us through this or the game's up. Why not hire the little miss out there to run the office? She can do dispatch, handle phone calls until we're able to take it on again. I wonder what kind of wage she wants."

"Well, she's pretty cute, but she doesn't have any work experience to speak of. So her wage won't be much, not compared to these truckers."

"See what I mean? It's better all the time. And you keep asking me, what's Paddy's plan for the business? Well, she does plans."

Brett blew out a surprised laugh. "She doesn't look like the type for a trucking office, Frank. She won't be able to handle the guys, the language. You know what it's like in here."

"Yeah, but still. The guys will tone it down a bit around her, is my bet. And she'll have to be tough. Maybe she won't last, who knows? But she doesn't need to stay long to get us out of this mess. Russell says five weeks in a cast, four in rehab, that's what the doctor's telling him. Meanwhile we can search for some temporary drivers. I'll make a few calls tonight. What do you think?"

Brett stared at him as if he'd sprouted feathers. Then he shrugged and said, "Well, it might work. Even if it's just short term. How long to learn the dispatch system? Half a day? A day? You could teach her today while I'm out at my meetings."

Frank nodded.

"Okay. It's a lame brained idea. Let's do it."

Frank chuckled and stuck the cigar in his teeth. "You hire her, I'll train her."

Brett brought Katherine into the office and offered her a seat. "We think we have something in the way of a job offer. It might not be quite what you're looking for."

The girl listened with a slightly horrified expression as he talked. Finally he came to a halt. "What is it?"

"Pardon?" she said faintly.

"You're looking at me like I eat small children."

She blushed. "I'm sorry. I just keep thinking about your eye. It must be painful."

He lifted his hand and gently rubbed a fingertip on the eyelid. "Yeah, but I've had worse. It'll be better in a few days."

"What happened?"

"Hockey. There was a game last night and I got involved in a fight." He didn't mention that once the fight started he had done his best to escalate the conflict, maybe tried to annihilate the other player. He figured he'd save that conversation for Coach.

She seemed a bit more comfortable at that explanation, less like she might be ill. "Oh," she said. "Hockey, of course." And that must have answered some question in her head, because she started to pay attention to what he said.

Fishing around in the back of the desk drawer, he found an employment form for her to fill out and went to talk to

Frank. "She's all yours," he said. "I'm off. I'll be back later and we'll sort things out."

Frank nodded and turned back to answer a call.

Brett suddenly stopped cold at the thought of what his father's reaction to hiring a woman was going to be. Paddy would have a bird when he found out. It might send his blood pressure into orbit.

CHAPTER FOUR

Driving away from the bank later that day, Brett headed for the arena and his next appointment with Coach Ruxton. He was a little surprised at the way his meeting had progressed with the banker, Lindquist. Dressed for the road, suit, shirt and tie, polished shoes, he knew how to present himself. Hockey had certainly taught him that. But he figured the bruised mouth, black eye and stitches would probably detract a little from the business-like attire.

Lindquist was surprisingly mild about the cuts and bruises on his face. "I've been to a lot of the games since we got a team in town," he said with a grin. "You guys won, it was great."

Brett laughed. "Yeah, we did."

"That was some fight. What started it?"

"Not too much," Brett said. "There are a few fights most games."

The banker looked curious. "Yeah, but this one really exploded."

"True." Brett eyed him, wondering how much to say. "I have an old injury in my left knee. And the Seattle forward was heading straight for it. I just reacted without thinking. I always protect that leg if I can."

Lindquist nodded, "Yeah, I knew that. It's what kept you out of the big leagues, right?"

Brett shrugged, feeling himself get warm. "Who can say?" Paddy must have been talking it up with the banker.

"Well, what can we do today?"

Brett produced the letter he'd gotten Paddy to sign giving him the authority to deal with the corporate account.

Lindquist read it carefully. "This is good, Brett. I'll call around the house and get Paddy to sign new cards for cheque signing authority. Then I'll come by the office to have you and Frank sign."

Coach Ruxton was on the phone when Brett arrived. His office in the arena was a small cubicle near the dressing rooms in the bowels of the huge building. Papers and play diagrams cluttered his desk and were piled in stacks on a bookcase behind him.

Waving Brett to a chair, he finished his conversation and swivelled round to face him. "Well, Mr. Rome. How are you today? How's the eye?"

Brett grinned, but his mouth hurt. "The eye's been better."

Ruxton chuckled. "Yeah, I guess it has. So how are you feeling?"

"Good, can't complain."

The coach eyed him. "Tell me about this fight. How did it start? Level with me, Brett. We're just getting to know you and we need to be honest with each other."

Brett shifted in his chair. "The forward Wasylyk headed for me at full speed right out of the gate. He was going to hit my bad leg, and I reacted by stopping short and getting my stick between his skates as he approached. I fell into the boards and took him down with me. When I got up, the fight started."

Ruxton waited for a minute. "Well, quick thinking and even quicker action. But that might be thirty percent of the story." He watched Brett without blinking.

Brett snorted. "Yeah, about thirty percent."

"Well? Let's hear the rest."

Rubbing his eyelid gingerly with the tip of his finger, he continued. "What do you want to know? I've been under some pressure lately. I don't want to begin a whining session here."

Ruxton just waited silently, finally motioned with a hand for him to explain.

"My father had a heart attack, a few months ago now. You may know this already." He glanced up but Coach nodded for him to continue.

"He's too sick to manage his business. For some reason his company is totally overextended and I've been left trying to prop it up. I'd just finished my stint as a player with the Vancouver team and was in line to become defence coach as well as doing some recruiting for Vance.

"I've had to turn my back on that and I guess it pinches a bit. Vance says he'll wait, but who knows how long before I can go back." He took a deep breath. "I love the game and I love to play, so this is a great chance here with your team. I know I felt pretty angry at Wasylyk, kind of out of proportion to the body slam I was about to get."

Ruxton was quiet for a few minutes. "Well, that's a bit more of the picture, I guess. Do you think this is the kind of thing that will recur?"

"No, Coach. It won't. I apologize for putting the team in that position."

Huffing out a breath, Ruxton swivelled back and forth on his chair. "What did Vance say when you told him you were turning down the position and coming over to the Island?"

"He was pretty good about it. Said skills don't disappear just because you don't use them for a year. Things like that."

"So he'd have you back if you were to go back to Vancouver?"

"He didn't really say." Brett was pretty sure he could have that job in a heartbeat. Vance had told him he was still the best choice but he didn't need to brag. Not when he'd screwed up so badly right out of the starting gate with this coach.

Settling his beefy arms across his desk, Ruxton leaned forward. "Here's what I see. I see a young man at a crossroads. You've got a few things in front of you, a possible continued career in hockey, a possible career in coaching, and a family responsibility to your father. I doubt if you can do it all. At some point you'll have to choose. But that point may not be yet."

He leaned back, eyed Brett for a moment. "So I'd like you to continue playing with us. You have the best defence record in the league for goal assists. The line coaches like what they saw last night, including the fight, if you want to know the truth.

"I know those kinds of fights aren't your style. You're a good player and we can use you. As long as our interests align, we'd like to keep you on board. Agreed?"

Brett rose and shook hands. "Thanks, Coach. I respect that, I'll do my best."

"I know you will, son. You'll play with your head as well as your heart. That's what everyone says about you."

Ruxton watched Brett Rome leave his office and reflected on what Vance had told him. Brett was dealing with his father's heart attack and demands to come home. Plus there was the girlfriend who picked out a different hockey player every few years and had recruited a new one while Rome was out of town playing the last games of the playoffs. Not easy for anyone to handle, let alone a young hot-headed player who already stood in the midst of a great deal of turmoil.

~~~

Brett got back to the office just as the trucks pulled in at the end of the day raising a small cloud of dust. He bounded up the stairs and immediately regretted it when the headache behind his bruised eye kicked up a racket. As he walked into the office, Frank was collecting the paperwork from the drivers and Katherine was being introduced to the men.

"Wow, the scenery sure has changed in here," Pete remarked to no one in particular as he took his leave.

The mechanic, Gert, leaned his big frame against the back

of the couch while he watched the action, his hands shoved in the front pockets of his overalls. Gert was from the Ukraine and still carried vestiges of a heavy accent. A big man, no taller than Brett but broad and heavily muscled, he'd been a fixture at Rome Trucking for decades.

Now he commented, "Things looking different in here than they did yesterday."

Brett nodded, and slapped him on the shoulder. "Whatever I can do to make things work better."

Gert gave a guffaw of laughter.

Wilf shook Katherine's hand. "Good to meet you, Miss." He glanced at Brett as he passed. "I don't know about this," he muttered under his breath.

Renwick drove the old trucks and had worked for Paddy for years. He nodded to Katherine and headed out the door. "Yep, things are sure getting shook up in the office," he offered to no one in particular as he descended the steps.

Brett watched Katherine's expression. The colour rose higher in her cheeks with each comment, her lips pressed more firmly together. She busied herself organizing the papers on the desk, gathering her portfolio and purse. She got her keys out and glanced at Frank.

"What time should I be in tomorrow, Frank?"

"Well, I'm in by six thirty to get organized but the trucks don't leave until seven, so come then."

She smiled. "Thank you for your patience today. I feel like I've learned a lot already."

"Hey, we're just getting started." Frank nodded at her and took the day's papers from Buster who had parked the last truck.

Katherine crossed the floor and passed in front of Brett to the doorway. "Good night, Mr. Rome."

"It's Brett. Good night, Katherine. See you tomorrow."

She gave him a guarded look. "You can call me Katy."

Her high colour only intensified as they both heard Buster saying to the room at large. "Boy, talk about a change in the view around here. This'll be trouble. Paddy's not goin' to like it."

She hastened down the steps.

Brett laughed to himself as he watched her walk away. That little suit sure moulded nicely to her shape, and her legs looked great. Nice ass, too. He could just hear the kinds of comments there'd be when she wasn't in the office. It was going to be interesting, for as long as she lasted anyway.

~ ~ ~

Sighing, Katy leaned back against the headboard of her single bed. She didn't have much furniture, but then this room didn't take much furniture.

Her dresser was the only thing she had brought with her from home. The gleaming old oak was lovely in the afternoon light. It had been hers since she was too small to reach the drawers.

She smiled. It may not be big but it was small. Dad always said stuff like that. He'd look at his car and say, "It may not be new but it's old", and they'd both laugh themselves silly at the obvious statement.

She sobered as she thought about her day. She still had her part time night job and now she had a new day job. It was exciting. Not the kind of place she'd expected to find work, but she'd be able to use her education there.

Bruno was her only concern now.

The first thing that had attracted her to him was his size. She'd been at a nightclub with the other girls having a drink, a few dances when she first met him. However, she found some guys too big, overpowering and she shied away from them. But Bruno was not much taller than her. He was slim and wiry with dark wavy hair and a nice smile.

When he'd asked her to dance, she gladly went onto the dance floor with him. He phoned her the next week and asked her out. They went to a movie and then for a drink. Just one drink. He was meeting some people, he said, so couldn't stay long. Their dates had been fun, casual, low key. He always kissed her when he took her home, soft kisses, kisses that didn't overpower her. Sweet kisses.

One day he'd talked about his investment strategies and a company called Rome Trucking. He described the huge yard, the big trucks that pulled in there at the end of the day, noisy, dusty. It sounded exciting. Mr. Rome was expanding, he said. She should see the new dump trucks with pups. It gave them a load and a half for each trip, raising their efficiency by fifty percent.

Katy had already confided to him that she'd saved money while going to school. Bruno talked about ways to make money work rather than leaving it in the bank earning next to nothing. If it was invested with the other money he gathered, there would be a monthly interest payment made to the investors.

Could she be a part of this investment, in just a small way? Bruno mentioned needing a hundred thousand dollars, but even sixteen thousand would contribute, wouldn't it? With quaking heart and nervous excitement, Katy transferred her money out of her savings account and wrote Bruno a cheque. Here was her future. She'd have her money working for her.

She hadn't told her father. This was something she wanted to do on her own. When she started receiving dividends, she'd tell him about her investment strategy.

Then Bruno stopped answering his phone. But not before he slept with her. Her heart stuttered at the memory. She couldn't believe she'd done that. It didn't seem like such a big deal at the time. It was over before she knew it. And then he stopped phoning.

That was when she'd called the swimming pool and found her summer job was gone. Well, she had another job now, even better than the last one.

~ ~ ~

Brett played three games in a row and slept the weekend away, doing workouts in between naps. He tried to arrange decent food for his father. Paddy's girlfriend, Dancy had disappeared from the house.

The night she'd crawled into his bed in Paddy's back bedroom still burned in his memory. It had only been a few days after Dad was released from hospital, still shaky and ill, spending most of his time sleeping.

In his sleep, Brett became aware of his girlfriend Marilyn moving against. Marilyn, who'd left him for another hockey player, Marilyn who he still thought about. He pulled her closer in his dream, breathed in her scent. It had been so long, too long since he'd been with her. She felt warm and welcoming and even below the sense of being asleep he missed her. His interest rose just from the feel of her in his arms. He wanted to kiss her, touch her all over. Her smooth hands moved across his back, her sweet mouth on his neck.

He woke with a start, totally disoriented, unable to identify where he was in the pitch black. His erection was painful. But Marilyn's scent wasn't right, there was something different, something wrong... This wasn't their room.

He froze in sudden uncertainty, then reality struck. Marilyn was gone from his life. And this was the single bed in the back bedroom of his father's house.

"Dancy!" Pushing her away, he leaped from the bed, hopping for balance as his foot tangled in the sheet. "What the hell?"

"Shhh," she whispered, her voice husky. "Don't wake Paddy. He's in a deep sleep right now. It's the best time of night."

"Get out of my bed!" His voice was a low hiss.

"This isn't your bed," she said scornfully. "We just let you stay here. Anyway, come back. You don't want to waste that nice hard-on, do you? I can put it to good use, I promise," she added.

Brett thought he might be sick. This was his father's woman, someone his father slept with. Feeling around in the dark he couldn't find his clothes and finally flipped the light switch.

"Ohhh, look at you. I thought so," she purred. "Come back to bed, baby. It won't hurt anyone. Paddy will never know. And I'll make it so good for you."

Brett scooped his briefs from his duffel on the floor and

pulled them on. His pants followed, then a shirt which he slung around his shoulders. "Get out of the bed, Dancy. Now!" His voice was low, frigid, demanding.

Pouting at him with red lips, her dark hair curling across her shoulder, she slowly pulled back the covers. At the sight of her naked body, Brett turned his back.

"It's okay, you can look now," she said a minute later, her tone mocking.

He turned slowly to find her wrapped in a housecoat, her face pale, expression contemptuous. Staring at her, he wondered what kind of woman his father had chosen. She lived here, didn't lift a finger to take care of Paddy, wouldn't ensure there was food for him but stocked the fridge with beer, the one thing Paddy couldn't have.

Walking up close, he put his face right down into her scowl. "Don't you ever do that again. Do you hear me?" he hissed. "He's my father. I respect him. And he doesn't deserve this. Get out of my room, Dancy. Don't come back, and you see that he gets lunch every day."

Her eyes narrowed, her mouth pouted. "I'll tell Paddy you tried to seduce me."

"He won't believe you for a minute. I can get women like you a dozen at a time after every hockey game. They're younger and they're prettier. If he ever hears of this, if you say one word, I'll tell him the full story, got it? Lunch, every day. I mean it."

Brett called Aunt Ray, his mother's sister, the next day. There had to be another way to handle his living arrangements.

CHAPTER FIVE

Bruno Morelli pulled his van up tight behind the low grey Mercedes parked at the side of the street. Tyler was home. He reached forward to grab the keys from the ignition and felt the lump of his cell phone in his front pocket.

Katy had called him twice today, three times yesterday. Luckily he'd seen the caller ID before answering, because he didn't know what to say to her. When he'd asked her to dance that night in the club, she'd just been up dancing with a burly guy in a tee shirt who was trying to snuggle her up tight. A fight had broken out, her partner turned to fend off another guy backing into him, and she'd run for her table.

He had to grin to himself. She was skittish alright, but when she danced with him, she seemed to relax. Maybe he wasn't big enough to overpower her.

She was so cute, he couldn't resist her. Mostly he went to the clubs to pick up a woman and sleep with her. But Katy was different, so he asked her out for a drink. She seemed naive, and naivety was something that was rare in his life.

In the end, he wanted to impress her. She was working hard, proud to be finishing her diploma courses and he had no education to brag about. So he trotted out the investment scheme. She was enthralled by the idea. Maybe he shouldn't have told her. Tyler certainly thought so. And Tyler was the boss. Bruno winced and climbed out of his truck.

Tyler should have been happy he'd talked Katy into putting some money in. Like she said, it wasn't much but sixteen thousand should help. Bruno had liked the argument and bounced it off Tyler but he had reacted badly. By then it was too late. Bruno had already cashed her cheque.

Now he was afraid to take her calls. He felt like a heel, because he'd seduced her before he dropped out of her life. And she'd been a virgin. What a fuckup.

~~~

Sitting at the office desk going through bank statements, Brett heard the sudden squealing of tires, then the heavy crunch of gravel. He looked out his office window in time to see Katy park her car and slam out of it in a tearing hurry.

Right behind her came Pete in one of the new trucks. He came in a little slow and very carefully parked against the fence. Brett frowned and walked to the front of the office.

Katy barrelled past him and seated herself at the main desk. As she gathered some papers together on her desk, he saw her hands were shaking. She glanced over at Frank, "Is everything okay there?"

At the dispatch table, Frank raised his head and nodded then went back to work.

"Good," she said breathlessly. "I just got to the bank in time to make the deposits."

Brett listened to this exchange while watching Pete head for the office steps in a determined stalk that had the hackles rising on the back of his neck. "What's up with Pete?" he asked of no one in particular.

Katy's head shot up, then she lowered it again to the schedules spread on the desk in front of her.

Pete took the stairs two at a time, walked right past Brett to stop in front of her desk. "Katherine," he said in a strained voice, "Do you know what could have happened? I could have hit you."

His face was florid, his neck corded with emotion.

Breathing heavily, he erratically waved his hands, one holding a bundle of delivery papers from his day's work.

Katy's face had gone ghostly pale. She stood slowly. "I'm sorry, Pete." Tears stood in her eyes.

"You damned near scared me to death! I thought my heart would stop."

Frank stood up from his desk, watching the drama. Cautiously Brett stepped closer. "Hold on now, Pete. Take it easy."

Pete glared at him. "Take it easy?"

"No, it's my fault. I'm really sorry, Pete." One tear fell and rolled down her cheek.

Pete lowered his arm, and flapped the papers helplessly. "Well, okay, but I have to say…"

Katy stared at the top of her desk. Pete gazed at the crown of her head wordlessly. Then she just stepped forward and wrapped her arms around his skinny waist. "I'm sorry Pete." Brett heard tears in her voice.

Pete stood like a statue, his hands held aloft as if afraid he might accidentally touch her, then slowly one hand came down and he patted her shoulder awkwardly.

"It's okay. Just watch what you're doing out there. I thought I'd die."

Disentangling himself as best he could, he handed his papers to Frank and stood there uncertainly.

"So," said Brett. "What happened?"

Pete glanced at him sideways. "I had just shifted down and gunned it to turn in the gate when she darted in front of me in that little car of hers. I'd already hit the gravel, there was no way I could slow down, no traction whatsoever. For a minute there I couldn't even see her. Scared the hell out of me." He shook his head. "I think I need a drink."

Brett slapped him on the back. "Pete, you're a good driver. If anyone could come out of that one okay, it would be you. And with the weight of the pup on too." Pete's face became slightly less flushed.

"And I guess Katy will be more careful. She's not used to

being around trucks like we are, right?"

Katy sat at the desk, her pen wobbling as she tried to write a note on the page in front of her.

"Come on everyone." Brett pulled a bottle of rum out of the bottom drawer of Paddy's desk in the office. "Here we go." Frank found a Coke and they splashed a bit of liquor in the bottom of four glasses and added the soda.

"Here, Katy. Now that Pete's lost his cool, you've been initiated. Not many people have been able to shake him." Grinning at her, he swiped her ponytail. She gave him a quavering smile and took a sip from her glass.

"That's better. Right, Pete?"

"Yeah, I gotta say it is. Here's to Katy. When I first saw her, I thought she'd change things around here. I just didn't know I'd blow a heart valve over it."

Katy gave a shaky laugh. "You must be tougher than that, Pete. One small scare."

Pete gave her a rueful grin. "Not so small, little girl. Keep that in mind."

When Wilf and Renwick arrived, everyone turned to the newcomers. Brett stepped closer to his newest employee and slid a hand under her ponytail to rub the tender curling hairs on her slender neck. Leaning down he spoke into her ear. "Are you okay?"

She glanced at him. "I'm fine." There was a light sheen of perspiration on her forehead. The hand holding the glass shook.

"It's okay, you know. We all make mistakes. And these guys have been doing trucks all of their adult lives. They're professionals, but this is new to you. It's okay."

Her eyes filled with tears and he tugged her against his side for a second in a one-armed hug. Just to reassure her, he told himself. Just to make her feel better. Eventually he had to drop his arm because he couldn't think of a good reason to keep it there.

CHAPTER SIX

Bruno listened to the phone ring. When it finally went to voice mail, he clicked it off and dialed again. Then he heard her breathless voice at the other end. "Hello?"

"Hi, Katy. I got your messages." She'd called him every day, leaving longer messages each time.

"Sorry about that." He heard the discomfort in her voice. "I'm just quite anxious. I need to know when I can get some of my investment back. Can we meet?"

"Yeah, that's what I'm calling about. I'm out of town for a couple of days, so let's meet on the weekend. Are you okay with that?"

He listened to the silence as she seemed to process his offer. Then he heard a smile in her voice as she replied. "Sure. I'd like that. I just want to know where the investment went. I'm very short of cash."

"I know," he said. "I know. Remember where the Lieutenant Governor's house is, along Rockland Avenue?"

"Yes. I've been there before."

"Good. Well, I'll meet you there. Just walk along in front

of the gates and I'll find you."

"Okay, Bruno. And thanks for calling me back."

There was a lengthy pause while he cleared his throat. "You're welcome," he said, his voice suddenly hoarse.

Clicking his phone off, Bruno glanced guardedly at his companion. "Does that work? She's going to meet me Saturday. That gives us a few days to get our plan together, right?"

Tyler smiled at him. Bruno had never been comfortable when Tyler smiled. It happened at odd times and out of all relationship to what was happening. He remembered him smiling late that night behind the Striders Club, before he grabbed the hammer out of the trunk of his car and nailed that bouncer in the side of his head.

The bouncer should have been around front doing his job to keep the lineup under control. But it was late on a weeknight and there was no lineup. He'd come into the alley to buy a little coke and Tyler had laced him.

Bruno wasn't sure why, nor did he have the nerve to ask. Maybe the guy didn't pay, or maybe he talked too much. Tyler was touchy that way. As long as Bruno had known him, things went Tyler's way or they didn't go any way at all. Tyler was an okay partner but he was no friend.

"That'll work fine," Tyler said. "Remind me before you go to meet with her. We can come up with a story that'll keep her happy and off our backs. Don't let your feelings for her get in the way, Morelli. She's just a girl."

Nodding, Bruno vowed to himself to keep that in mind. She was a sweet girl and he had a real fondness for her. But Tyler kept him in coke. He wasn't hooked, he wouldn't allow that to happen but he did like it. Reaching for the small bag Tyler had put on the table, he stood to go.

~~~

Katy shut off dispatch and shuffled the papers together. She giggled softly.

Passing behind her, Brett laid his hand lightly on her shoulder. "What's so funny?"

She looked up at him, smiling. "Well, I'm not sure you even need me here. The drivers ask me questions and then tell me they had it right in the first place."

He grinned at her. "With Frank out driving, they're trying to break you in easy."

"Yeah." She sobered. "What happened to your face?"

"You know, hockey."

"Don't you wear a face shield?" She hesitantly ran her fingertips over his cheek. He felt his neck get hot.

"Mmm hm, but someone got their stick handle up under it."

"Oh." She quickly dropped her hand in her lap. "Okay."

Brett examined her face for a minute. "Are you going to do a set of books for us?"

Very businesslike, she straightened her back and he had to smile to himself. She twitched like a cat, he'd swear.

"Of course," she said.

"Good. There's a laptop in my office with some kind of accounting software on it." Fetching it, he set it up on the main desk. "You could start from last month and fill in the rest when you have time. I need to get a handle on the cash flow."

"Of course," she said again. "Let me see what kind of programme it is."

Later, when he heard her talking in the main office he thought she was on dispatch. But he soon recognized the tone of that gravel voice responding to her questions. Rising, he walked around the desk.

"Hi, Dad. I wondered when you'd show up here." Paddy was standing straight and that was all that could be said for him. His face was pale, almost grey and covered with a film of sweat. His hand shook on his cane as he stood unsteadily in the middle of the room.

Katy jumped to her feet and extended her hand. "Oh, I'm so sorry. I didn't know. How do you do, Mr. Rome? I'm Katherine Dalton." Paddy stared at her outstretched hand for so long that she was beginning to retract it before he finally reached to shake hers. Her cheeks turned a becoming pink.

Brett scowled. Why was the old man such a Neanderthal? This whole industry was like that. It was a wonder their own truckers had accepted Katy as well as they had.

"Dad, Katy's the office manager. She handles dispatch when Frank isn't here and does the invoices and bookkeeping."

"Bookkeeping?" Paddy walked slowly into the inner office and collapsed in the chair, his cane leaning against his knee. "We've never had a bookkeeper. Why do we need one now?"

Brett closed the door and sat in a chair facing his father. "How did you get here?"

"Dancy's waiting out in the car."

Brett raised his eyebrows. "She won't come in?"

"I don't think so."

"Do you want a coffee or a soda or something?"

"No thanks." He heaved a breath. "I won't stay long. How are things going?"

"Well," Brett paused. "They're definitely coming along. We've got the three new trucks rolling. Frank is driving almost full time. When I can, I drive. With Katy in the office it frees us both up."

Paddy nodded. "Yeah, that's about what I figured, although I don't hold with having a female in the office."

Brett felt his jaw tighten but Paddy didn't give him a chance to react. "I had a call from Claude Mikkleson," he continued. "He's got a big project coming up. He'll give us a crack at it. I'll help with the quote. Should be able to handle it."

"That would be good. We can use the work." Brett rubbed his chin. "How are you feeling? What does Doc Wilde say?"

"Not much. Listen, I've been meaning to talk to you about something." He had to pause to catch his breath. "The thing is, Dancy isn't too comfortable with you staying at the house. So it might be better, you know…" He made a rolling motion with his hand.

"If I got myself another place to stay."

"Yeah, that's it. Get your own place."

Brett examined his father closely. "Not a problem. I've already put out feelers on that."

There was a knock at the door. Brett pulled it open to see Dancy standing there. She gave him a sly smile. "Hello, Brett. Long time no see."

"Dancy." His voice sounded cool even to his own ears.

She lifted her brows and swung her gaze to Paddy. "Ready? I've got things to do."

Paddy got to his feet and slowly headed out of the office. "Sounds good. I'm about finished anyway."

"Nice to meet you, Mr. Rome," Katy called as they moved toward the door. Paddy waved without turning his head. Dancy gave her a knowing look and followed him, her hips swinging.

~~~

Katy slowed her car as she drove down Rockland's narrow winding streets past the high gates of the Lieutenant Governor's house where Bruno had promised to meet her. Continuing on to the end of the block, she pulled a U turn and squeezed her car into a tight parking space.

She was early but didn't want to miss him. She might be close to getting some of her money back and that desperate feeling in her stomach was starting to ease. Climbing out, she walked back to the ornamental gates.

The gardens were lovely this time of year. Katy had taken a tour of the grounds once. They were magnificent. Groups of gardeners volunteered, adding fresh new flower beds with the seasons. Peering through the grill she saw banks of roses in full bloom. Every colour of the rainbow, they were displayed like jewels in the expansive gardens.

She heard a car coming and glanced to the street to see if it was Bruno but it was just a little moped going slowly by. She turned back and got absorbed in the view.

Startled by the roar of an engine, she glanced around. A low grey car was coming fast down the winding street. Tinted windows blocked her view of the driver. The sidewalk was very narrow here. Katy tried the gates but they were locked. The engine revved louder.

Looking over her shoulder, her heart clenched in her chest as she saw the tires of the car jump the curb, hopping onto the sidewalk. In a sudden panic she leaped, grabbing the metal work of the gate as high as she could reach and jerking her legs up, her feet tangling in the bars.

The bumper of the car scraped the gate just below the soles of her shoes. The gate jerked and shuddered at the impact and she almost lost her grip on the iron bars. Bouncing back onto the road, tires squealed and the vehicle roared around the corner out of sight.

Katy hung there, paralyzed with fear. Then her grip suddenly gave way and she fell to the concrete on her hands and knees. Crouching, she gasped and panted in pain, her whole body shaking.

Tears came thick and fast, running down her cheeks as she fought for breath, her mind whirling. *Was that car trying to hit her?* She didn't know. *Would they come back?* That thought galvanized her into action and she grabbed the grill of the gate with bleeding hands, pulling herself awkwardly to her feet.

She stood for a moment, swaying, before she staggered across the road toward her car. An elderly lady, ramrod straight with white hair dragged tight back in a tiny bun, waited on the sidewalk, her dachshund on a leash.

The woman was shocked. "I saw that!" she said. "Are you alright, dear?"

Katy peered at her through her tears. "I don't know," she managed.

"What was that driver thinking?" the woman scolded, glaring down the street through her thick glasses. "It's outrageous. He shouldn't get away with something like that." Then she looked back at Katy. "Do you need help?"

"I think I'm fine. Did you see the licence?

"No, I didn't, I was too shocked to pay attention, I'm afraid." Her face was pale.

"Did you see the driver?"

"Not a thing. Those windows were dark as night."

"No," Katy said faintly. "I didn't see him either."

Back home, she poured a hot bath and carefully lowered herself into the tub. Now if only she could relax without one of her roommates banging on the door wanting to use the bathroom. The hot water laced with bath salts crept over her tender knees and she winced in pain, sucking in a breath.

That felt better. As the heat seeped in and began to do its job, she relaxed against the slanted end of the tub and let out a sigh. She had stopped shaking a while ago and now the muscles in her shoulders and neck began to let go. She lowered her tender hands into the water, hissing air between her teeth as the water stung the scraped spots.

Ahh. It was a relief to just relax and soak her stiff and aching limbs. She knew she'd have to think about it soon, think about what had happened, but not yet. Just now she wanted to take care of her sore body.

Could that have possibly been an accident? Well, logically it was possible. But was it probable? No, she didn't think so.

If it wasn't an accident, then Bruno must have had something to do with it. She shuddered at the thought but forced her reasoning forward. If he did, was he the one driving the car? That wasn't his car, he drove an old van. But he could have borrowed it or even stolen it.

Her thoughts stopped at that. She couldn't see him stealing a car. But if he had borrowed it, could he give it back to the owner with the front bumper all smashed?

She circled back again. Maybe he did steal it. If he stole it, he wouldn't care what the owner thought when he found it with the front bumper destroyed.

Letting out a pent up breath, she sagged back in the water. This was getting her nowhere. It was pure speculation. But what she did know was Bruno had set up the meeting with her and he didn't show. But a car came along that nearly hit her. She couldn't sidestep that.

She was afraid, shaking with fear. Bruno was no longer her

friend, her one time lover, her investment counsellor. Bruno was dangerous. Her insides seemed to contract and a shiver spread outward. The water was too cold. She jerked forward to turn on the tap.

CHAPTER SEVEN

Bruno left Vancouver, catching the last ferry back to the Island. He tried Tyler's number again but there was still no answer. By the time they docked, he was in a frenzy. Damn Tyler. He'd sent Bruno out of town the very day he was to meet with Katy.

"Don't worry about it," Tyler had said. "I'll meet her. I'll explain the situation, that we can't pull money out just because she's short of cash."

"That isn't the issue. She lost her job. Maybe we can give her back half of it." He knew he sounded weak and that was never a good thing when dealing with Tyler. But he couldn't hide his worry.

"Why don't I call her and postpone the meeting? She'll understand. I can meet her tomorrow."

"No, this works. I'll deal with it. Don't you trust me?" Tyler smiled and Bruno shuddered.

"Of course." He'd had to leave it at that. He wasn't going to challenge Tyler. He was sure he wouldn't win.

Now he drove down a dark street in the lowlands and stopped at the last house on the block. The front windows were blacked out, so no light showed. But Tyler was meeting him here. Grabbing the duffel bag, he walked up the steps.

He didn't stop to knock, just opened the door and went in. There was a lamp on in the front room, Tyler slumped in a chair, the TV flickering in the corner.

Tyler looked up and motioned him to the other chair. "How'd it go?"

Bruno nodded. "Good. Here's the stuff." He shoved the duffel across the floor.

Tyler took his time opening it up and inspecting each package carefully. Finally he zipped it and shoved it back. "Give it to Balson. He's in the back room." He jerked his head toward the hall.

"Okay." Bruno sat for another moment. "How'd it go with Katy?"

Tyler just stared at him. Bruno squirmed but kept his gaze steady.

Finally he smiled. "It went fine. She didn't show."

Bruno felt the tension he'd been holding all day leave his shoulders in a rush. Nothing had happened. That was good. That was the best outcome he could have hoped for. He'd wait for her call, set up another meeting.

Leaving the house later that night, Bruno spotted Tyler's grey BMW parked across the street. As he passed it he noticed a deep dent in the front fender. Running his fingers along the depression, he found fresh gouges and scrapes in the metal. Those hadn't been there yesterday. Tyler had been up to something.

~~~

Katy poked her head around the office door. "Someone named Lionel is on line one."

Brett jabbed the button. "Uncle Lionel," he said. "I wondered when we'd hear from you. Have you talked to Dad?"

"Hi, Brett. Yeah, I just talked to Paddy. It sounds like he's coming along, doesn't it?"

"Well, slowly. He still can't drive and he's taking a ton of pills. Have you been down to see him?"

"Not yet."

Brett heard his heavy breathing over the line. "How're you feeling these days?"

"I get by. Betty does a lot, of course. I should come down and see Paddy, catch up."

"Yeah, you should. Why don't you drive down this weekend? Dad's got a spare room." Brett chuckled to himself at the thought of that little bed in the back bedroom. "In fact, you can stay with me if you like, I have an extra bed that's better than Dad's."

Brett had found the main floor of a house to rent, two bedrooms that suited him fine for the moment. Aunt Ray had had a friend who knew someone. He smiled to himself. Aunt Ray had been his rock over the years since his mother died. "You can drive down island in the daylight, go back the next day."

"Well, let me talk to Betty. The reason I called was about your spare room. Randy just finished his cooking course and he's got a job in a restaurant in Victoria. Paddy mentioned you had your own place and I wondered if Randy could bunk in with you for a while. He's supposed to start work next week."

Brett rubbed his chin, an alarm sounding in the back of his skull. This sounded like the family trap, as Aunt Ray used to call it. But what the heck. He wasn't home that much with the number of hockey games he was playing and Randy probably needed to get away from the folks. He didn't have to stay forever.

"That might work," he said cautiously. "Why don't you come down this weekend, bring Randy. We can talk about it."

Uncle Lionel laughed and broke into a wheezing cough. "I'll call you back."

~~~

That day Brett went to get a case of beer for his Thursday night meeting with the staff. It was a way to connect with the drivers and help them buy into the future of the company, kind of like how any group worked. He'd been on enough teams to know exactly how they functioned. When he stopped in to see Paddy on the way, the TV was on in the living room but Paddy wasn't there.

"Dad?" He walked into the kitchen to see his father pull some toast out of the toaster and drop it onto a plate.

"How you doing, son?" Paddy picked up a knife. "What's up?"

"Not much. Just hadn't heard from you for a day or two."

"Yeah, been busy." They looked at each other and both burst out laughing. Paddy's laugh was weak, slightly hoarse.

Brett leaned against the counter, still chuckling. "That was a good one. Haven't heard you laugh in a while. How are things with Dancy?"

"Dancy who?" There was a different, terse note to Paddy's voice.

"Oh, oh. What's happened? She gone AWOL?"

"You might say. She'll be back. She'll probably run out of money shortly."

Brett opened the fridge door and took stock. "I see sister Liz has been by." There were containers of homemade soup in the fridge.

Paddy grunted. "I'm getting mighty tired of that soup."

"Well, why not freeze one and eat the other. I can get you some different stuff." He turned from the refrigerator. "I just had a call from Uncle Lionel. I gather he's been talking to you."

"Yeah, did he ask if Randy could stay with you?"

"Yes, thanks a lot. Why can't he stay with you, you're his uncle. He could be helpful and he cooks."

"Yeah, but I'm waiting for Dancy to come back. She didn't like it when you were here."

Uneasily, the men eyed each other then let the topic drop. "Well, I think I've talked Uncle Lionel into coming down to see you this weekend."

"What?" Paddy stopped with the toast halfway to his mouth. "What for?"

"Because he's your brother, Dad. What do you think?

When's the last time you saw him?"

"I don't know." He munched thoughtfully. "A year, maybe."

"Yeah, you aren't very well and he sounds like hell. His emphysema must be worse because he was wheezing away on the phone. No need to wait till he keels over. And Randy's coming down anyway."

Paddy nodded. "Okay. Actually it'll be good to see him. Betty, not so much."

"Come on, Aunt Betty's a nice lady. She's cared for him for years. And done a fine job of it."

Paddy grunted.

Brett decided to take that as agreement.

"Listen, do you want to come over to the office this afternoon? We have a beer or a soda at the end of work some Thursdays. I use the time to get everyone caught up on what's happening in the company and what's coming down the pipe."

Paddy bit into the toast and chewed slowly. "Maybe next time. How's it going over there?" Sitting at the kitchen table, Brett filled him in on their progress.

"I've been out to Sooke to see Clyde Mikkleson's big project." He thought about the road north of Sooke, winding and narrow, with cement curbs placed over the crumbling edge of the pavement. There was sheer cliff down one side and steep treed bank up the other. Add world class rainfall and there wasn't much that couldn't go wrong out there. It was a challenge for any trucker.

"A hundred and thirty-two homes," he said now, "each on a half-acre, plus services. So about eighty acres in total. The logging roads are in fair shape, they say the dispatch operator is good and can handle the traffic, so wait time shouldn't be too bad.

"Yeah," Paddy chewed his last bite of toast. "They got a deal on the land from a logging company. Mikkleson is friends with the CEO of Timber North."

Brett nodded. "They say they'll get access off Clutesi Road

as soon as the permits are issued."

Paddy shook his head. "Nope. That won't happen, not for the gravel and sand components."

"Yeah, that's what I thought. So the wait time is the main issue. I'll make sure it's covered." Brett ran his thumbnail along the edge of the table, then levelled a look at his father. "What I still don't understand is why you bought three new trucks. I could see one."

Paddy shrugged and sipped his coffee. "Dancy wanted me to have a bigger, fancier company. She wanted to brag about the big trucks, the company was a little small for her taste."

Brett stared. "You're joking. For Dancy?" He shook his head, then grinned at his father. "The things we'll do for women. We never outgrow that, huh? I'm disillusioned."

Paddy shoved his son's elbow off the table with a weak jab. "You're never too old to cater to pussy. Remember that."

"Yeah, well. Let's hope."

~ ~ ~

Katy yawned and shuffled down the hall to the kitchen. Her roommate Sid sat at the table doing a crossword and drinking a cup of tea. "Hi, Katy. How are you this morning?"

"Good." She yawned again. "What are you doing home? Don't you work Saturdays?"

"I got a day off."

"A day off? Who ever heard of such a thing?" She plugged the kettle in and dug a grapefruit out of her drawer in the fridge.

Sid laughed. "Yeah, for once. I heard you have a new friend."

Katy gave a start of surprise. "I do?"

"Don't you know? Sherry said he was so good looking she thought she'd drop her drawers on the spot."

"Oh, Brett. He stopped by to give me a lift yesterday morning. My car needed gas. Yeah, he is good looking. But he's not my special friend or anything. He's my new boss."

"How's the job going?"

"Pretty well. I've learned how to use the dispatch, it's a

radio system to communicate with the drivers. And I've started doing the company books. They've never been done, can you imagine? The owner just took a stack of paper in a box to his accountant at the end of the year. But now the owner's had a heart attack and that's his son who's come to run the company. Trying to put a set of books together is a challenge. I've been referring to my textbooks, I just don't let anyone catch me."

"So, you're telling all the drivers where to go and what to do on the dispatch system?"

Katy laughed. "Well, kind of. Mostly they already know. But during the day things change." She finished dissecting her grapefruit and plopped down at the table beside her friend.

"What's he like?" Sid raised her brows suggestively.

She giggled. "I do seem to recall that Sherry tried to climb all over him." Just then Sherry's door opened and their heads turned in unison to watch her walk into the bathroom. Katy swivelled back to face her friend.

"He's really tall and you know I don't like big guys. They're intimidating. Anyway, he's a hockey player, so that probably explains all the muscle."

"A hockey player? Hang on." Sid ran from the room and returned a moment later with a coloured brochure in her hand. She folded back the cover.

"Here he is." The page showed a full length photo of Brett Rome in uniform, hockey stick in hand. Katy couldn't see his face because of the helmet and shield but she recognized that stance. "Yeah, that's him."

"Good God, Katy. You don't like him?" Sid was positively flabbergasted.

"No, I didn't say that. I do like him. He's been very nice to me. I was just saying he makes me nervous."

Sid laughed. "Look at this." There was another picture, head shots of all the players. "You don't find this face attractive?" They both stared at the large hooded eyes, straight blunt nose and full lips emphasized by a set of dimples in his cheeks. His hair was a shade of dark tawny blonde, his face arresting and handsome, determined.

"Yeah, I do. He's good looking. But he's… I don't know. Very muscular, I guess."

"I'll bet. He'd make me nervous too. No wonder Sherry was all over him."

Katy smiled. "Yeah, she was. She wanted us to meet her and Pat at a nightclub later. But I came home instead, had a big weekend ahead."

"Yeah, you always do. Listen, Mike likes hockey and he has season's tickets to the Victoria games. Why don't you come with us one night? You can watch your boss get beaten up out there on the ice."

Katy laughed. "That would be fun. Dad and I used to watch hockey a lot. I'd love that."

"Okay, it's a date. I'll find out when the next at-home game is that's not on the weekend. That way you can fit it in around your work schedule." Sid grinned impishly at her. "By the way, how's your Dad?"

"Good. I'll see him tomorrow. We're going to church then lunch at his place before I go to the hotel."

"Say hi for me."

~~~

Brett pulled his house key from the lock and pushed the door open. The smell hit him right off. Burned something. He threw mail on the hall table and went into the kitchen.

Their toaster didn't work and Randy had obviously been making toast in the oven. Instead of cleaning up, he'd thrown it into the sink. Randy himself was nowhere to be seen but he followed a trail of towels and underwear to his bedroom door.

"Randy, you in there?" He heard a groan and pushed the door open. Chaos, everywhere he looked. What the fuck?

"Randy, you've only been here a week. What the hell are you doing?" He glanced over at the bed to see the naked muscular chest of his younger cousin emerge from a nest of bedding.

"What?" Randy rubbed his eyes and ran his hands back

through his hair. "What's up?"

"Not much. You can't leave a mess like this in the house. If you cook, you clean. Surely they taught you that in cooking school."

Randy laughed, then coughed. "Well, now I cook but I don't have to clean. Someone else does that."

"Here you have to. Come on man. I don't want to come home to a mess like this. Your clothes are in the hall and your burned toast is stinking up the kitchen. Clean it up." He shut the door and shook his head. Aunt Ray was right, this was a family trap.

He found some dinner and changed for hockey practice. Afterward he invited Jerome and another team member, Hart Tremblay back to the house with a case of beer and a pack of cards. Hart brought a fourth guy for poker.

Brett walked around the flat and cursed under his breath. The toast had been cleaned up in the kitchen but different clothes now decorated the hallway floor. He caught them with the toe of his shoe and shot them into Randy's cluttered room, slamming the door. Then he swished the whiskers from the bathroom sink and dug around for a new roll of toilet paper.

This was not going to work out. He'd have a serious talk with junior when he had a chance.

The next morning he sat in the office arguing with Paddy on the phone. "Dad, I'm totally serious. If you're going to write cheques on the company account, you have to let me know."

Brett listened for a minute, his fingers drumming on the desk. "You're still getting your wage, Dad. It's hard enough trying to sort out this situation without surprises coming at me. What do I tell the banker when the truck payments aren't covered? You either have to work with me or find someone else to clear this up."

He paused. "No, I'm not trying to put pressure on you. Have you got any more company cheques at home? Well, I'm coming to get them. Seriously, Dad, this can't happen. We're walking too close to the edge as it is."

Brett put down the phone and banged his fist on the desk. He felt like banging his head. It was only five thousand dollars, but when things were this tight, it might as well be fifty thousand.

Paddy's credit card statement had come in as well, and it was higher than it had been since before the heart attack. Was Dancy back, or was his old man feeling well enough to go out drinking again? If so, he was buying for the crowd.

Brett put in a call to Lindquist at the bank. The truck loan payments would be late, he informed him. Because of Paddy not being here, things were still in a bit of an uproar. They were doing the best they could, etcetera. He felt like a liar, but got agreement to delay the payment by a week. He hung up.

"Katy," he called. She poked her head in and smiled. He immediately felt himself relax.

"Have you got Paddy's credit card bill? Make the minimum payment."

"You told me to keep it paid in full."

"I know, but things have changed. Without wrestling it out of Dad's girlfriend's grimy paws, the only way to keep the charges under control is to keep it high."

"Okay." She saluted.

She collected invoices owed to them faster than Paddy used to and Brett was hopeful they could dig themselves out of this quagmire. He relaxed back in his chair.

Now if he could just get Katy to go out with him. He knew she was more comfortable around him now but he wanted more. He wanted to hold her close, inhale her scent. He felt a rising interest below his belt and decided he'd better think of something else.

Leaning forward he put in a call to Claude Mikkleson. He needed more information before he sent in his bid on the Sooke project.

That afternoon Brett took the steps to the office two at a time. "Katy, there should be a delivery later today, a new file cabinet."

She frowned. "We already have one."

"I know, but this one has a lock on it. We can put the chequebook and bank statements under lock and key."

"Okay. Wow, you look great."

Brett stopped his progress across the office floor and turned to face her at the dispatch desk. "That's a nice suit," she added, her eyes wide.

He gave a little bow. "I'm glad you like it. Bank day today. What have we got that's going to make Lindquist happy?"

She handed him the day's schedule. "It's jammed with jobs. The trucks have been running busy. The drivers, I should say. We still have a couple of trucks that could work, I guess."

Brett examined the paperwork. "Is Frank out for the day?"

"Yes, he's driving No. 2."

"I could drive this afternoon, as soon as I'm finished with the banker. That will put another few loads on the bottom line."

Katherine bent over the schedule and pencilled in truck No. 5 for Brett, four loads of top soil.

"Top soil?"

"That's what we've got." She pressed her lips together. "And the others have already been given their assignments."

Brett frowned. "Topsoil's dirty."

She snickered. "Topsoil's dirt."

He grinned. "Want to go out to dinner tonight? I can put my nice suit back on for you."

Her smile dimmed visibly. "I don't know."

"Come on. I won't keep you out late. I have a hockey practice at ten," he wheedled.

"I'm not really dressed for it, I'd have to go home and…"

"That's okay. You leave here at four, I'll pick you up at six thirty. Okay? Nothing fancy."

"Well, it is a nice suit. I guess I could." She turned back to dispatch and Brett hesitated. Had she just agreed to go with him?

"So that's a "yes"? Good. I'll make a reservation." He

walked into his office. That was a "yes"! He'd given up hope. Now what? He'd made arrangements to meet Jerome for dinner and go to practice with him. Heart beating faster, he grabbed his phone.

CHAPTER EIGHT

Katy left right on the button at four o'clock. She needed to shampoo her hair and paint her nails. What outfit would she wear? She hardly dated.

On the other hand, this wasn't a real date. This was a quick dinner with Brett before he went to hockey practice. She wouldn't worry about her nails.

She was almost ready when the doorbell sounded. Quickly she grabbed her jacket. Coming down the hallway she heard Sherry chatting enthusiastically in the living room and slowed for a moment to listen. It was always bad news when Sherry got involved.

"… so we sent a note in for you but I guess you didn't see it. Maybe we can arrange to get together after a game and go out for a drink. You could always bring a friend, Pat and I would both be there."

Brett smiled over Sherry's head as he spied Katy in the doorway and put out his hand for her.

"Uh, usually I'm pretty busy after the games, Sherry," he said, turning back to her. "We have a wrap-up afterward going over the plays, not really free to head out. But thanks anyway."

"Bye, Sherry," Katy waved as they went out the door, feeling some tension relax in the pit of her stomach. She was glad Brett was too busy to go out with Sherry. The sudden thought of that possibility had made her distinctly uncomfortable. "Tell Sid I'll see her tomorrow. I left her a note."

She started down the steps as Brett closed the door.

"Hey, hold on." He caught up with her and took her elbow. "You have to give me a chance here. I'm not that quick." He leaned down to open the door of the Corvette. Once they were both seated, he started the engine and let it idle for a minute.

"I have reservations at Fireside Bistro but we can go somewhere else if you like. The food there is good as well as pretty fast."

Katy hummed with the sound of the engine and gave a delighted grin. "Fireside Bistro sounds great. I like it there."

"Okay." He revved the engine and she gave a little shiver of anticipation.

"You like the sound of that, don't you?"

She laughed as they took off down the street.

~~~

The restaurant was busy and their table had been reserved beside the cold fireplace filled with flowers overlooking a tall narrow window into the garden at the side of the building. The muted clatter of knives and forks, the low conversation of diners blended with the blues music played by a duet set up on a low platform in the corner.

Brett watched Katy dissect her salmon. She took a tiny piece of it and put it in her mouth. Then she took a tiny bite of the rice pilaff, a minute piece of grilled asparagus. These were child sized bites. His own plate was nearly empty. Her hands appeared too small to handle the heavy restaurant cutlery. She struck him as fragile, almost defenceless and he wanted to be the one to defend her.

He chuckled at her stories of Frank's idea for rotating the old trucks, Pete's penchant for correcting grammar and spelling mistakes on the daily sheets, Wilf's need to phone in to the office hourly. She was observant of the drivers yet forgiving, clever yet kind hearted.

"What about the perfume?"

"What perfume?" she asked, tilting her head to the side.

"Your perfume."

"Pardon?"

"Didn't you notice? Yesterday, every one of them made a remark at the end of the shift. Boy, sure smells good in here. Didn't used to smell like this, stuff like that. I noticed it at lunchtime, too."

Her cheeks went pink. "I didn't hear that. I guess I was busy."

He laughed. "You must have been. Then there was the day you wore those little white sandals. I must have heard ten remarks about those sandals."

She blushed now, using her napkin to wipe her mouth as she glanced away and focussed on the fireplace.

"I'm not embarrassing you, am I? You know they're going to notice things. There's never been a woman working in a trucking company in the history of the city. I'm amazed the men haven't protested more than they have."

"Seriously? No women at all?"

"Maybe one. And she was fifty with a heavier beard than I have."

Katy burst out laughing.

He loved her laugh and smiled ruefully. "There were some husband and wife trucking teams who did just fine," he finally admitted, "and women drivers as well."

"One thing I can't figure out," she said.

"What's that?"

"I've done month-end statements for the whole year now but I can't find an investment that was made in Rome Trucking by a friend of mine. I asked about it the first day I came in but it got lost in the shuffle when you hired me."

"What friend?" Brett bristled, he couldn't help it. "What investment? I don't remember you talking about it that first day."

"If you remember what that day was like. You had this

huge black eye and a giant cut with about a dozen stitches across your eyebrow."

"I did not!" His chest shook with laughter. "A dozen stitches? There might have been three or four. And a black eye is a black eye. They don't get any bigger or smaller." He self-consciously rubbed his eyebrow where the pink scar was still visible.

She grinned cheekily. "You know what I mean."

"Okay, so I looked a little alarming."

"Yes, and you hired me without even interviewing me, let alone phoning my references."

"Yeah, I was surprised myself. That was Frank's doing. So, what investment are we talking about here, who is the friend?" He hoped his voice didn't betray his rising discomfort.

"My friend, Bruno Morelli. He raised money to invest in Rome Trucking. He'd been talking to the owner, and I assume that was Paddy. Bruno offered him a hundred thousand dollars in exchange for shares. But I don't see any record of it. I can't find the deposit in the bank."

Brett shook his head. "I've never heard of anything like that. I doubt if it happened. Dad wouldn't want to dilute the shareholdings for a hundred thousand dollars. He's got a line of credit a lot bigger than that."

"Yes, I know that now. It's just that Bruno was going to deposit it with Rome Trucking. I saw him the day before he met with the owner."

"When was that, do you remember?"

Katy dug out her phone and paged through the calendar. When she named the date, Brett shook his head emphatically.

"Dad had his heart attack. There was no such meeting. Frank and I have been managing things since then. What's your interest in this?"

Her eyes shifted toward the fireplace again.

"Is Morelli a boyfriend or something?" She didn't answer, moving a piece of red pepper around the plate with her fork. He waited, a tight feeling squeezing his chest.

Finally she said, "I invested in that fund. And if it didn't go to Paddy I'd like to find out what happened to it, that's all."

Brett felt the muscles in his chest start to relax. "What does Morelli say?"

She glanced at him and then quickly away. "I haven't spoken to him in a while. I'm not sure what he'd say."

"He's not answering his phone?"

She shook her head. "No. Anyway, I just wondered if you knew anything about it."

Brett reached forward and took her hand, massaging the fingers clenched tightly around the handle of the fork. "I'll ask Dad about it. Maybe he knows what happened."

Her face brightened for a minute. "Okay, thank you."

"You look beautiful tonight, Katy."

Disbelief flashed across her face.

"You always look great, but that dress is really nice. I like your hair down like that."

She seemed confused for a second, then smiled.

"Would you like some dessert?"

"No, thanks. You don't have time anyway. We should get back."

Brett walked her to her door and took her hand before she could step inside. "Wait a minute, Katy. I just want to say I enjoyed dinner very much. You've turned me down so many times that I began to think I'd lost my touch."

"So many times?" She giggled. "You've only asked me a couple of times, and then only because it was convenient. We don't date."

"No?" He pulled her closer and held her loosely in his arms. She felt wonderful against him and she smelled even better. He lowered his head to rub his cheek against her hair. "Well, it was nice, anyway. Can we do it again?"

Her smile was tentative as she pulled back. "Yes, it was nice. Do you have time to come in?"

"No, I'd better get going for practice. Besides, Sherry's in there."

Katy burst out laughing then quickly sobered. "She likes you, Brett. You'd make her day if you answered one of her notes after a hockey game."

Brett shuddered dramatically. "Are you trying to set me up with your roommate?"

"Well," she commented, her voice lower. "I don't think she's very nice. I hate to say it, but you should be careful."

Oh, man. Here she was watching out for his interests. He couldn't stand it. "Come here, Katy."

He tugged her up against him. "I know who I want to date, and it isn't Sherry." He laid his mouth over hers. Immediately he had the strongest feeling of recognition. This is how he'd known it would be. She tasted like heaven, she tasted like home. She tasted like more.

She hesitated but he pressed further, running his tongue along her bottom lip. She sighed, opened her mouth and he took full advantage. She seemed to melt against him, turning liquid at his touch, but only for a moment. He was just getting comfortable when she began to pull back. He loosened his hold but didn't let her go.

Before she had a chance to bolt, he said, "Thank you for a wonderful dinner." He kissed her temple where the fine hair curled, held her a moment more and released her before she could protest. "I'll see you at work," he said and bounded down the stairs.

Man, he had to tread lightly. She was skittish as a colt. Better not leave an opening for her to turn him down before he even got there. More gentling, he figured.

But he'd gotten somewhere tonight. Her kisses were dynamite. He hoped he could concentrate at practice. He was the new man on the team and he didn't need to look like a moonstruck idiot out there on the ice.

~~~

Brett watched the last pickup leave the lot at the end of the day, then glanced over at the workshop. Gert was still banging away at something but he'd be gone soon. He walked back toward the office. There were a few things he should finish before he left. As he went down the side path he passed the bathroom window and some small movement caught his eye.

He turned his head and there was Katy standing in her skirt and bra, leaning in toward the mirror. There was a warm flash of smooth skin and rosy flesh before he finally jerked his head away, stalled on the walkway. His heart jack hammered in his chest and his breath came fast. He felt like he'd taken a check to the ribs.

Keeping his head averted, he started slowly up the steps. He never imagined someone could see in that washroom window from outside. Good God. Anyone could have caught her there!

He looked back. The window was fairly high, but any tall man could see in. Did the drivers know that? Who was tall enough? Gert for sure, probably Renwick. Maybe even Russell, the bastard.

He'd better get a cover on it, at night it would be even worse. Hell, it would be like watching a movie, looking from the dark into the lighted room. He stood on the top step until he caught his breath, waved to Gert as he left the mechanic's shop for his truck and stepped back into the office.

There was a cake on the table in the kitchen, a bowl and spatula discarded nearby. Curious, he went closer. She'd just iced a cake on a fancy plate. There was a plastic bag on the counter beside it.

"Whoa, who's this for?" he called.

The washroom door snapped open. "Don't touch that!" He saw her tousled hair and one bare shoulder as she leaned out the door. "Leave it alone, I'll be out in a minute."

He grinned as she disappeared behind the door. Damn, his temperature had shot straight up again. The glimpse of bare skin just reinforced the sight he'd caught through the window. This woman was murder on him.

A few minutes later, she reappeared. Her makeup was different and she had on a pretty sweater with pearl beads across the front.

"What's the occasion?"

"I made it for Dad. It's his birthday and he always wants an angel food cake. I'm just going to take it over to him."

"And what's in the bag?"

She smiled. "You've been peeking, haven't you? It's raspberries and whipping cream to go on the cake."

"That's lemon icing, right?"

She frowned at him. "Did you touch the icing?"

He tried to look innocent. "No, I just stuck my finger in the bowl, there's a tiny bit left. Or there was."

She giggled. "You're a big baby." She took her jacket off the hook and shrugged it on. "See you tomorrow." Grabbing her purse, she went over to balance the cake in one hand and grip the bag in the other.

"Here, you need some help." He deftly lifted the cake out of her grasp and headed toward the door. "Come on, I'll carry it." She walked out onto the top step and Brett engaged the alarm, locking the door.

"I'll come with you to your Dad's, okay?"

"What? No, you don't need to do that. I can manage."

"Well, I'll bet you have a present for him, right?" He loved teasing her, she always rose to the bait.

"Yes." Her expression turned mischievous. "I got him an eReader, bought it on sale a few months ago. He's such a geek."

"Whoa, that's a nice gift. Well, you'll need help carrying all this stuff in."

She glowered at him. "I don't need help. I can manage just fine."

"No you can't. Come on, where does he live?"

"Are you wrangling an invitation to some cake? Because if you are…"

Brett grinned. "Of course not. My mother would never forgive me for being so - ungentlemanly. I'm just making sure you can get everything there safely, so I'm going to follow you in my car and help carry the stuff in. Besides, I'd like to meet your father."

Katy eyed him for the longest time. "Well," she finally said reluctantly. "He might enjoy meeting you as well."

He laughed. "Thank you, Katy. That was very generous-hearted," he teased.

Katy's father was a surprise. Younger than Brett had imagined, he was probably in his mid-forties, in very good physical shape for someone who walked with arm crutches. Brett figured he worked out pretty heavily, although his legs appeared to be more wasted than the rest of him.

Les Dalton eyed him carefully when they were introduced and gave him a very firm handshake. Brett knew he was being scrutinized. Well, that was okay. The man cared about his daughter and that ranked well with him.

He'd like to find out the story on his injuries, but more importantly he wanted to get to know him. Les Dalton might be the key to finding a way into Katy's life. He shook his head as he headed out to his car. When had he started thinking like that?

CHAPTER NINE

Next morning the rush was over and Katy was in the office alone when Brett came in.

"Hi there, you're early."

He stopped in front of her desk and leaned a hip against it. "Were you, by any chance, at the game last night?"

Her face lit up. "Yes, I was. It was great. I went with my roommate and her boyfriend. He has tickets for all your Victoria games."

"I thought so." He gave her a measured look.

"You thought so? How would you know I was there?"

"I saw you."

Her mouth opened then closed. "When did you see me? I never saw you anywhere. Well, other than on the ice. It was a great game. I'm sorry you didn't win. And you got banged into the boards so hard! How's your neck? That must have really hurt. But Mike said you guys are used to it, so I thought…"

Brett's dimples were showing deep in his cheeks and Katy had learned that meant he was hanging onto his temper or some emotion. "What is it?" she asked hesitantly.

"You were jumping up and down, yelling." he said.

"Well, I guess. I mean, yes, I was, but…"

"That's why I got hammered into the boards. I thought I

saw you and I just turned my head to check when someone nailed me."

She covered her open mouth with her hand. "That was my fault?" She seemed horrified.

He laughed ruefully. "No, that was my fault. I'm supposed to pay attention to the game, not the fans." He gave her another look. "Why didn't you send a note into the locker room? We could've gone for a drink somewhere."

"Really? But you told Sherry that you don't have time to come out after the game, you have to go over all the plays, and meet with…"

He knocked on the top of her desk to get her attention. "That was Sherry. This is you. Let me know if you're coming and we can do something after." She watched him walk into his office.

"You didn't say how your neck is," she called after him.

"It's good," he shot her a grin.

When Frank returned from a run, Brett emerged from his office. "Frank, are you in for a while?"

"Yeah, the rest of the day."

"Good. Listen, I need you to put some kind of cover over the bathroom window. At least the lower half, so you can't see in from outside."

"Really?" Frank gave him a surprised look. Brett jerked his head toward Katy who was seated at the desk at the other end of the room, and nodded. "Yeah, for privacy."

Frank's gaze shifted to Katy. The back of his neck went red. "Okay, I'll take care of it."

Brett nodded and turned around. "Katy, want to come with me?"

She popped out of her chair. "Where are we going?"

"Just over to see Paddy."

"Oh," she seemed doubtful. "You need me to come with you?"

"Yeah."

She gave him a studied look. "Alright." Grabbing her purse and sweater she walked with him to Paddy's pickup that he drove most days to work. "How come?" she asked as she climbed into the truck.

"How come what?" He stood holding her door.

"How come you need me to come with you?"

"Just because."

"Oh." She seemed to be thinking that through. He hid his smile and slammed the door.

Climbing into the driver's seat, he fired up the engine. "I just get in wrangles with him. We don't always see eye to eye. If there's someone else there he's sometimes a little easier to get along with."

Her eyes widened as she stared at him. "I hadn't noticed."

"Now you're being sarcastic. Well, I guess he was a bit snarky in the office when he came in to visit last time. Let's hope he's in a better mood today. We need to sort out this issue of the truck being impounded and Frank's ticket. It'll be good to have you there."

When they pulled up in front of Paddy's house, Katy burst out laughing. "Is this your family home?"

"Yeah, why?"

"Because I grew up one block over, right down there." She pointed.

"You did? Where?" He put the truck back in gear and moved off down the street. "Down here?"

"Yes, keep going. There, the second house." He stopped in front of a yellow bungalow in the middle of the block and she stared for a minute. "Yes," she said faintly, "right there."

"It looks like a really nice house."

Oh," she smiled at him. "It was. I loved it in this neighbourhood, didn't you? It was a great place to grow up. Lots of kids."

"How come your father moved?"

"Umm." She shook herself. "It was best. It was time I moved out and so he sold it."

Paddy was dozing in his chair when they knocked on the door and walked in. He woke with a start and frowned at Brett. "What are you after?"

"Just come to see what's going on," said Brett. "You remember Katy."

Paddy switched his gaze to her and glared but didn't speak.

Brett waved at the couch. "Have a seat, Katy. Would you like a soda?"

"Yes, please." She smiled at him, that light in her eyes again and he grew warm. She must be a witch, he mused as he pawed through the fridge door. All she had to do was smile and he warmed like melting wax. Her face was so bright and full of joy, he found it hard to look away.

Like today. He didn't really need her with him, he just wanted her here. He found three cans and came back into the living room in time to hear Katy say, "You must be very grateful, Mr. Rome."

"What for?" Paddy barked.

"For your son coming back from Vancouver to run your company for you."

"He didn't have a choice, did he?" he growled.

"Of course he had a choice." She took the can of soda from Brett. "He could have stayed where he was. Your drivers have a choice too. They stay, at least partly out of loyalty to you. You must be very grateful."

He stared at her and she held his gaze. Finally he gave a reluctant grunt. "Yeah, I'm grateful. Things would have fallen apart if he hadn't come."

"You're right. You must have been a good father, for him to be willing to do that for you." She took a sip of her soda.

Both men stared at her for a moment then looked warily at each other. Brett popped a can and handed it to his father. He cleared his throat. "The cops will release the truck tomorrow."

Frank had been arrested for going through a yellow light the day before. When they pulled him over and searched the truck, the police found cannabis in the pocket behind the driver's seat and immediately impounded the truck along with the load it still carried. Frank had been furious.

Brett continued. "We searched all the other trucks at Katy's suggestion" He gestured at her with his can. "We didn't find anything else."

"How's Frank?"

"Pretty upset. He keeps talking about if he hadn't gone through that yellow light."

"Everyone goes through yellow lights," Paddy grumbled.

"That's what I told him. And his argument was a good one. Sometimes it's safer to go through than try to stop, especially with a heavy load on like he had. So we're challenging the ticket in court. It'll take some of Frank's time but he wants to keep his record clean."

Paddy nodded. "Yep, a trucker's only as good as his driving record. That had to be Russell's pot."

Brett nodded. "That's what I think. Russ is too stupid for words sometimes. It's a good thing he's off with a broken leg."

Paddy laughed, "Or you'd break his other one, right?" He took a sip of his drink and gazed at Katy with speculation.

Brett hastily jumped in to prevent some kind of awkward question from his father. "Katy raised an issue, Dad. She has a friend named Bruno… uh…" He looked at her for help.

"Morelli," she said. "Bruno Morelli."

"Yeah, so?"

"Well, he told her he was going to invest some money in Rome Trucking, a hundred thousand dollars. Have you been talking to anyone about investing in the company, or even buying shares?"

"Don't be stupid, Brett," Paddy scoffed. "A hundred thousand dollars wouldn't touch the debt or make a dent in the line of credit. And shares of the company? Not on your life."

Katy cheeks were pink. "I just thought I'd ask."

"Okay. You asked. So, what do you think of the trucking industry?"

"Oh, I love it," she exclaimed. "Everyone has treated me very well. While I'm here, can I get credit card receipts from you? We don't have many and you're going to need them for the accountant at the end of the year."

Paddy gave her a flinty-eyed glare then jerked his head toward the bedroom. "Go look on the top of my dresser. What I have will be there."

Paddy gave a grimace as she left the room. "She's a bulldog, is she? She won't be happy till she gets all the receipts. Well, good luck with that. Dancy has most of them."

Brett laughed quietly. "She's not a bulldog but she does try to do things right. She's been a real asset."

"Has she? Does that mean you're screwing her?"

Brett flushed darkly. "Will you for once speak with respect about an employee? And keep your voice down." His own voice was strained. "No, for your information I'm not sleeping with her. She's doing a great job, although I'm sure you find that hard to believe."

Brett stalked into the bedroom, anger seething under his ribs. "Did you find anything?" His throat felt so tight he could barely get the words out.

Standing very still by the dresser, she slowly turned her head toward him. "I couldn't help but hear what he said," she murmured softly. At the suddenly stricken look on his face, she quickly added, "But he's your father, don't leave here angry. I think he's forgotten how to behave. Maybe you can remind him."

He stared wordlessly down at her for a moment, then reached out and pulled her against him, burying his face in her hair and wrapping his arms tightly around her waist. "I don't know if I can," he muttered. "He doesn't seem to listen."

"He does." She rubbed his back. "He's hurting too." She hugged him tight for a minute. It felt so good that when she stepped back a pace he could barely let her go.

"Anyway," she turned to the dresser. "I've found some receipts. I guess that's a start. If he gets audited it will be his problem, after all."

CHAPTER TEN

The next day Katy listened to her cell phone voicemail, then eyed Frank. "I thought you were driving this afternoon, Frank."

He held up a finger while he answered a call. When he flicked the dispatch switch, he turned to her. "I was going to but Brett called and said he needed me in here. He has to take you to some meeting."

Katy cheeks went a dull red. "So he says," she muttered. Pushing the delete button to erase the message she clicked her phone off. It embarrassed her to be at Brett's beck and call. She always felt off kilter. Her stress level seemed to escalate when she spent time with him. He was her boss, yet she was attracted to him. She didn't know how to handle it. Her friend Sid would advise her to just relax and enjoy it. She smiled to herself. Sid was all talk and no action, she was just as up tight as Katy herself.

The papers in front of her were starting to blur. Balancing month-end was driving her crazy. Pushing them aside she pulled the file for the Claude Mikkleson job out of her drawer. Frank was here to catch the dispatch calls so it was the perfect time to try to organize the work.

As she laid out the file, she thought of the phone call she'd made first thing this morning to Bruno. He'd answered on the first ring. "Bruno, I need you to talk to me," she started.

"I can't talk now." His voice was muffled as if his nose was blocked. "I'm busy, Katy. And I already said I'll call you when I have some news."

"I know that, but just listen. You made an appointment with me to meet at the Lieutenant Governor's House and you didn't show."

There was a long silence. "What do you mean I didn't show? You weren't there."

Katy shook her head. "I was there. I mean, I was there for a while. Did you come?"

Bruno sniffled into the phone. "You didn't show, Katy. I did my part."

She closed her eyes. Did Bruno arrive at the Rockland address after she left? Gripping the phone tighter she talked into the silence. "Bruno, I've talked to Mr Rome at Rome Trucking and he said you didn't invest with him. If you didn't invest in his company, where's my money? I need to know." Maybe she sounded slightly breathless and desperate, but that's how she felt.

There was a pause then Bruno said, "Katy, if you mess with this you'll be in trouble. Stay away from Mr. Rome. I mean it. There'll be repercussions."

"It sounds like you're threatening me." Her heart stopped beating at his tone, and her voice cracked.

"Katy, I'm telling you as clearly as I can. Don't get in the way. Don't step into the middle of this. Do you understand? You'll get hurt." The phone went dead in her hand.

Bruno had sounded scared, which made her even more frightened. She'd never been afraid of Bruno. He wasn't big and dominating. He didn't loom, or push his weight around. But this morning he'd had a steely note to his voice that she'd never heard before.

And she still had the scabs on her hands and knees from her encounter with the car that afternoon. What had Bruno done? She couldn't believe he was the driver of that car. Because if she believed that…

"What's that you've got there?" She jumped and turned to see Frank leaning over her shoulder.

"Oh… It's the Mikkleson file. Did you say those two owner-operators were committed to working on that job?"

Frank scanned the column in front of her. "One is, Hans Marshall. He's a good guy. The truck's a bit older, kind of like ours and he's reliable. The other one is still thinking about it, he might have another job. We should probably start searching for someone else."

"What do you think if they work out at Sooke? It's really easy to organize, simply pick up and deliver. That way our guys will be doing the other jobs that require shifting around."

Frank patted her shoulder. "That's probably a good idea. So we definitely need another truck and driver. Let me see what I can do."

"Okay. What if we put Buster out there too? He's really cranky when his jobs get changed around during the day. It might suit him better having a steady day to day project."

Frank grinned to himself. Buster hadn't been cranky before she arrived. He objected to having a woman give him orders. "Sure, that makes sense," Frank said. "Serve him right for being so irritable."

Katy laughed up at him. "Yeah, absolutely. Who else?"

Frank bent over the roster. "Don't forget Gert is getting No. 4 running, which means we can use another casual driver. Russell isn't ready to come back, with that leg."

They were still puzzling over the file when Brett took the steps two at a time and walked through the open door. He slapped his hand on the desk. "Thanks for holding the fort, Frank. Katy, are you ready? We don't want to be late."

Her mouth set but she stood and grabbed her purse. "How long will we be?"

He shrugged. "A couple of hours. Frank, we should be back before two."

Frank nodded and answered a call on dispatch as Katy took her suit jacket and shrugged into it.

~ ~ ~

Brett drove straight to Swan Lake and pulled into the parking lot. Katy stared around and her head swivelled back to eye him. "Where are we?"

"This is Swan Lake Park."

"I know its Swan Lake Park. What are we doing here?" She turned back to examine the view of the little lake. Brett unclipped his seatbelt and stepped out of the car. He opened her door and offered his hand. Hesitantly she put her fingers in his, he tugged and she stepped cautiously out of the Corvette. "Why are we here?" she asked.

Closing the door behind her, he gritted his teeth. She couldn't be dragging her high heels any harder if she tried. "Because we're going to eat lunch here." He opened the trunk with more force than was necessary and pulled out a food hamper and blanket.

Her jaw snapped shut. "Lunch?"

"Lunch. It's lunch time. We're going to eat it here." She looked down at her suit and heels.

"It's okay," he assured her. "There's a paved trail and a nice grassy patch. We won't have to go far." She narrowed her eyes against the sun as she gazed up at him. He held his arm out and slowly she reached forward and put her fingers hesitantly in the crook of his arm.

He felt a zap as her hand made contact. He tried not to show his reaction but he knew he had it bad. She just touched him and he reacted like a kid with his first girlfriend. His cheeks flushed and he did his best to ignore it.

"This way." He led her toward the path and along the shore of Swan Lake. The birds sang in the trees, the ducks twittered in the sedge grass at the edge of the water. He felt her begin to relax and tugged his arm closer to his side to anchor her hand against his ribs. By the time they reached the spot he'd chosen, her face had softened and she watched the water birds with undisguised interest.

Spreading the blanket beneath a big old twisted Garry oak he set the hamper down in the shade. Katy stood in a moment of apparent indecision, then sighed, slipped her heels off and sat on the blanket, her legs to the side. She motioned to the hamper. "What's for lunch?"

Brett grinned. "Hungry, are you?" He wasn't sure what was in there, he'd ordered it from a local deli, but pulled out salad, sandwiches and fruit, chocolate squares. There were small bowls, plastic utensils.

"When I was a kid," he said as he pried the lid off the salad, "we used to come here on our bikes. My friend Robbie and I. We'd be gone all day. Mum made us a sandwich to put in our backpacks and we just took off. It's such a shallow lake that I guess she didn't worry we'd drown.

"But the birds are phenomenal. Do you know how many types of ducks come here? Mum found us an old bird book and we'd make a note of each type we saw. There must have been twelve or fifteen different varieties."

Katy fished an olive out of her salad and put it carefully between her teeth. Brett watched it disappear and had to look away. She didn't try to attract him but apparently all she had to do was breathe. "Anyway," he continued, "we spent lots of time here. The swans are huge, especially to a small boy."

"Were you ever small?" she asked.

Brett glanced at her sideways. "What do you mean?"

"Well, you're quite large. I don't know many men as big as you. Were you always big for your age or just when you grew up?"

He frowned. "I'm no bigger than the average guy. I was kind of typical as a kid, I think. Robbie was bigger than me one summer but I caught up the next year." Watching her carefully, he wondered where this was going but she turned her head to gaze at the lake.

"Have you been here before?" he prodded.

She nodded. "Mmm hmm. My mother brought me here a few times when I was small."

"How old?" He grabbed a sandwich.

"Six and a half."

"Six and a half? That's pretty specific. How can you be so

sure?" he teased. But her expression was sober when she turned her face back to him.

"Because she left right after."

He paused, the sandwich halfway to his mouth. He lowered his hand. "What do you mean, she left?"

"Oh, it doesn't matter." She fiddled with the cucumber in her dish and tried to spear a piece of tomato with her plastic fork.

"No," he stilled her hand. "Tell me."

She pierced him with her clear-eyed gaze. "She left. One day I came home from school and she was gone."

He stalled for a second. "There was no one there to take care of you?"

"The neighbour lady was there. She'd waited for me at our house and took me over to her place until Dad got home. But Mum never came back."

"Did she disappear? I mean was she kidnapped, or something?"

She choked out a laugh.

Brett shook his head. "Well, how do you know she wasn't captured by someone?"

"I guess she left a note for Dad. I didn't see it. But he heard from her a couple of times after, so I gather she left under her own volition."

"Volition, huh?" He pondered that as he watched a pair of Canada geese herd six or seven gawky goslings out of the grass and down to the water. "I can't imagine what that would be like." He thought of how it had been for him, with a father who didn't seem to care a whole lot about his family. But to be just abandoned…

He caught the glint of moisture in her eyes and laid his sandwich on the blanket. "Ah Katy, come here." Shifting closer he pulled her against his side with both arms. He just sat there holding her, inhaling the faint perfume that rose from her hair. She made a muffled sound into his shirt. "What?" He craned his neck to see into her face.

"I don't know how we got onto that. I didn't mean to ruin

lunch."

Brett just tugged her back against his chest. "You didn't ruin it. I didn't know that about you and now I do. I feel privileged to know you better, Katy."

He felt some of the tension leave her and slowly he pressed her nearer to his side. This was not how he imagined lunch going but he welcomed it with his whole heart. To have her in his arms, even like this to give her comfort, was amazing.

Pulling her back against the wall of his chest, he dragged some of the food forward. She ended up leaning against him as if he were a tree trunk while she ate her salad and a piece of sandwich. There was a bottle of light wine in the hamper and he poured them each a glass, unwrapped the chocolate squares.

"So who took care of you?"

"Well," she licked her finger slowly and Brett felt his whole body respond. He shifted uncomfortably. "The neighbour lady I just mentioned, Mrs. Hannam, took me after school. She was really nice and used to make dinners for us sometimes.

"Dad had his accident before Mum left, so he went every day to rehab and then his job with the Navy. He was a landlubber after that, he said, because of the injury. So it was easier than it might have been if he was a single parent and still going to sea."

"How did he injure himself?"

"Oh, he always explained that the ship took a sharp left turn. You see, the captain is supposed to sound an alarm when he is about to change direction, and he failed to do that. So Dad didn't know it was coming. He was thrown across the engine room and hit his back on some equipment."

"That's a serious injury."

"Yes. They've looked after him well. In those days he was home by four-thirty or five every day. As I got older, I was able to come home on my own."

"A latch-key kid."

She paused a second. "That's what they called it. There weren't many of us then. It meant you couldn't have a friend over because parents wouldn't let their kids go to a house without an adult there. Not until I was older anyway."

"You've got a good dad."

She nodded, her hair rubbing his chin. "Yeah, I do."

Brett let his chest expand against her back and watched the side of her cheek as she ate. "He asked me to come out and visit him."

"He did?" She turned her head to squint up at him. "When?"

"When I helped bring his birthday cake over, remember?"

"Oh. You mean the time you invited yourself along."

He laughed silently at her sarcasm and knew she could feel his chest shaking. "Yeah, that time. That cake was worth inviting myself along for. I wonder if I'll get a cake like that when it's my birthday."

"Depends," she said and took a sip of wine.

He laughed again, out loud this time. "On what?"

"I haven't decided."

He smiled and lowered his face into the curls at her temple, took a deep breath. He wanted to lay down with her on the blanket, just hold her close, cradle her in his arms. He ached with need for her. He breathed her in again and eased back. She was so skittish and this was going well. He wouldn't do anything to jeopardize it.

"Look, a hummingbird." They watched it hover in the air above a patch of yarrow, going flower to tiny yellow flower with its long thin beak probing the depths. Its throat glittered ruby red and green feathers shone on its back.

"Oh," she breathed, "they're so beautiful." He realized he watched her more than he watched the birds. Time to get back, before he forgot himself and lost what little ground he'd gained.

Katy helped him pack the lunch away, pushing the cork back into the bottle. "This was very nice, Brett. You could have just asked me if I wanted to have a picnic lunch."

"Really? You would have said yes?"

She blushed and glanced away. "Well..."

"Mmm, that's what I thought. I had to pull rank to get co-operation from a reluctant employee."

Smiling, she began to gather the picnic things together. "It was nice. The picnic, I mean. I haven't been here in a long time. It was good to see the park again but I'd better get back to work."

"Maybe we could do this again?" He gave her a hopeful look.

She laughed. "Maybe."

He nodded and snapped the hamper closed with a satisfied thud.

CHAPTER ELEVEN

Thursday night at the office had become something of a ritual. Once or twice a month, Brett bought a case of beer and put it in the fridge. The men came in dirty and sweaty. They knocked the dust off their boots, washed their hands under Katy's watchful eye and sat around the kitchen of the old office to talk.

Russ was there tonight and Brett wasn't happy about it. He'd poured a big rum and coke for Katy at the beginning of the evening and Brett was even less pleased, his anger a hard lump in his chest. "No hard liquor, Russ. I mean it. This is a driver's thing and we all have to get home afterward. One or two beers, that's all."

The little bastard denied any knowledge of the cannabis in the cubby of truck No. 11. "No way, Brett. I wouldn't do that. My driver's licence is as valuable as the next guy's."

Brett glared at him. "No one else drove that truck, Russ. I'm having a hard time believing you."

He managed to appear mightily offended. "Paddy wouldn't doubt my word," he boasted loudly, looking around for support from the other truckers.

"Paddy was the first one to suggest you put it there. You jeopardized everyone's job and the future of the business. I'm trying to imagine why I'd take you back on as a driver when your leg is healed." He felt an irrational anger churn in his gut. *I don't need this right now.*

"You bastard! It won't be your decision. Your father was a better manager than you'll ever be!" Russ leaped up, stumbling on his leg cast. The other men grabbed him and threw him back into the chair.

"Leave it alone, Russ," Frank barked, leaning over him and waving his cold cigar. "Sit down and shut up."

Rage simmered in the air. The men knew they were working with a delicate and unstable situation in the company. They didn't need this guy throwing his weight around and tipping things out of balance. Making an effort to move on to other topics, Brett ignored him as Russ glowered around the room.

Katy had brought chips and salsa, which were soon gone. The conversation ranged mostly around the new contract he'd finally landed that week with Claude Mikkleson. The drivers talked about which trucks to handle such a big construction site, who should drive, what the conditions would be like on logging roads if it rained heavily, which it often did in Sooke.

Now that Katy worked here, Brett was much more aware of the physical habits of the drivers. The scratching while they talked, the shifting of body parts provided a constant noisy background to the conversation. Katy usually ignored it, although he'd seen her yank her gaze away to stare out the window or across the room if the crotch adjustments became too obvious.

By the time the beer was gone, most of the drivers had filed out, heading home.

"Come out with me, Katy," Russ pleaded, trying on his most engaging grin. "There's a bar just down the road."

Katy smiled. "No thanks, Russell. Not tonight."

The young driver finally limped out in a huff under Brett's dark glare. Picking up the empty cans he stacked them back in the beer case while Katy rinsed out the coffee cups in the kitchen sink. She was always so willing to help.

"Thanks for that, Katy."

"Oh, you're welcome." She sat down on the couch again, heaving a big sigh, her cheeks bright pink. "I must be tired tonight."

He crossed the room to sit beside her and took her hand in his, stroking the pretty slender fingers. "Tired, huh? Or was it that big rum that Russ poured you?"

She giggled and leaned into his side. "Well, it might have been that."

He put his arm around her shoulders and pulled her next to him. She felt so right nestled against his side. "How do you feel? Do you want to go for dinner somewhere now that all the rowdies are gone?"

She looked up at him with big eyes, then simply moved forward and placed her mouth on his. He stilled momentarily, then kissed her back, carefully at first because she'd been so cautious with him. But she was wide open for once and he quickly deepened the kiss. He moved his mouth to her temple where the fine hair curled, then down to her ear lobe. He sucked on her little earring, his need mounting rapidly.

"Katy?"

"Yes?" She kissed his neck.

His temperature shot straight up. Burying his face in her hair, he breathed deeply, taking her in. Her kisses were like a drug. He felt himself losing touch with reality, focussed on her mouth and then her throat. She panted lightly in his ear.

"Brett," she whispered.

"What," he said. "Do you like that?"

"Yes, oh yes." She tugged at the top buttons of his shirt and he felt them give.

The little sweater she had on just melted away under his fingers and he was touching bare skin. "Katy, you aren't drunk are you?" He peered doubtfully into her face.

She laughed lightly. "No, of course not."

"Good."

Her hands fell to her lacy bra and it came off under her fingertips. Oh God. She was beautiful, her little rosy nipples pouting up at him. She fell back against the sofa as his mouth went down to devour her. He heard her panting lightly in his ear.

She tugged, ripping at his shirt.

He reached to help her get it off. Yanking the buttons free, he tore it off his shoulders. Then he pressed against her, skin to skin. Now he wasn't thinking clearly, simply swamped with need, but it didn't matter. He knew where this was going, he hoped he knew where this was going. And he was on fire to get there.

Her hands dropped and she pulled at her skirt, struggling to get it off.

"Katy, just a minute." His head shot up, his gaze taking in the view out the windows with the floodlights bright in the yard. He strode over to the door and locked it, snapping the interior lights off at the same time.

Anyone could look in the windows or come through that door and see them together, see her naked like this. Turning around, his breath stalled as her skirt went sailing through the air and landed on a chair. Oh, man. He grabbed her sandals, unbuckled the straps.

Then he kissed her feet, each little toe. "Oh, baby. You are so beautiful. You've got me all tied up in knots." She sighed and writhed against the ancient upholstery.

"Baby, don't lie there on that old couch against your bare skin. Here." He lifted her, grabbing up his shirt to spread over the cushions. "That's better." She relaxed back with a sigh, her hands coming down to tug at her lace panties.

"My God." He covered her fingers with his to slow her down. "Are you sure? Baby, you have to be sure." Sweat popped out on his forehead. What if she wasn't? It might kill him to stop now.

Her palm caressed his face, her fingers threading back through the hair at the nape of his neck. "I'm sure, Brett."

He hesitated. "Are you on the pill? Because I don't have any..."

"Um hmm. I am. Don't worry."

All hesitation fled. He kissed her again on that lush mouth, along her throat as he eased the lace down her legs. His breath was tight in his chest. He fought the rest of his clothes off and placed himself carefully against her length.

"Oh, baby. You feel like satin." She opened her mouth and he sank into her kiss. Her hands moved on his chest, rubbing the hair and snuggling in the warm hollows under his arms.

He touched all the places he'd thought about, that he'd envisioned. He touched what he'd seen through the bathroom window that day, the brief glimpse of bare skin that had haunted his every waking moment.

When he settled between her legs, she tugged on the small of his back pulling him down against her. She was wet and ready, he couldn't stop himself from pressing into her, all the way in. She stiffened in his arms, made a sharp little cry in her throat and her fingers clenched and tangled in the hair on his chest.

"Easy. Easy, it's okay." Covering her hand with his, he stroked her fingers to ease their grip, then slowly began to move. She was so tight, so hot, and he'd wanted her since the first day he saw her. She'd been out of his reach, all this time. But not out of his sight. That glimpse he'd had of her stayed with him.

Now she was his. He took possession. He took control. Her muscles relaxed around him and his hands soothed her, smoothed her beautiful skin, marked her as his.

He was in a rhythm now. He gazed down at her lying in the shadows of the couch, her face turned slightly away, her hair in tangled curls, hands palms up beside her head on the old sofa cushions. Angling his head, he lowered his mouth to cover hers and she just took him in, her lips soft and clinging. When he felt her stiffen at the start of her climax, it finished him. He pumped himself over the edge, sweat running down his back and pooling at the base of his spine. Burying his face in her throat, he smelled her, tasted her, memorized her.

~~~

Katy stirred and pushed against the weight of his arm lying across her breast. "Brett, maybe we should…"

"No, it's okay baby. It's okay. You're stunning." He ran his hand across the firm swell of her breasts, the smooth skin of her abdomen and down between her legs.

She stiffened.

"Shh, it's alright. You're so silky down here." His fingertip slid over her clitoris, back and forth and then just inside her secret place.

She caught her breath.

"You like that, don't you?"

She watched him, her eyes wide and child-like. Leaning forward he pressed a gentle kiss to her lips, stayed and lingered on her mouth. He squeezed her breast and moved his head to suck that rosy nipple against the roof of his mouth.

The second time was even better, if that were possible. She relaxed, she welcomed him. His fingers were everywhere and he felt hers slide down his back, feeling him, learning him. Her touch nearly undid him. He gritted his teeth, anchoring her to the couch with his palm.

This time would be slower, he thought, not as frenzied, not as rushed. But she rose up, arched up to meet him as she came. Pounding into her, he gripped her hip to keep her from sliding up the couch, pumping his way to completion.

He must have dozed. He became aware that she was pushing on his chest. "Brett, let me up." Slowly he came awake, one hand cupping her breast, his face in her hair.

"Sorry," he laughed low. "I fell asleep for a second."

"I need to use the washroom."

"Yeah, okay." His grip tightened. "Okay," he said again.

She pushed once more and he lifted his arm away. Carefully she sat up. He ran his fingers down her back to her buttocks. What a lovely body she had, so womanly, rounded.

Blindly she felt around in the darkness for her clothes and he reached to hand her the sweater he'd removed earlier.

"Thank you," she whispered. In the dark she tiptoed

across the floor, switched on the light in the bathroom and closed the door. He had a quick glimpse of sleek skin and rounded breasts, then heard water running. The toilet flushed.

The afterglow was so powerful he had to force himself to sit up. In the dark he found his underwear and pants, his belt clanking as he picked them up. He slipped his shorts on. She was prim in some ways, hesitant, and he didn't want to embarrass her. When the door opened, he stood.

"I'll just get cleaned up. I'd take you back to my place and we could shower, but I have my cousin living with me right now and he isn't house broken."

He studied her face, the shadowed eyes. "There's no privacy and it's a disaster. I guess we can't go to your house."

She shook her head, and he smiled. "Yeah, do you want to go get some dinner?"

"Okay," she nodded after a moment.

"I'll only be a minute." He paused to tip her face up. In the light from the bathroom her mouth was rosy and a little swollen, her hair a curly froth of dark brown that she'd tried to tame with her fingers.

"You're so beautiful, Katy. So..." He kissed her before he could finish the thought, a kiss that lingered and deepened. "Okay," he said, his voice strained as he forced himself to lift his head. "I won't be long."

The bathroom smelled like her, like woman. He peered in the mirror and couldn't stop the grin. He'd better wipe that off his face before he went back out there. Washing himself, he dried with the stiff paper towel and put his pants on. He left the belt undone, his shirt had been left spread out on the couch cushions. When he opened the bathroom door, it was still dark in the office.

He groped on the wall for the light switch, flicking it on. Katy was nowhere to be seen. Glancing around, he noticed the front door of the office was open. What the hell?

He strode across the floor to the open doorway. Hearing a car door slam he looked out in time to see the taillights of her little car come on. "Katy?" he called. The car backed up and spun in the gravel as it shot forward and out the gate.

"Katy! Katherine!" he bellowed. "What the fuck!" He watched in astonishment as the tail lights disappeared down the dark road.

Standing there, he stared at the road for a long time as if he expected her to come back. As if she'd just gone to get something and would return any minute. Glaring down at his clenched fists, he slowly straightened his fingers. What the hell had happened?

Brushing a mosquito off his arm he turned back into the office. His shirt was still spread across the cushions of the couch. He grabbed it up in a ball and threw it across the room in a sudden fury. What was that all about? *She'd* come on to *him*. He never would have dared take it that far. Not when she backed up every time he came close. So what had just happened?

His gaze roamed the office, bouncing off the furniture. He had nothing to compare this to. He didn't know what to think or how to handle it. Should he go over to her house, see if she was alright?

Did she have a phone call, telling her about some emergency? That was too ridiculous for words. She'd have told him about it, knocked on the washroom door. No emergency was that immediate, was it?

He touched the cushions where they'd lain. Damp had penetrated his shirt and wet the fabric of the sofa beneath. Picking up his shirt from the floor he held it against his face. It smelled of sex and of her.

Had he been too rough? Had he misjudged her intentions, gone all the way when she just wanted to play a little? That thought made him sick to his stomach. Yet, that couldn't be right. She'd been taking her clothes off as fast as she could.

Buckling his belt, he grabbed a sweatshirt off the hook by the door and tugged it on, jamming his balled up shirt in the pocket. When he drove by her house her car wasn't there so he finally went home.

CHAPTER TWELVE

Consumed with frustration and confusion, Brett got into the office next morning before anyone else. The first thing he did was search the place. A fancy comb that Katy used to hold her hair back had been kicked under the couch. He stuffed it into his pocket.

Hurriedly sponging off the cushion on the couch he flipped it over, wet side down. A pair of lace panties were stuck between the cushions. He held them tightly in his hand, his body flooded with heat. He wanted her back on that couch, ready for him, not running as fast as she could in the other direction.

Frank arrived and they were well into organizing the loads when Katy's car finally pulled into the lot. Brett felt his body go rigid as he watched her climb out of her vehicle and wait to walk in with Pete who had arrived right behind her. His face flushed. She was deliberately avoiding him!

"So, are you ready for the day?" he heard her ask Pete as they came up the steps. Pete smiled and mumbled a reply. She didn't meet his gaze when she stepped into the office, just called out to Frank as she put her purse in the bottom drawer of the desk. "Have you got that under control? I'll get busy on the invoices."

"Sure, go ahead," Frank muttered and pointed at the

schedule. "Right here, Brett," and Brett was pulled reluctantly back into the discussion.

As the drivers picked up their delivery lists, took their keys from the cabinet by the door and filed out, Brett watched Katy. She studiously ignored him, saying goodbye to the men and bending intently over her papers.

Going into his office, he firmly closed the door. If he didn't simmer down, he was going to say something he shouldn't. He was ready to explode, to bellow, to demand answers and he knew he couldn't do any of that. He made a few calls, got his mind on work and cleared his desk.

When he quietly opened the door again, Frank was gone and Katy was on her knees, her head pressed under the end of the couch. Her bottom stuck up in the air and her skirt had pulled up showing an enticing length of thigh.

He stared hungrily as a possessive feeling rose in his chest. *This is mine to look at.* His temperature rose at the same speed as his interest.

He slipped his hand into his pocket, fingering the soft lace of her panties. He knew he should give them back. She'd be worried about where they were, if they might unexpectedly surface when the drivers or some customers were in the office.

"What are you searching for, Katy?" Brett heard the anger in his voice even though he tried to control it.

Jerking back, she hit her head on the arm of the couch and leaped up. "What?"

Her face red, she returned to her desk and sat down, pulling a stack of paperwork toward her, staring at the top sheet for a long time.

Brett grabbed the keys to truck No. 2 and as he walked past her desk he paused, then laid his hand palm down on her papers. She watched, transfixed. When he moved his hand, her hair comb lay there like an offering. Fingers closing over it, she slowly lifted her head, her face pale and set.

Brett eyed her with hope and anger warring in him. "Katy, we have to talk about last night." But she rose and went into the washroom, closing the door.

Watching her retreating back he knew he should have given her the panties. But he was too angry, too confused to be generous. He promised himself he'd be back in time to talk to her before she went home. But after a long day of deliveries he walked into the office to find Frank answering the phones and Katy nowhere in sight.

He bent down to speak in Frank's ear. "Where's Katy?"

Frank covered the receiver. "She had to leave early but I was here, so it was okay." He returned to his conversation.

Brett shoved his hand back in his pocket and felt the lace of the small garment there. This was madness. She was going to have to speak to him sometime. She worked for him, for God's sake!

He immediately cringed. For the first time he had a glimpse of understanding about what it might mean for a woman to have a relationship with someone she worked for. Yes, he'd taken the university courses like everyone else, Human Resources Management, Business Ethics, but it had never really sunk in at a personal level.

Now he understood with a vengeance what happened in this situation. It put a woman in a position of utter powerlessness. He saw that, he understood that. And yet, that's exactly how he felt right now. Powerless.

~~~

The next morning when Sid sleepily made her way down the hall, Katy was in the kitchen munching on a bowl of cereal. Sid stopped in the bathroom, then emerged and headed straight to the coffee pot. It was dry.

She stared at it forlornly. "Why is it always empty?" she whined, but settled for boiling the kettle and making a cup of instant. "So, Katy. What's up with you?"

Katy hesitated. "Not much."

"Did you work last night?"

"And tonight too."

"Yeah, every weekend's the same story, right?"

Katy smiled. "Pretty much. It's the weeks that are

different."

"Yeah, those are work as well." They both laughed. Sid still worked for the community centre as a lifeguard. It's how the friends had met.

"How are things going with Mike?"

Sid gave a slow smile. "They're going just fine, thank you."

"Is that right? You look like the cat with the cream. Good for you." Katy patted her arm feeling lost next to her friend's delight. "He's a nice guy. I like him."

"Hmmm. Me too. He's been wondering when I'm going to move in with him."

"Seriously? Wow. Things are moving along pretty quickly. Are you going to?"

"I don't know. I don't want to jump into anything, but he's been really good to me. And he's a good guy. Solid you know?"

"I know. Lucky you. Hang onto him, eh?" She stared into the bottom of her cereal bowl. Why did she always make such bad decisions about men? First Bruno, who dumped her and wouldn't return her calls after she'd given him all her money. And now Brett, her boss, at a job she desperately needed. By contrast her friend's life was moving along just fine.

Sid nodded. "I intend to. Did you know your friend called around yesterday?"

Katy stopped chewing. "My friend?" Tension tightened her shoulders.

"Your hockey player friend."

Katy felt the blood leave her head. *Brett was here? What for?* Maybe he wanted to fire her, she'd stepped way out of line. Or he was so angry he couldn't wait till she was back in the office to deal with her.

Sid chatted on, "I finally met him. Katy, he's so handsome. Don't tell me you don't like him, because I won't believe it. He seemed to think you'd be home. Anyway, Sherry came right out and asked him for a date, if you can believe it."

She did? Katy tried to manage a semblance of a smile. "Yeah, I believe it. What did he say?"

"He turned her down. He said he was already seeing someone."

"Seeing someone?" She stirred the cereal in the bottom of her bowl, her appetite gone, then rose to empty it in the sink. What little she'd eaten felt like it might come back up. *Was Brett seeing someone?* If so, what they'd done on the office couch was even more out of line than she'd imagined. The thought made her cringe, and she felt a pang behind her breastbone. "Well, he probably is." Trying for nonchalance, she dropped her dishes in the dishwasher.

"He left a message for you to call him. Didn't you get it? I taped it to your door last night."

A shot of alarm zinged up her neck. *She was supposed to call him?* He was probably going to fire her. "There was nothing taped to my door last night, Sid. What are you talking about?"

"I'll bet Sherry took it down. I wouldn't put it past her. She gets downright mean when she doesn't get her own way."

Katy's head turned toward the hallway, sudden animosity rising in her throat as they both heard a door open. Sherry came into the kitchen, lifted the coffee pot. "Where'd all the coffee go?" She frowned accusingly at the two girls.

Sid shrugged. "There wasn't any there when I came in. And you know Katy doesn't drink it."

Sherry filled the pot, poured it into the machine and began rummaging around in the cupboard for the coffee.

"Sherry, did you take the note I taped to Katy's door yesterday?"

"Don't be ridiculous. Why would I do that?"

"Well, she didn't get it, and it's gone now. How do you explain it?"

"I don't. It's none of my business if she hangs out with rude hockey players."

Sid smirked. "Katy, come and see my new jacket, you'll love it."

~~~

In her room, Sid flopped down on her bed. "Close the door."

Katy glanced around the room. "Where's your jacket?"

Sid waved the comment away. "I don't have a new jacket. Now tell me what's going on with the hockey player."

"Sid, that's totally unfair!" She felt cornered.

"I know, don't you love it?" Her friend grinned unrepentantly, then sobered. "He really wanted to see you, wondered if anyone knew where you were, which we didn't." She shot a questioning glance at her, but Katy flopped down on the bed and clamped her mouth shut so she continued.

"He repeated a couple of times that you should call him, it was pretty important to call that afternoon. Where were you?"

"I was riding my bike on the Trails," Katy said. She'd really been escaping and the Trails were an easy place to go, to break away. "Randy called so I met him for a couple of hours."

"Who's Randy? Honestly, Katy! You have more men crawling around than anyone I know!"

Katy gave a choked laugh. *Was Brett crawling around?* If so, it was because he was angry with her. She'd made him look foolish and he wouldn't appreciate that. "Don't be silly, Sid. Randy's the assistant cook at the restaurant. He's new in town and doesn't know anyone. He's nice. Not interesting in that way, but nice."

"Hmm. Well, anyway. Mr. Rome was insistent. So what did you need to call him about?"

"Well, I don't suppose I can call him now anyway," she said with profound relief. "He left town yesterday evening. They have back-to-back games in Winnipeg. He won't get home till Monday."

"Oh, you don't think his cell phone gets any reception in Manitoba?"

Katy felt a blush rise up her throat.

"What's the big secret, Katy? Are you seeing him?"

Katy shook her head, confusion threatening to swamp her.

"I know you went to dinner with him a few times."

"The first time it was Frank, the manager at the office who

invited me over to dinner with him and his wife. That wasn't a date. Brett just drove me there, that's all."

"Oh, so the other times were dates."

Katy felt trapped. "I don't know. I didn't think so."

"You didn't think so? You think a guy asks you out to dinner but he doesn't want a date?"

"Well, I work for him! He wouldn't date someone who works for him. And it didn't seem like a date. He just asked me… I mean we were at work and he said…" She buried her face in her hands. "It's complicated."

Sid put her arms around her and hugged her hard. "Yeah, I know. And you don't have a Mum to talk to, so I'm going to be your Mum."

"I've got a Dad," she said defensively.

"Uh huh. And are you going to tell your Dad about this?"

She balked at the thought and shook her head. "No."

"That's what I thought. So tell me what happened."

Katy collapsed back on the bed and closed her eyes. "I'm so tired."

"Yeah, I know the feeling." Sid lay down beside her and held her hand. "So, what happened?"

"I slept with him." Her voice shook.

"Seriously?" Sid shot back up. "You did? I'll bet he could give you a wild ride." She laughed. "When?"

Katy eyed her nervously. "On Thursday night."

"But you didn't have a date Thursday night. You were home by about eight o'clock."

"I know. I don't understand it. I don't understand *me*."

"Tell me, Katy."

"Well, I'd had a drink. Brett has a meeting for the drivers every other Thursday night right after work and he told everyone no hard liquor, just beer, but one of the drivers brought some rum and poured me a big drink. Brett got mad at him for it. And it seemed to take away all my fears. I mean, I really like him, you know. He's been good to me. And Bruno's been gone for quite a while, he's the only one I've ever fooled around with. And I thought, why not? Lots of other women want Brett, why shouldn't I have him? So I took my clothes off."

"At the office?" Sid appeared shocked.

"I know. It was stupid. I can't believe I did it." She closed her eyes, hoping to drown out the memory.

Sid gave her a nudge. "Tell me what happened."

Katy took a deep breath. "The drivers were gone, Brett and I were just cleaning up. He sat down beside me on the couch and held my hand." Her voice wobbled. "He asked me if I wanted to go for dinner and I just started to kiss him. One thing led to another. I more or less attacked him."

"Holy shit!"

"Yeah, I know. That isn't what a Mum would say, by the way."

Sid giggled and tugged at her hand. "So, how was it?"

Astounded, Katy gaped at her friend. "How was it? You want me to tell you how it was?"

"Yeah. Something's wrong, Katy. If it went well, he wouldn't be over here trying to find you and you wouldn't be hiding out avoiding him. So how was it?"

"It was awful. It was kind of wonderful."

"Why awful?"

Tears stood in her eyes and she began to shake. "It hurt, and I didn't expect it. I was right, you know. He's too big for me. It hurt, and then there was a kind of clenching and it was over. I tried to get up, but he said, 'no', and just kept me there and did it again."

"Kept you there? Did he force you, Katy, did he?" Sid sat straight up on the bed and leaned over her friend to peer into her face. "Tell me the truth."

"No, don't be silly. I pretty well forced him. I took all my clothes off and then tried to get his off. No, he didn't force me."

"So how did he keep you there?"

"He kissed me and his hands were gentle. His hands are big and calloused but they were so caring." Tears leaked out of the corners of her eyes.

"Was he rough?"

"No, not rough. I don't know. He was persuasive." Katy covered her mouth with both hands.

Sid lay back down beside her and patted her arm. "So you liked it, and it spooked you."

Katy turned to her, a dawning awareness in her eyes. "I just didn't know it could be like that. He was looking at me and touching me like I was precious or something. And we didn't even date. I don't know what I was doing. *What was I doing?*" Her voice rose higher as tears poured down her cheeks.

"But why did it hurt?"

Katy hesitated, obviously fighting with herself, then her voice dropped to a whisper. "I think he's just too big for me. That's why I like smaller men."

They lay there in silence for a while, then Sid sat up. "Katy, I think he really cares about you. Brett, I mean. You didn't see him when he came here. But he wanted to see you. He was adamant that you get the message to call him."

Katy shivered.

"I think you should call him."

CHAPTER THIRTEEN

Katy laboured over the forms on her desk, trying to produce a prototype for an interim billing invoice.

"It's not a good idea, Katy." Frank poked his finger at her nose, his cold cigar clenched tight. "We've never billed like that. Once the job is finished, fine." He slashed the air with his hand. "It's the honour system. When the job is finished, the bill is due. But we don't bill interimly, or however you say it. We just don't."

"I understand, Frank. But this job coming up is too big for us to carry financially when we're so short of cash. More than half our trucks will be diverted out there, and if we don't do interim billing we won't be able to meet payroll. Mr. Mikkleson will understand. This is a big job and it'll go on too long for us to carry it. I think we should bill every week."

Frank braced his hands on his hips, looking belligerent. "Paddy won't like it. It's the honour system. It'll embarrass him."

"Well, he should have thought of that before he bought new trucks he couldn't afford," she muttered. "We'll see what Brett says."

She quaked at the thought of what Brett might say on that or any other topic. She still hadn't talked to him. Knowing he'd be on the ice playing hockey, she'd finally called him last night. Then like a coward she left a short message and turned her phone off.

She didn't know what time he'd get into Victoria, maybe not today at all. That would be better, for her at least. She'd have one more day to fortify herself before having to face him.

The dispatch squawked and Frank went to get it. While he was busy the phone rang. The banker, Lindquist, wanted to talk to Brett. When he found out Brett wouldn't be in until late today, he said he'd call Paddy at home.

"Is it an emergency, Mr. Lindquist? Perhaps I can help you. I'm the office manager." She made a face at Frank who was now listening to her side of the call. Katy hung up and frowned at a worried Frank.

"He said it wasn't an emergency but he wouldn't wait to talk to Brett. He'd call Paddy at home. And Brett should call when he gets in. What's that about?"

He shrugged expressively. "It must be an emergency, right?"

"Sounds like trouble with the account, doesn't it?"

Frank had a grim cast to his face. "I'd bet on it."

"Well, I can go online and see what the balance is. But it should be okay. I've been very careful to give us some leeway for an emergency." Frank hung over her shoulder as she opened up the company bank account.

"Here it is. So, it seems like... Oh, no, Frank. There's nothing in the account. What happened? What do I tell Brett? We've got payments coming out this week. And payroll is Friday. What are we going to do?"

Frank stared at the column. "Can you tell what that one big withdrawal is?"

Katy clicked on it. "It's a cheque, cheque number 1422. Let me see." She darted across the office, taking a ring of keys with her. Unlocking the filing cabinet she pulled out the heavy company cheque book.

"Number 1422. Why, it doesn't say anything. It's the next cheque in the book after I finished paying all the bills last

Thursday. You remember, you and Brett signed them. Do you think Brett…" She let the question hang.

"No, I don't," said Frank. "But I have an idea about who would."

"Oh, this is bad. What can we do?" She fumbled in a file and pulled out a sheaf of papers. "I can do interim billing for some of these bigger jobs. That would bring some money in, even if we can just cover the expenses for this week."

"Yeah, good idea, Katy."

She gaped at him.

"Well," he said awkwardly, "now that I think about it, interim billing may not be such a bad idea after all. You get started on that, I have to go out for a bit. I'll be back later." She watched him bound down the stairs.

Reaching for the phone she called Brett's number. When he didn't answer, she left a message telling him Lindquist from the bank wanted him to call. She thought she knew what it was about and it would be better if he called the office before he called Mr. Lindquist.

~~~

Katy worked through the morning, monitoring the phones and the dispatch, adamant the job schedule would be completed on time. They'd need every dime.

Just as she launched into schedules for the following day, Brett walked through the door, so handsome he took her breath away. He was dressed for travelling with the team, trim and powerful in a tailored charcoal grey suit that fit him to perfection, showing off his broad shoulders and lean waist.

"Katy," he said.

"Brett!" Katy jumped to her feet. "Did you get my message?"

"Yeah, just got it when we landed so I thought I'd come over straight away rather than stop in at home." He bent a piercing gaze on her. "Did you get my message?"

"Uh, the one from Saturday?" she stuttered.

"Yes, Saturday. Did you get it?"

She couldn't hold his gaze and had to glance away. "I got

it on Sunday. Sid left a note taped to my door but it disappeared. She told me Sunday that you'd been over."

"Then why didn't you phone me?" His face was stern, his eyes fierce on her face.

"I did."

"Not till evening when you knew I'd be playing. You couldn't call me when you found out I'd been by to see you?"

She felt like a deer in the headlights. "Uh, Brett…"

Just then, to Katy's vast relief Frank strode through the door. "Have you told him yet?"

Brett whipped around. "Told me what?"

"No, I haven't had a chance. Brett, it's not good news. The banker called."

"Yes, you said."

"Well, he wouldn't say what it was about but he wanted to speak to you. When he found out you weren't here, he said he'd call Paddy at home. Frank and I thought it might be about the bank account. So we checked."

She took a deep breath. "The account is empty. A big cheque went through on Friday afternoon and emptied the account. I've been trying to…"

Bret's gaze swung from her to Frank and back. "What does that mean? A big cheque, how big? Where would such a cheque come from?"

Frank motioned to him. "You better come in here. We'll be a minute, Katy." Pulling his boss into the inner office he closed the door.

Katy stood, undecided. Finally she sat back at her desk and immediately leaped to her feet again at the sound of shouting from the other side of the office door. She stared at the door for a minute, then glanced out into the yard. The first truck was coming through the gate signalling the end of the day.

Knocking on the office door, she opened it quickly and stuck her head in. "The drivers are just starting to come in." Without looking at either man, she closed the door again and went out on the front steps.

Pete was the first to arrive. He parked No. 10 in the yard and climbed out with his lunch pail, water bottle and sheaf of papers. She delayed him for a moment, taking the receipts and examining them, questioning him about his day. By then the second truck pulled in and Wilf climbed out of No. 9. The two men kibitzed together.

When the office door behind her opened, Frank emerged. "Well, about time," he said to the drivers. He gave Katy a pointed look and jerked his head toward the inner office. She handed him the stack of papers and went in.

Brett stood with hands braced low on his hips staring out at the chain link fence that ranged around the perimeter of the property. It was ten feet high and topped by three strands of barbed wire, designed to deter intruders from entering the yard and vandalizing the equipment.

She stood in front of his desk uncertain what to do, but he didn't turn around. His jacket hung on the back of the chair, his shirt sleeves rolled up his forearms. She felt herself grow warm as she admired his broad shoulders and slim waist, the deep muscles moving and bunching under his clothes as he shifted.

"Did you want to see me?" she murmured.

Slowly he turned a stern face and she could see he was pale. "Yes, I need to see you. Sit down, Katy."

She sat, her hand trembling as she smoothed her skirt. He watched her for a few minutes.

"Why did you run away?"

Her eyes darted up in alarm to meet his and then down again. "I don't know," she whispered.

"Were you afraid?"

She nodded.

"Did I scare you?"

She pressed her lips together. "I can't talk about it here."

"Okay." He took a deep breath. "But just for the record, you started it. I didn't pressure you to make love with me. Did you think I pressured you?"

She shook her head.

He sighed and shifted his feet. "I might not be here tomorrow. I'm about to have the showdown of my life with Paddy. Can I call you?"

She regarded him for a minute, instinctively knowing this was a turning point for him, for them. "Did Paddy take the money?"

He nodded. "Frank went to see him."

"Does Frank know that you might not be here tomorrow?"

"Yes."

"That's sad," she said, feeling her heart squeeze in her chest. "The company will stop. Frank can manage the office but it needs someone like you to run the company." How would she bear it if he didn't come back?

"Well, the thing is, I'm not running the company. I'm a temporary overseer with no authority to make the type of decisions that need to be made. Paddy still has that power and he's making bad decisions, based on what Dancy wants from him."

Katy nodded. "I wondered," she said.

"Did you?" He crouched down in front of her. "You're such a clever girl. Katy, I need to talk to you. Will you please answer my calls, make a time to see me?"

"Yes," she whispered, holding his gaze with effort. He made her nervous with his size and powerful presence but she longed for him, too. She was caught.

"Thank you." He took her hand in his and stared at it, smoothing her fingers. She felt a jolt in her breast. He'd done that the night after the truckers left, the night she seduced him. That simple motion is why she'd first kissed him.

"You won your last game," she said softly.

He gave her a ghost of a smile. "Yeah, we did."

"No, I mean *you* won it. You scored the last goal and broke the tie."

He narrowed his eyes as he scrutinized her face then rose to his feet. "You were paying attention, were you?"

She smiled shyly. "Maybe."

He huffed out a laugh. "I don't know what to make of you, Katy."

~~~

Brett went straight home. He was brutally tired and figured it didn't matter if his talk with Paddy happened now or later. Dropping his bag in his room he took a long hot shower. Stepping over the clutter in the hall he opened an empty fridge. Randy was out and he had the whole mess of rumpled clothing, dirty dishes and scattered items to himself.

He called for some Chinese, then tiredly dialled his sister's number. On the third ring, she picked up. "Brett, we watched your Sunday game. How exciting is that? You scored the winning goal. The coach must be glad he took you on, even for a limited engagement."

Brett gave a ghost of a laugh. "Thanks, Liz. That's nice to hear. Listen, we've got a problem."

"About Dad?"

"Of course." They both laughed. "Of course."

Brett told her what had happened. There was silence for a minute while he could hear her kids shouting in the background.

"Let me call you back, Brett. I won't be long."

"It's okay. You don't have to do anything tonight. I just thought I'd let you know. This whole situation isn't tenable. Never was, I suppose."

"I know, but don't do anything just yet. I'll call you back."

The food arrived and Brett had just served a plate of Gai Ding chop suey, steamed vegetables and garlic ribs when his phone rang. It was his sister. "We're coming over, Brett. We'll be there in about twenty minutes."

"Liz, you don't have to do that. Tell Ed there's no rush."

"No, we've got a sitter. We'll be there shortly."

By the time Brett had eaten his dinner and picked up most of the clothes in the living room, piling the stuff on Randy's bed, his sister was at the door. Her husband Ed stood just behind her right shoulder.

"I refuse to apologise for the mess," he said, waving them

in. "Randy isn't house trained apparently, at least not yet. But my patience is pretty well shot, on this and everything else."

Liz laughed and gave him a big hug. "You poor guy. You've got Dad on one side and Randy on the other. How do you hold up?"

Reaching past her he shook End's hand. "It's not as bad as all that. Sit down guys, can I get you something?

Ed followed him into the kitchen. "Good God. Does it always look like this?"

"No, it started out pretty regular and it's gotten steadily worse. I can't tell if he's trying to piss me off or if he's depressed. But we'd better get this sorted. I can't even have the guys over let alone invite a woman back here."

Ed raised his brows. "Have you got a woman already? How long have you been in town, you hound?"

Brett laughed. "Well, if I did have one. You have to plan ahead."

"Too right. Although from what you've said in the past, you only have to wait until your next game."

Liz was seated on the couch in the living room when they made their way back bringing a few soft drinks with them. "I'm sorry, Brett. You've been carrying the main burden of Dad since he had the heart attack."

Brett held up his hand to stop her while he finished swallowing. "That's not true. Hell, you've been over there every second night since he got home from the hospital. You've brought him food that you made yourself, done his laundry. You've done more than your part."

"The fact is," said Ed, "it hasn't been easy for anyone, including your father."

The others turned to him in surprise.

"Well, you know how proud he is. He can't be proud in this situation, and he's having to accept help instead of being the big man."

"True. But he could try a little harder," Liz said.

Her brother laughed and wiped his mouth. "That's for damn sure."

"So, what do you want to do?"

Brett stared into his sister's eyes, relief warring with anxiety in his gut. "I think I'm finished. This isn't the first time he's taken money out. Although last time he didn't totally empty the account, just took enough that we were scrambling to cover payroll. Do you know what that would be like? Embarrassing as hell. Employees who have been with you for years and you shaft them?" He shook his head in patent disbelief at his father's irrational actions.

"Anyway, the only way I can stay is if he hands over control and he's not going to do that. So I think, in the end, the bank will foreclose on the new trucks. Frank can keep the old trucks running. Unless Dad gets well really fast. Not likely is it?"

"Well," said Ed. "No one needs to face him alone. I say we all go."

"You want to come?"

"If you think I'm letting Liz go over there to face him without me there, think again. He can be damned brutal. If she goes, I go."

"I know what you mean. He doesn't pull any punches." Brett pushed his hand through his hair in frustration, knowing he was too tired for this but it had to be done. "So, is it tonight?"

"I think so." Liz's mouth was firm. "No point in wasting a good sitter. This has gone on for how long? He won't accept help but let's us do everything for him. Maybe it's time to face facts, for all of us."

"Yeah, I guess. I just hope Dancy's not there."

She looked surprised. "I understood she'd left him."

"You're joking. I thought he took the money for her."

"Well, maybe he did. Maybe she came back for it. She'll stay until it's all gone, I suppose," said Ed. "Is that why you moved out, because of her?"

Brett studied his face, wondering how much he knew. "Dad asked me to leave," he finally replied. "He said Dancy wasn't comfortable with me there."

His sister snorted. "He was afraid she'd go after you."

Brett turned his head and stared at her, trying to school his expression. "You think so?"

Something in his expression sent her into gales of laughter. "That's what happened, isn't it? She came after you."

"It wasn't funny." Brett ground his teeth, a wave of embarrassment rising in his chest.

Liz laid her hand on his shoulder. "I'm sorry about all this, Brett. It hasn't been easy, has it?"

"Not so much," he smiled ruefully. "Not for any of us." He reluctantly grabbed the phone.

"Dad, this is Brett. How're you doing? Yeah? Well, I want to come over to talk to you. Yeah, tonight. Liz and Ed are here with me and we think it's time for a family council. No, it can't wait. Now or never. But we hope you say now."

Brett listened for a few minutes. "Well, Dad, the thing is, I'm not going back to the office. But I don't want to leave without telling you to your face. That's right." He watched Liz wrinkle her brow while Ed patted her hand. "We'll be there shortly."

He stopped pacing and put down the phone. "Okay, guys. Let's go. He took a little persuading, but it's better if he has notice of what I'm going to say before we get there. Shall we take two vehicles?"

Ed stood up. "Let's go in one car. We can come back here afterward and regroup. I'm sure we'll need it." Liz gave a weak laugh.

CHAPTER FOURTEEN

When they walked into the family home, Paddy was alone watching television. He turned the sound down and waved them to seats.

Brett stared around at the others, wondering how they'd come to this, a showdown with their father. It didn't seem right, any of it, to pressure a man who was still trying to recover from a heart attack. He felt that suspended animation feeling again. They went round and round the same issues without resolving anything, never moving forward, never making progress. It was like running in place.

He cleared his throat and leaned forward to speak.

Paddy lifted his hand to stop him. "I know what you're going to say, Brett."

Immediately Brett felt a surge of impatience. "Actually, I doubt if you do."

Paddy narrowed his eyes. "Let's just say I have an idea, okay? We don't need to get into details."

"I was going to ask if Dancy's here."

Paddy's mouth tightened. "No, she's not."

Brett sat back in his chair, crossed his ankle over the opposite knee. "Okay."

"You don't have to get all defensive," charged Paddy. No one answered. He hung his head. "Okay. Okay. I'm the one who's defensive."

Lifting his head, he glared at Brett. "You're here because I've cleaned out the company account. Frank already came to see me about it."

Liz raised her hand for permission to speak as if she were at school. "Not just that, Dad. We also have issues with what kind of care you're getting. We can't manage it by ourselves and you won't cooperate in organizing something else."

Paddy nodded. "I see. Anything else?"

Brett pursed his lips and blew out a breath. "There are probably a dozen things but those are the main ones."

"Well, I have a proposal," said Paddy. He scanned the quiet room. "I'll put back what money I have left and I promise to consider letting hired help in here a couple of times a week. How's that?"

"What is it you want from us, Dad?" Liz was pale but determined. "What you've just offered doesn't even begin to address the problems."

Paddy seemed surprised. "Why not? I've given both of you some concessions."

"What do you want in return?" Brett leaned forward, his hands on his knees. "What do you expect?"

"I want you to run the company for me till I'm better, till I'm able to run it myself."

Brett leaned back again and shook his head. "Not a chance."

Paddy frowned. "Why not?"

"I wouldn't go back there without a whole bunch of fundamental changes. Putting back half the money doesn't cut it."

Paddy spread his hands. "So, what is it you want? What would it take to keep you here to run the show? Getting too big for this kind of action, is that it? You have a good hockey game, score the winning goal, and suddenly your priorities change?"

"Dad," Liz interjected. "Stop it. You're digging a deeper hole for yourself. It becomes harder and harder to forgive that kind of talk."

Paddy swung back to Brett, his neck a deep red, the colour climbing the long planes of his face. "What will it take to keep you here?"

"I don't know. I haven't even thought about it. This arrangement doesn't work and I've decided to let it go. Frank can keep things going for a while. Maybe you'll be back in the saddle in a couple of months and you can do what you like with it."

"What about if I rescind my signing authority on the bank account? That way I won't be able to take any money out without your consent."

Brett simply shook his head, his mouth a straight line.

Paddy bent a piercing gaze on his son. "You want control of the whole thing? You want to own the whole thing? What?"

Brett spread his hands. "Stop it, Dad. It doesn't work. I don't draw a paycheque. I can't make the decisions that need to be made. I can't stop you from raiding the company. What am I doing there? It's a waste of time."

"I'll pay you."

"Well, if you're going to pay me, then pay someone else. Hire yourself a manager and pay him. Same difference."

Paddy's face flushed a darker red. "You know it's not the same. Family cares about these things. A hired manager wouldn't."

"Sorry, Dad. You've used me up. I'm sure you can find someone who could run it at least as well as I can. And there wouldn't be this tug of war between us. You could have a professional relationship with a different person."

"You want to go back to Vancouver and get your coaching job back." Paddy rose slowly from his chair and stood over him, wavering uncertainly on his feet.

"Dad, you don't listen." Brett stood and faced his father toe to toe. Anger burned in his throat. Suddenly this wasn't just about today, it was about all the years of drinking and neglect, about ignoring his kids, about how he'd treated their mother.

"You put me in there and treated me like some kind of lackey. You expected me to drop my own plans and take care of yours and then you abuse that relationship. What do you expect? Do you think we'll keep taking your shit, the way Mum did? It's not going to happen!"

Liz leaped up between them, laying a hand on each chest. "Come on, don't go there, Brett. Mum wouldn't want us to."

He turned away and paced the room, thinking he'd like to throttle Paddy. "Right. You're right, Liz."

Paddy sat again, breathing a little heavier. "Okay. Let's all calm down." He ran his hands up and down his thighs, took a deep breath and let it out slowly.

"I have a different proposal. I talked to my lawyer tonight to find out how to go about it. What I'll do is turn the company over to your management. I'll sign half the shares into your name. You'll get a salary equal to mine. I'll give up signing authority on the bank account and we'll share the profits fifty-fifty."

Brett just stared at him.

"Well," Paddy motioned with his hand. "What do you say?"

"I say, what's the catch?"

~ ~ ~

Gathered back at Brett's house an hour later, Liz looked curiously at her brother. "Are you thinking of taking that offer, Brett?"

"Aren't you insulted by that offer?" he said bitterly. "The company is your inheritance as well as mine. And right in front of you, he offers me half the business. He doesn't think. He has no clue how his actions impact his children. He never did." Brett's mouth had a sardonic twist. "I don't honestly know why Mum stayed with him. He treated her like dirt."

"It wasn't quite as bad as that, Brett. She gave as good as she got. And she loved him. He loved her too, in his own way."

"Yeah, and what way was that?"

His sister laid her head on his shoulder. "You weren't here after you were fourteen. You missed a lot that you would have noticed if you'd been older. They had a good relationship. Mum was happy. Most of the time, anyway."

"Most of the time?" He looked at her aghast.

"Well, you can't ask for much more. Can you, Ed? You're not going to be happy *all* the time."

Ed nodded. "Your father changed quite a bit after Marie died. But he didn't cheat on her or treat her as badly as you seem to think he did."

"As far as the company goes," Liz continued, "he can do what he wants with it. It's only when he dies that I have any claim to what's left and I don't even want to think about that. I don't begrudge you getting paid to run the company but I'm surprised he was willing to go that far. Weren't you?"

"Flabbergasted." Brett fell back against the couch, all the air knocked out of him. "My jaw must have hit the floor."

Ed laughed. "No, actually, you were pretty cool."

"Well, that's not how I felt. I was getting so close to grabbing him by the lapels and lifting him out of his chair. Then he backs up and goes in the opposite direction."

"I could see that need in you to slap him around a little." Ed chuckled. "I mean, I was pretty sure you weren't going to hit him. But after watching that fight in your first game with the Victoria hockey team I have a new respect for your ability to use self-control during confrontation."

Brett burst out laughing, feeling the tension slowly leak out of him. Liz chuckled and hit Ed on the shoulder. "You bum. We weren't going to go there." She bent a searching gaze on her brother. "That was some fight though, now that we've brought it up."

"Oh, we've brought it up now, have we?" Brett was still chuckling.

"Yes, we have. What happened?"

"Well, a lot was happening, wasn't it?"

"Was it about Dad?"

"Partly." Brett lowered his lids and contemplated his

coffee cup.

"Liz, leave it alone. His girlfriend had moved on."

Brett's eyes flashed. "Is there no privacy in this family?"

His sister laughed. "Not a shred. Someone has to hold your feet to the fire or you'll get too big for your britches. Besides, I never liked her. I didn't think she was good for you. So," she continued, glancing round the living room, "what are you going to do with cousin Randy?"

He sighed and surveyed the clutter. "What would you do? Is he just a total slob? Surely he didn't get away with this at home."

"Maybe that's what this is. He can finally rebel. I suppose you have to explain that he has a week to move out. That might get his attention."

Both men turned to her in astonishment.

~ ~ ~

Katy said goodbye to Randy in the kitchen, gave Juno her tips and dug her purse out of the locker. The fact that she'd put her job at Rome Trucking in jeopardy just added to the weight she carried on her shoulders tonight. Not only was the company close to bankrupt, she'd taken the unforgiveable step of sleeping with the boss. There was no going back from an action like that. She was bone tired.

Her car stuttered, then started and she backed carefully out of her space in the parkade. It would be good to get home.

Traffic was heavy around the downtown area bars and hotels but once she turned off the main streets, it quickly died down. Driving on auto pilot, she was nearly home when lights flashed from behind, blazing suddenly into her rear view mirror.

Was this a police blockade? She shielded her eyes as the lights quickly gained on her. Beginning to panic, she hit the gas to get out of the way but the vehicle kept coming fast. Fear climbed her throat. She wasn't going to be able to escape if she didn't do something fast. The lights loomed closer and there was a loud bang. She felt the sudden impact as the vehicle smashed into her rear fender.

The power of the crash jerked her backward against the seat, then threw her forward onto the steering wheel. The seat belt snapped across her chest, wrenching her shoulder as her car swerved toward the ditch.

Damn! They must be drunk. Traffic was so light, they had all kinds of space to get around her if they were in that much of a hurry. She managed to steer onto the verge at the side of the road and the bright headlights followed, tucking in so tight behind her she couldn't see the vehicle.

At least it wasn't a hit and run, she thought frantically. She'd get their insurance information and everything would be okay. As she struggled to unfasten her straining seat belt, in the rear view mirror she saw the truck door open. A tall figure stepped out and moved swiftly forward toward her side window. The speed of the approach took her totally by surprise.

Now she was nervous. There was no one else on this road. Should she get out of the car or lock her door? They were coming up on her awfully fast.

A dark hooded figure approached her driver's door just as more headlights appeared from behind and a second vehicle hove into view. He darted forward. There was a cracking sound and her driver side window shattered as the glass splintered in a million particles. Had he banged on the glass, to break it like that?

The driver of the truck whirled in her rear view mirror and retreated swiftly as the second car passed them. Then the truck gunned its engine, pulled a U turn and disappeared.

Katy sat there for a moment, her breath coming fast. Her side window sagged in its frame beside her, the glass opaque with pebbled bits clinging to the film. She had no idea who had hit her, not even the make or licence of the truck.

With unsteady fingers she grabbed her cell phone and dialed the police. After she breathlessly told the operator what had happened, they put her on hold. Her hand shook as she waited. What if this guy came back? She was a sitting duck parked here alone.

Someone else came on the line and she told her story again just as a loud truck roared up and passed her on the road, making her jump in her seat. The tension was too much. After being put on hold a second time, she clicked the phone off and pulled out onto the street. All she wanted to do was get home.

Katy didn't sleep well. Every time she dozed off she was jerked awake by the sound of the truck hitting the back of her car or the shattering of the window.

In the early light of dawn, her car was a disaster, the rear lights broken out on the left side, the driver's window opaque. Opening the door, she brushed glass particles off the driver's seat.

When she started it up, she realized she couldn't see out the window or into her side mirror. She glanced at her watch. She was going to be late if she dithered any more. Brett didn't need another excuse to fire her.

Driving slowly, she planned her route to avoid turning left and pulled gratefully into the trucking yard twenty minutes later. As she climbed out, Wilf drove up beside her.

"Whoa! What happened to your car?" He bent down and ran his hand over the broken light. "When did this happen?"

Before she knew it, there were three drivers standing around her vehicle, examining the rear bumper and side window. Pete thought the car was a write off but Katy was determined that wouldn't happen.

Someone went to get Gert and he examined the rear end thoroughly. "I can fix," he said, fingering the dent in the fender. "I make lights fit."

He leaned down to peer under the bumper while Ollie poked at the broken window. Gert dusted his knees off.

"Two days," he predicted. "I need window from junkyard and new light. Two days."

CHAPTER FIFTEEN

Brett rolled over and was instantly awake. He punched the pillow under his head as he relived his dream. Katy had been running through a field and he was chasing her. It was playful, she looked so pretty and he was laughing.

He called to her but she didn't stop. Then she turned her head and it was Marilyn, smiling slyly and beckoning him on. He slowed his pace, confused and then angry. Where was Katy and why would he go after Marilyn when she'd discarded him like a used condom? Then her face changed again and somehow he knew it wasn't Marilyn at all, it was Dancy, Paddy's girlfriend.

Rubbing his hand over his face he blew out a frustrated breath. He didn't want to even try to figure out what that was about. Throwing back the covers, he slapped off the alarm before it rang and headed down the hall to the bathroom. This morning he had an appointment at six with the hockey training coach but his focus was on Katy, specifically why she wouldn't talk to him. It irritated him, irked him, made him damned cranky.

As the shower pelted down, he grinned wryly to himself. It wasn't as if it was the first time in his life that he'd slept with a woman and moved on. Although he wasn't the one who'd moved on this time.

Was that why he was so irritated by it? He shut the faucet down, shook some water off and rubbed his chest with the towel. Part of it was that he worked with her in the office, she spoke to Frank or one of the other guys instead of him. Yet he wanted her, longed for her. He was angry over this ridiculous mess they were in.

When he'd fucked her on that couch, it meant both less to him and more than it appeared. Less because he hadn't initiated it, it had taken him totally by surprise. He was unprepared in mind, if not body. And more, because she didn't sleep around, he knew that deep down.

She'd wanted him, and she'd seduced him. And he'd damn sure wanted her. Up till then, he'd been thinking about the logistics of dating her while she worked in his office. But she took the issue right out of his hands, escalating the action so quickly his head was still spinning. And then she walked away.

He threw the towel on the rack in disgust at himself. He wanted her, damn it! Longed for her, ached for her. And she'd turned her back on him, wouldn't give him a chance to recover from whatever offence he'd committed.

It hadn't been very romantic to make love to her in the office. If he had the chance to do it again, he'd do anything but that. Take her to a hotel, even bring her back to this pigsty, but not on the office couch. No wonder she was upset.

Pouring cereal into a vaguely clean bowl he shoved pizza boxes aside to sit at the kitchen table. The milk still smelled good so he added some to his breakfast. As he munched he studied his dilemma from every angle.

He'd asked her to call him when she was free, but it hadn't happened. He'd left her two messages on her cell phone yesterday, both during office hours and admittedly it was only one day since he'd seen her. Apparently she didn't answer her phone while at work, which was good from an employer's point of view, but at the same time irrationally angered him. Moodily he concluded that this was not a rational issue, it was emotional and the main emotion on his part seemed to be lust. Well, and maybe ego. He was damned mad she was ignoring him.

She'd be sleeping now. He glanced at the clock and moved to dump his bowl in the sink which he discovered was overflowing with dirty dishes. Sighing, he opened the dishwasher and began to stack the racks. He added soap and turned it on. Then he found a piece of paper and left a note for Randy to clean the kitchen before he left for work.

As he went back to his room for his wallet and keys, he pondered what Coach had always said. "If you want it, Brett, you have to go after it. No one's going to hand it to you. You can practice and work out and get strong and train. But in the end, you have to go after it. It's the most important thing you'll bring to the game, the will to go after the win."

Okay, so he'd go after her. She wasn't going to come to him, so he'd go after her. Yes she worked hard. She worked two jobs for heaven's sake. Who did that? But she also had time to do things. He knew she went out, so he'd be the one she went out with. Here, kitty, kitty, kitty. He jingled his keys in his hand as he jogged down the front steps.

When Brett got into the office that afternoon her car wasn't in the lot. "Where's Katy?" he asked as he walked through the door. Then he stopped short in surprise because she was sitting at the desk, head bent over her work.

She glanced up as Frank pointed at her.

Brett felt the colour climb his neck. "Sorry. I didn't see your car out there."

She went back to her work but seemed to keep him in view from the corner of her eye.

Frank finished his call. "I'm out of here." He grabbed some keys and headed for truck No. 2 parked in the yard.

"Where's your car, Katy?"

She glanced past him at the door. "Gert has it in the shop. He's repairing it. I hope you don't mind." Her gaze for once was directed right at him.

"Why? What happened to your car?"

She faltered. "The bumper is smashed and the driver side window."

"Good God! When was this? "

Her face paled. "I got rear ended last night."

He crouched down in front of her, took her hands in his. "Were you hurt, Katy? What happened?"

"No. A truck rear ended me, and then the driver walked up to talk to me and he must have hit the window, because it shattered. Then he ran."

Brett frowned. "He ran? So you don't know who it was."

She shook her head.

"Did you get the licence plate or the make of the truck?"

She only shook her head again. "His lights were really bright. They blinded me. I thought it was a police blockade at first. When I reported it to the police, they put me on hold for so long that I finally gave up."

"Call them again. Some maniac is running around rear ending people."

"Yes. I will."

"Call them now. Make a report."

Taking the steps two at a time, Brett went out to the workshop. Gert lay on the floor under the rear bumper of Katy's little car using his feet to push on the back fender. A new light cover lay on the floor beside him.

"What do you think happened here?"

Gert grunted, gave a harder push and the plastic popped out, slightly misshapen. He got to his feet, wiping his hands on a rag. "I think he hit her pretty hard. The bumper was dented too, I had to bang it out. Looks not too bad."

Brett bent down. "It's good, Gert. And those lights will sit properly?"

He shrugged. "Passable."

"What about the window?"

Gert surveyed it for a long moment. "Hard to break one of these. Safety glass."

"Yeah." The window was totally shattered, the splinter pattern spraying out from a small round centre of impact in the upper right portion of the glass.

Gert shrugged. "I got new one coming. Tomorrow. She can't drive tonight. Frank told her already." He grinned. "She don't like it, being told."

Brett could only nod in frustration. That was for damned sure.

~~~

"Bruno, you're going up Island today." Tyler's face was strained this morning, no smile in place.

Bruno shrugged. "Any time."

"Good. Balson will get you the stuff. You know who to see. He's expecting you about five this evening. So better get a move on."

Bruno stood and pulled up his pants. He seemed to have lost weight. Maybe he wasn't paying enough attention to what he ate. He realized he hadn't eaten yesterday at all. In fact, he didn't remember much about yesterday.

Coke took away his appetite, took away all his urges. Checking his pockets for cash, he decided to stop on the way and get a takeout meal at some drive through place

"By the way," Tyler interrupted his thoughts. "I've changed your phone."

Bruno turned toward Tyler in confusion, his brain wasn't working too well today. "My phone?"

"Yeah, here's your new one. The number's on the paper."

Bruno took the paper and examined it for a long time. "Okay." He turned the phone on. "Is it ready to go?"

Tyler nodded. "She won't bother us anymore."

Bruno's head jerked up. "Who? You mean Katy? What... happened?" He'd almost said, "What have you done?" barely catching the words in his throat before they were spoken. Sweat popped out on his forehead.

"I heard she was in some kind of accident. So she won't be bothering us, calling all the time and trying to get her money back. She wasn't a good idea in the first place, Bruno. You made a bad decision. This was our game, not something to be shared and spread around to a bunch of people. Think better next time. Now get going before you're late and they get upset with you."

Bruno moved slowly toward the door. An accident? He'd listen to the radio on the drive up. Maybe even stop and get a newspaper. He hadn't heard about any accident. But he'd been sort of out of it yesterday. He should try to pay a little more attention.

~~~

That afternoon, Brett and Paddy signed papers that transferred half the company into Brett's name. Brett shook the lawyer's hand and walked him to Paddy's front door.

His father stood beside his recliner, his shoulders stiff as he watched Brett come back into the house. "There, son. Now that couldn't be clearer."

Brett eyed his father thoughtfully. "It's interesting that you've done this, Dad. I have to say I'm surprised. Why now? Why not when you first got sick?"

Paddy heaved a sigh. "I thought it'd be temporary, the heart attack thing. People bounce back. I expected to be on my feet in a couple of weeks. But it hasn't happened that way."

He shrugged eloquently, his face set in stern lines. "Time to face facts. Dancy's gone anyway, she took off with one of the guys from the Moonlighter that she used to flirt with when we drank there. I don't expect her back."

"I'm sorry about that, Dad. I really am."

Paddy's eyes glinted wetly. "It's okay son, she wasn't a keeper, was she? She even made a try for you."

Brett blanched. "I didn't do anything to lead her on." His lips pressed in a firm line and the dimples in his cheeks deepened.

Paddy waved his protest away. "I know that. That was just how she was. Anyway." He turned back to his recliner. "What do we do now?"

"Well, I'm not ready to give up hockey, so I still have another commitment. We need to talk about that." Brett lowered himself onto the couch, lifted an ankle over the other knee and leaned back.

When he left Paddy's house, he was more confused than ever. Paddy was cooperating. He'd given a lot of ground and seemed committed to making the company financially sound. Obviously he envisioned himself being well enough to spend the income.

Yet he'd just spoken to Dr. Wilde earlier this morning and Paddy hadn't even gone to his last doctor's appointment. He was drinking and he refused to do physiotherapy. How did he think he was going to get well?

Brett shook his head in astonishment. As a hockey player, he'd been injured often enough to treat his body as a machine. If something wasn't working properly, he took it to the mechanic. And then he did what he was told, because the mechanic or the doctor knew what to do to make him heal the fastest and get the best results. He didn't ignore that advice, he treated it as part of his job.

He'd better have another meeting with Liz and find someone who could help them get this thing rolling with Paddy.

CHAPTER SIXTEEN

The first rush of diners had slowed and Katy took stock of her tables. The couple against the wall and the party of four in the booth were both working their way through their dinner, the party of six was ready for their plates. She'd better check with Juno, the cook.

It was the middle of her Sunday night shift. The dining room stayed open until eleven tonight and she was the opener. She'd be first off as the customers dwindled in numbers. She had a lock on that shift due to her longevity here. Often the later customers had more to drink and they might tip better but they could also be a challenge to deal with.

She backed into the dining room through the double hung doors of the kitchen carrying three plates of steak and crab followed by a busboy carrying three more dinners.

"There you are." She dropped the dinners, two steaks done medium rare, one rare. She directed the busboy to drop the others at the appropriate places, two pasta and chicken and a salmon, and checked the table to make sure nothing was missing. She took a follow-up wine order, told the busboy to bring another basket of bread and whisked the large pepper grinder off to a side table.

Then she took a breath, visually checked two more tables in her section and came to a stop. The maître'd had just seated a couple of men and she recognized the back of that neck instantly.

Brett Rome sat comfortably, his suit jacket fitting immaculately across his broad shoulders. Recently brushed, his slightly wavy tawny coloured hair fell just past his shirt collar. She recognized the shape of the big ring on his right hand as he turned his water glass and leaned forward to say something to his companion. Another hockey player, Katherine figured, given the breadth of the shoulders and lean build.

The other waitresses were eying them curiously and one grinned at Katy, raising her eyebrows. As she went by she gave a big smile and whispered, "Want me to take that table? It's no problem, really."

Katy felt herself flush. What was he doing here? He knew this was where she worked on the weekend. Well, she couldn't just ignore them.

As she approached the table, Brett glanced up. "Hi, Katy," he smiled, his dimples showing. "I wondered if I'd see you here tonight."

"You *knew* you'd see me here," she said, her eyes accusing.

"Well, maybe." He laughed. "Meet my friend, Hartford Tremblay. Hart, this is Katy Dalton. She works at Rome Trucking when she has the time. I guess we don't pay her enough, though, because she has this second job."

Hart stood and shook her hand. Katy blushed harder. He was handsome in a hard-boned, muscular way. Katy brought their drinks order and surveyed her other tables.

One table was just finishing up. She did a final check to make sure they had everything they needed and brought the bill. When she rang it through on the credit card, the tip showed up at a healthy twenty-five percent.

She'd noticed the husband eyeing her all evening and she always found it was best to ignore that. It caused tension between spouses and she worked hard to ensure everyone was satisfied with the service. But this tip was pretty rich and she thanked him enthusiastically.

When she looked across the room, she found Brett frowning at the customer. She sighed. *Why was he here?* Well, he probably ate out a lot, it was just a matter of time before he ended up here on her shift.

Hart ordered steak, Brett the salmon and they shared a bottle of wine. They both turned down salad but ordered extra vegetables. No dessert for either of them. They dawdled over their wine and then coffee until Katy's shift was over. The other wait-staff were picking up any new customers that came in.

When she went by Brett's table for the third time to see if there was anything else they wanted, Brett waved at an empty chair. "Why don't you sit down with us, Katy? Are you almost finished work for tonight?"

"Sorry. We're not allowed to do that. I am finished my shift, though. I'll get another waiter to take over your table, if you like."

"No, no." Brett reached for his wallet. "We'll settle up." Katy handed him the bill and he slapped a credit card on it. "Do you need a ride home, Katy?"

"No, thank you. I have my car. I'm in the parkade down the block."

"I see." He punched in his code numbers to authorise the credit transaction and added a tip. Katy examined it for a moment, her cheeks turning rosy.

"Brett, that's too much."

"How do you mean?" He stared at the slip. "Looks okay to me." She could see Hart smirking into his fist.

"There you go." Brett handed it back to her. She frowned, flustered, and then gathered some glasses from the table. "Thank you, then. I'm off shift now. Nice to meet you, Hart." Hart nodded and gave her an admiring look.

"Care to join me in the bar for a nightcap when you're through here?"

"Uh..." she hesitated.

"Not for long. I have to get going myself. Just a coffee or a drink." He smiled disarmingly.

"Um. Okay. I'll need a few minutes to finish." She headed to the back, flustered again. By the time she had tallied her tips, given her portion to Juno and checked the schedule it was quite a bit longer. Brett was still sitting at his table, swirling the last of the wine in his glass. He stood as she came out.

"I thought you might have gone out the back way," he admitted, smiling wryly.

"Oh, I'm sorry. It always takes longer than I think to wind up the shift. Where did your friend go?"

"He had other business to attend to."

~~~

Brett put his hand at the small of Katy's back and steered her across the lobby into the bar, a sense of satisfaction settling in his chest. Finally, he had her to himself. It was dim and quiet in there on a Sunday night. Settling her in a small booth he went up to the bar and returned with wine for her and a soft drink for himself.

"You're not having a drink?"

He shook his head. "I already had some wine. I'll do better with this." He sat down beside her and leaned back, giving her a slow smile. "How long have you worked at the Regent Hotel?"

"More than two years. All through college."

"That's good. You must be their star performer."

"What? No, don't be silly. They have full-time people, then a few of us part-timers to fill in on the busy nights. But I do get to choose my shifts."

"You must have your favourite customers as well."

She grinned. "A few come in pretty often. It's nice."

Like that guy sitting with his wife, he thought, *the one who left the big tip and couldn't keep his eyes off you.* His lips compressed and Katy shifted uncomfortably. Reaching to take her hand, he rubbed his thumb across the backs of her fingers. "Do you like working here?"

"Yeah, I like it pretty much."

"That's good. It's nice to work in a place where you like the work and the people."

She glanced sideways at him. "Don't get me wrong. I like working at Rome Trucking as well."

"Do you?" He turned his head to smile into her eyes. "What do you like about it?"

"Well." She wriggled to get comfortable and he watched her breasts bounce in that little blouse. His grip on her fingers must have tightened because she tugged at her hand to free it from his grasp. When he'd first caught sight of her in the restaurant, his heart had given a soft jerk, like it had been shot with an electric prod.

Hart gave a low whistle. "Is that her?" He gave her a slow once over. "Very nice, Rome."

"Keep your eyes to yourself, Hart," he barked. But he couldn't really blame him. She was wearing the traditional black and white of any classic wait-staff, but on her it seemed different. That blouse, just slightly low-cut with the tucks across the tops of her breasts had fired his imagination. He knew intimately what those breasts felt like, tasted like. He hadn't forgotten a single detail. He wished he'd been able to see her that night, see her body, but it'd been too dark in the office.

He'd noticed other men in the dining room eyeing her. It drove his temperature up. She wore a short tight black skirt with a slit up one thigh. He'd had to look away. Thank God she dressed professionally at the office or the younger truckers would get out of control.

He tried to pry his mind off her breasts and pay attention to what she was saying. "I like using the skills I got at college," she continued. "It's really nice to be right out of class and already using them. And most of the drivers are nice. Gert is really kind and Frank has been so patient with me."

"Yeah, Frank's one of the good guys." Brett flattened her hand on his thigh and covered it with his own. "I wanted to tell you, I've settled things with Paddy. I'll be back in the office tomorrow."

He watched the smile bloom across her face. "Oh, that's great! I'm so glad for you." She gave him a serious look that somehow went straight to his belly. "I wasn't sure what the future of the company was going to be without you there. That must be a relief for your father, as well."

Brett was surprised. "Yeah, I think it was. He seemed different. He talked business as if it's important how the company fares." He squeezed her fingers. "All we need to do now is get his physiotherapy organized and convince him to attend the sessions."

She nodded in understanding. "Not too easy to get that done, right?"

"No. He's one stubborn man."

"But he's got you and that counts for something."

"Well, we try. My sister, Liz and I, we try."

She smiled softly and patted his arm. "That's nice," she said. Oh, man, he could hardly do this. When she went soft on him like that he just wanted to pull her onto his lap and kiss her senseless.

His eyes must have gotten a bit intense because her expression became wary and she looked down at her empty wine glass, moving it an inch to the left with her fingers.

"Did you want another drink?"

"Oh, no thank you. I have to go home now."

"Okay. I'll follow you home."

"Pardon?"

He glared ferociously around the room. "You got rear ended last week. I'm following you home."

CHAPTER SEVENTEEN

Cradling his beer, Brett leaned back in the heavy chair in his favourite bar. He shook his shoulders out and cranked his neck. "That was a good game, Jerome, but we could have played better. I think the ice was soft. It must be this heat." He lifted the front of his shirt away from the sweat on his chest.

Jerome nodded. "I know. It was a shame the win came so easy." Shaking their heads they both laughed.

Hart snorted. "You don't know what you're talking about. They never come too easy. It's when we play Edmonton next week that we're going to have to dig deep to keep ourselves from looking like fools."

"Maybe. They have a better win record and their player ranking is higher. But we almost got them last time and our defence is tighter now. Could be we'll run right over them."

Brett twisted around as he saw his driver Russell limping toward them, weaving between the overstuffed leather chairs. There was a walking cast strapped to his leg. As he approached, Brett turned his head. "How's it going, Russ? When's the cast coming off?"

"Ten days. Not long now. Then two or three weeks of rehab."

"I think you said four to five, last time I saw you." Brett

narrowed his eyes.

"Maybe. I'm optimistic." He glanced around the table. "Care to sit?"

"Well, I'm wondering why you guys are in here when your new office lady is dancing up a storm in Strider's down the street."

Brett stiffened. "How do you know?"

"I was just there. She's with a few girlfriends and the guys are tripping over each other trying to get near them."

"Why did you leave, then?"

Russ flushed a dull red. "Well, I can't dance. And it's too loud to sit and talk."

Brett looked around at his buddies. "I think I'll have to take a stroll down to Striders. Anyone in?"

Hart and Jerome pulled up short at the long line-up in front of Strider's nightclub but Brett kept walking. When he reached the doorman he clapped him heavily on the back. "How's it going, Brad? I don't think I've seen you since Prince George, third year with the team."

The doorman's face split in a huge grin. "Rome! Hey, man! How's it going? I knew you were here playing with the Victoria team. How's that working out?"

"Not too bad. Not as good as the big leagues, but we both know that."

They laughed together. "You can say that again."

"So, did you go on after Prince George or go back and pick up life at home?"

His friend sobered. "Home for a bit then trades training. I'm a carpenter by day but this fills the bill for a bit of excitement at night."

Brett examined the long lineup at the door and then into the club doorway. "Any chance of sneaking in? I've got someone in there I need to see."

"Male or female?" Brad raised his eyebrows.

"That's right."

The doorman laughed. "Okay, you and your buddies."

"Come over and see me one day," said Brett. "I'm

working in my father's company, Rome Trucking. You can find the office in the phone book."

"Will do."

They squeezed past the crowd to press into the busy entry.

~ ~ ~

Katy straightened her blouse and adjusted her pendant necklace. She grinned at her friend. "It's so good to see you, Erica. When was the last time you came over? It must be months." She had to speak directly into her friend's ear to be heard over the din.

Erica laughed, throwing back her long blonde hair. "It is months. University classes will start soon. I took a few days off to see everyone before I get bogged down in coursework again."

The song ended and it was quieter for a few minutes. "Sid's doing the same thing." Katy motioned to her roommate.

Katy turned at a tap on her shoulder. A young man stood before her, long hair, engaging grin. "Care to dance?" He held out his hand. Katy studied him critically for a second. He really was the right size for her, not too big and pretty good looking. Just then the waitress arrived with their tray of drinks.

Katy smiled and shook her head. "No thanks, not right now." She fished in her purse for some bills to pay for it. Gazing around, she sat back and sipped her cranberry martini. There was another tap on her shoulder. The same young man was behind her, leaning down. "Would you care to dance now?"

She turned fully around and smiled again. "No thank you. I'll dance later. Not now. Sorry."

He bowed and turned to Erica. "Care to dance?"

Sid and Erica both shook their heads.

"Wait till they do a line dance. We'll all go up then." Erica nodded and blotted her lipstick. Sid grabbed Katy's arm. "There's your hockey player," she hissed.

Erica leaned in. "What hockey player? Where?"

Just then Katy felt a tap on her shoulder. When she turned her head, the same fellow was there, grin firmly in place. "Care to dance now?"

"No, really. I don't want to dance now. Thank you," she said firmly, shaking her head. She saw a movement from the corner of her eye and Engaging Grin took a few hurried steps backward.

"She doesn't want to dance now," she heard a determined voice say. She turned fully to see Brett holding the fellow's arm in a tight grip. "Back off. She said no. She said no, twice. Give it a rest."

Her would-be dance partner took a wild swing and Brett jerked his head back but not quick enough. He grabbed his face with one hand and she saw a narrow ribbon of blood drip down the front of his shirt. His eyes held a disbelieving look as he turned and faced the other man. "Are you kidding me? Just leave her alone!"

Hart muscled in between them and herded Brett back while Jerome grabbed the assailant and shoved him toward the front door. Before she knew what was happening, three men converged on the table and over it went, drinks flying.

She felt her cold cranberry martini slide down inside her blouse sticking the material to her breasts like a second skin. Then she staggered as two bodies flew past in a fierce clinch. Erica grabbed her arm and tried to tug her out of the way as chairs were shoved and more men dove into the fight.

~ ~ ~

Brett felt a shot of alarm. Katy had just been body slammed by some bandit in a golf shirt. Picking her up under his arm, he pushed Sid and Erica before him toward the door of the club as Hart fended off the mob. They struggled out onto the hot sidewalk.

The doorman turned in surprise. "Whoa, Brett. Didn't take long. What's going on?"

"Sorry, Bradford. We had a persistent dancer in there and he wouldn't take 'no' for an answer."

Katy beat on his back. "Put me down," she hissed. He let

her slide down his chest until her toes hit the pavement.

"What were you doing?" Face flushed, hair wild, her shirt had damned near disappeared.

"What the fuck?" He pulled her back firmly against his body. "You're naked," he gritted. "Where are your clothes?"

Katy glared at him in apparent disbelief. "What are you talking about?" She pushed on his chest to make him back up and glanced down at her blouse. "Oh, okay."

"Yeah, okay." He pulled her back against him and sheltered her with his arms. "I'll take my shirt off, just hang on."

"Here, Katy." Sid shoved a cardigan at her and Katy struggled into it, Brett tugging the sleeves up, and buttoned the single button at the waist. "That's better."

"Barely," Brett muttered. "I can see damned near every ..."

She glared at him. "Be quiet!"

He glared back. The trickle of blood had slowed and he could feel it on his top lip. He sniffed and wiped at it with the heel of his hand.

"Well." She looked at her girlfriends who stood for a minute with straight faces staring at each other and then began to laugh. As the laughter grew, even Jerome started to grin. The girls were hanging onto each other, howling and struggling to talk at the same time.

The men looked bemused and shifted their feet. "Shit," muttered Brett. "I guess that worked out well."

Katy choked back another giggle and turned to Brett. "What were you doing?"

"What do you mean, what was I doing? That jackass wouldn't take 'no' for an answer. He kept bugging you to dance."

"I know, but I could have handled it."

"I saw you handle it. You said, 'no'. He should have accepted that."

Her eyes softened as she gazed at him. "I guess I should thank you for rescuing me." The other girls broke into more giggles and Brett could felt the heat climb his neck.

"Yeah," he said gruffly. Jerome snorted.

Katy looked at the other men. "Thank you for rescuing us."

They grinned back at her. "You're welcome," said Hart.

Jerome nodded. "Why don't we go back to the lounge, maybe have a drink there," he said, slapping his chest. "We need hydrating, we just finished a hockey game."

Hart laughed.

Brett seated Katy beside him and pulled her chair closer to his. "Maybe you can pull that sweater closed a bit more. It's not really…" Katy tugged her blouse away from her skin and it became less transparent. "It's still pretty low-cut," he grumbled. She gave a little smile.

He saw it, relaxed back in his chair and sighed, reduced to glaring at Hart when he happened to glance down at her cleavage. He watched as she introduced her friends to the other men and contributed comments about working at a trucking company.

She just made him feel good, even if he did blow it sometimes. He really shouldn't have overreacted to that guy. He was just asking for a dance. Any man would want to dance with her. But he didn't want her bothered like that. When she said "no", that guy should have taken it at face value and bowed out.

Aw, shit. Looking down at his hand, he clenched his fist and relaxed it. He'd gotten a bit belligerent in there. She seemed to inspire that in him. He was always trying to defend her and maybe she didn't need defending. There was nothing like coming on like a Neanderthal to turn a woman off. Glancing at her sideways he saw a little smile on her lips.

He leaned toward her. "What?"

"Nothing."

He flushed.

~~~

Erica arranged the foam mattress and blankets on the floor beside Katy's bed and punched her pillow into place. "Well, that was a fun night, but not quite what I expected."

Katy burst out laughing. "No, not quite. But it turned out okay, after we all settled down. Or after the men settled down. And luckily it wasn't a real fight. That would have been embarrassing."

"Yeah, a group of handsome guys, though. Too bad I don't live over here. Three hockey players in one room, how can you get so lucky?"

Katy grinned down at her. "You can always come back for a visit. I can't guarantee things will be quite as exciting." She held up her blouse. "I'm glad this blouse was already the colour of a strawberry because I don't see how a white blouse would survive a cranberry martini."

"Yeah. Things just exploded in there. That Rome guy wasn't going to put up with someone asking you to dance if you didn't want to dance with him. He's quite an employer, very protective." She gave Katy a speculative look.

Katy coloured. "Well, don't read too much into it. He just seems to be like that. Have you seen him play?"

"Yeah, when the Victoria team were in Vancouver last month but nothing like that happened."

"Well, here's what he was like the first day I met him." Erica's eyes got bigger as Katy described the scene. "And I thought the older guy was Mr. Rome. I didn't know the son was running the business." They both subsided into giggles.

"Is he nice to work for?"

"Oh," Katy glanced down at her friend. "He lets me run the office the way I want to. Can you imagine? I've been out of college for two months. But really its Frank who runs things, I just ask him for direction. Most of the drivers are really nice too. I couldn't have been luckier."

Erica watched her face for a minute. "I think you like him."

Katy flushed. "Well, of course I like him. He's just quite big, and I prefer smaller men, really."

"You have to be joking. What's not to like? He's good looking, he's strong, he's sexy. And he leaped to your defence, even if you didn't need it. Come on, Katy. This is me, your friend, Erica."

She laughed. "Well, I'm working on it."

Katy lay in the darkened room listening to her friend's deep breathing. Erika was asleep already. She shifted to get more comfortable. Why did she protest so much about liking Brett? It was like a reflex, someone mentioned Brett and she protested that he was too overwhelming for her. But he wanted her, he'd made that clear and she was infatuated with him.

Those feelings made her feel vulnerable in all kinds of ways. She worked for him, and her life balanced delicately on her work right now. But also his size made her feel insecure and she wasn't sure why. He didn't try to overpower her. Was it because she didn't think she could control him? Possibly. Taking care of herself was her job, had been since she was six, and Brett threw it all out of balance.

She could keep lying to her friends but not to herself. She wanted him.

CHAPTER EIGHTEEN

Katy fretted about the beginning of the big job this morning. Frank tried to calm her down but he was excited as well. If they pulled it off, the company would be well on the road to recovery.

She radioed to Buster as soon as she was in. The drivers had all left the gravel yard in East Sooke at seven, starting with their first loads. She talked to Renwick and then called Ken, the owner-operator that Frank had hired. She liked him. Middle aged and professional, he had a quirky sense of humour.

Then she called Sterns, the second man Frank had recruited. "He's good and can do the job," Frank warned her, "But he gets cranky so don't take any guff."

Organizing her day sheets for the Mikkleson job, she added them to the stack Frank had already created and went in to put them on Brett's desk. It was finally quiet in the office, everyone out and no one calling on the dispatch radio.

Sighing she sank into Brett's big leather chair. Her feet barely touched the floor but she gave a push and it swung around. Laughing she pushed again and had to grab the edge of the desk to slow down. The blotter flipped onto the floor.

Oops. She giggled to herself. If she was going to play around in the boss's office, she'd better not disturb anything.

Picking it up, she tossed it back on his desk, then grabbed her papers and stacked them together before laying them in the middle of the blotter. Then her hand stilled.

There was a note on the blotter in Frank's handwriting, 'Bruno', with a phone number. It wasn't the number she had for Bruno Morelli but he didn't answer that one anymore, it had been disconnected. Could be a coincidence, there was more than one man named Bruno in town.

But it was odd, the name written there like a note to call him. Slowly reaching for a pen she wrote the number down on a square of paper, tucking it into her pocket. The dispatch squawked and she ran into the outer office to answer it.

~ ~ ~

"I'll pick you up at eleven."

Katy glanced at him from lowered lashes, then straightened the phone on her desk. "Well, it's just that I'm usually busy on Saturday. I have stuff to do to get ready for work and then…"

"What time do you work?" He had a patient look on his face and she blushed.

"I start at six," she said, stacking the papers in front of her. "I leave home at five-thirty."

"Okay, so if you're home by four, does that give you enough time?"

"Well…"

"Three. How about if I guarantee to have you back home by three?"

She glanced at him, a small smile on her face. "Okay. Three will work. Thank you."

He smiled in return. "You're welcome. I just want to spend a little time with you."

She blushed.

"Good. So, let's look at the Mikkleson job. How are we doing?"

She was immediately more at ease. Brett grinned to himself as her spine straightened. Bristling with efficiency, she pulled the schedules across the desk. "The main problem right now is the length of wait time for our trucks on the logging roads. It'll be good when we can access the site directly through Sooke when they open up the route off Clutesi Road."

"Hmm. Well that's never going to happen."

"What?" Her head jerked up. "Mr. Mikkleson told me last time I called him. If we were just patient, it'd get better with new access. I was going to start the extra billing and he said there was no need, it would open up shortly."

"Yes, but the municipality of Sooke doesn't want that kind of heavy traffic through a residential area. They had a hearing on it early on and it was revisited last week at the Council meeting." Brett shifted his feet. "Mikkleson knows that. How are you billing? Let's have a look."

As Brett headed home that evening he pondered the message Frank had left on his desk. Bruno Morelli had walked into the office a few nights ago just as Frank was locking up. He asked to see Mr. Rome and Frank told him Rome was gone for the day. Morelli left his phone number and when Frank asked what it was about, he mentioned an opportunity to invest in the business.

"Do you know what that's about?" Frank had asked.

"Not really," said Brett, "but I've heard about this guy. What did he look like?"

Frank gave him a level stare. "He was about twenty-eight, thirty. Kind of average size. Lean and sinewy-like, black hair cut on the long side. And he didn't strike me as on the up and up, know what I mean? Something about him. Why, are you interested in finding investors?"

"No, but I'd like to meet Morelli."

Frank watched him but didn't say anything.

Brett grimaced. "What? I think Katy knows him and he talked to her about an investment. If he comes in again, I'd like to talk to him."

Frank pressed his lips against his teeth. "Are you thinking of messing in that little girl's business? Because I have to say..."

He put up his hand. "No. Okay? I'm not messing in her business, not really."

His foreman snorted.

"But I want to meet him."

"Okay." Frank shrugged.

~~~

Brett parked Paddy's truck at the side of the trail and walked around to open Katy's door. Pulling a backpack from behind her seat, he dropped the tailgate to let his dog out of the truck bed. Boots immediately sniffed around Katy's feet then stood with his head conveniently positioned right beneath her hand so she could pet him. Brett watched his manoeuvre with amusement. He knew exactly how the dog felt, he'd been there himself.

"Oh, I love your dog. He's so nice. Hello, Boots. Aren't you pretty?"

Brett snorted. "He hasn't been pretty in quite a few years. Probably not since he was a pup."

"No, he's lovely. Does he need a leash?"

"He's fine. He'll explore a bit but doesn't wander. Come on, this way." Brett took her hand and headed down the trail.

"Where are we going?"

"Not far, less than a mile. There's a nice meadow full of plants and tons of blackberries. Boots and I came down here last week to check it out and it hasn't changed much in ten or twelve years. Are you okay to walk that far?"

"Yep. I wore my walking shoes, like you said." Brett glanced down to see slightly worn runners on her feet. He looked back to his own hiking boots and realized she must not have a lot of financial resources to work with. No wonder she worked two jobs. He wondered what she was paying for with those two paycheques.

Yet she always looked beautiful, her hair brushed till it shone and pulled back into a ponytail or held with combs, sometimes just down on her shoulders. Today she had tiny heart earrings in her ears and a buttoned blouse tucked into shorts that reached halfway to her knees.

"How did you find this place?" She chatted as they walked along the trail and followed him through the trees up the bank and down again into a pretty sunny meadow. Boots bounded ahead, snuffling through the shrubbery. Brett stopped at the edge of the clearing. "What do you think?"

She took in a breath of surprise. "It's beautiful!" They faced a small dish-shaped field of grass bordered by shrubs and trees. Rhododendrons grew along two sides blooming in white and pale pink, daisies thickly dotting the expanse. The sun was captured in the space giving it a warm glow like a private garden.

He smiled down at her in satisfaction. "It is, isn't it? I thought you'd like it."

"I love it. Look at Boots. What's he found?" A chipmunk chattered madly and dashed for the nearest evergreen.

"Boots! Come here. Leave it alone." Brett pulled a blanket from the pack and spread it in the shade near the rhodos.

"You can even smell them," she enthused. "Their perfume is just lovely."

"Yeah, they're really something. Unique to the west coast. Here, Boots." He pulled a dish out of the pack and poured water into it, setting it aside for the dog. Katy grabbed the dog's toy on a rope and threw it with all her might, Boots bounding off to fetch it.

Brett grinned to himself. That was definitely a girl throw. He grabbed it from the dog's mouth. "Here, do it like this." He seized the end of the rope and slung it across the grass. "It'll go farther that way."

"Okay. Come here, Boots." She chased the dog and wrestled the toy from him, leaning back to heave it as far as she could. Her ass looked so good in those shorts. They showed her shape in a way that grabbed his total attention, and when she bent over to ruffle Boots ears, Brett tried not to let her see his stare. He laid out the food and called her over. Katy sank down on the blanket beside him.

"How old is your dog?"

He glanced up in surprise. "Boots? He's about twelve or

thirteen. He's really slowed down in the last couple of years, used to run like mad after the chipmunks. But he's getting old, aren't you boy?" He rubbed the dog's head.

"Did he live with you the whole time or did he stay at home with your parents?"

Brett smiled slightly at her probing. "Well, he stayed home with me when we first got him but when I left I was boarding in folks" homes so I couldn't take him with me. I'd see him when I came back to visit. But later when I got to university, he came with me. I've had him for the last five years now. Mum died four years ago, so it's just as well he was with me."

"That was hard, to lose your mother so young."

He stared into her eyes. "She *was* young. She had cancer and they found it too late."

"Oh, my." She patted his arm. "People think it's harder on daughters, but I think sons miss their mums just as much."

He examined his sandwich. She was right, he still grieved. Boots galloped past and he tossed him a crust of bread.

"It must have been hard to leave home so young."

He shook his head slowly, glancing back at her. "No, not really. I was pretty keen to get going on my career."

"At fourteen?"

"Yeah, why so many questions?" He reached over and pulled her toward him. "What are you thinking?"

"Just getting to know you. You don't like questions?"

He looked straight into those clear light grey eyes. "You can ask me anything you want. I'm not hiding anything."

She turned away. "Okay."

"Here, have a sandwich." He pulled out a pack and put it in her lap, grabbing another one for himself and tearing the packaging off it.

"You like picnics, don't you?" she mumbled around a mouthful.

Brett squinted up at her. "Yeah, I do. You?"

She nodded thoughtfully. "Yes, I do, actually. I just haven't been on many lately but you seem to know a lot of nice places."

He watched her eat, passing the cut vegetables and container of pickles when she slowed down, then some grapes. Tossing a biscuit to Boots he placed the package beside Katy.

"Are you trying to fatten me up?"

"Yes," he growled, his voice low, "and then I'm going to eat you up."

"Oh, the big bad wolf!" And she burst into gales of laughter. He grinned and shoved the food out of the way, pushing her down on the blanket.

"Yeah, the big bad wolf. And you're my little piglet." He tickled her and she laughed, writhing to get away from him. His hands gentled as his mouth found hers. His kiss was careful, soft on her lips. She stilled beneath him but he kissed her again, firmer this time and she slowly opened for him.

Lifting his head he found her watching him with that wary stare. "Did you like that?" She nodded, her body tense. So he kissed her again, more insistent this time, more sure. Slowly her eyes closed and he kissed her eyelids, her cheeks. He heard her sigh as he nuzzled her ear and down her throat.

She was lax in his arms. Returning to her mouth, he gave her long slow sucking kisses that nearly undid him while his hand was busy on the buttons of her blouse.

Carefully he spread the lapels and lifted his head to look down at her. She was beautiful. He'd known she would be, but he'd been driven to see her. That glimpse he'd caught through the office bathroom window had just whet his appetite. And the one night they'd made love, he could feel her flesh in his hands but he couldn't see her in the dark. The memory of that night had driven him mad, the need to *see* her was like an obsession. Her breath caught when he unsnapped her brassiere.

"It's okay. It's okay." He gazed into her wary eyes and then back down as he lifted the cups of her bra away to bare her to his sight. His heart hammered in his chest.

"You are so lovely." He stroked her silky skin. "I needed to see you. You're beautiful, Katy." He put his mouth at the top of her breast and licked his way down to the nipple set in a delicate circle of pale pink, a little pebble on his tongue as he drew it in. Tense under his hands, her breath came quickly.

"It's alright." He stroked her, watching her breast change shape under the pressure of his fingers. He looked back at her face. "Are you afraid of me?"

"Uh..."

"What are you afraid of?" He kissed the side of her mouth. "Tell me. You look at me as if you're not safe. Is that how you feel, unsafe?"

"Uh, no. It's just..."

"Just what?"

"I'm not sure what we're doing together. Are we dating each other?" Her eyes were wide with confusion.

He stalled for a minute. "Yeah, I think we are. Don't you?"

Her pupils dilated. "I wasn't sure. We don't seem to go on traditional type dates, and I work for you so I thought..." The colour climbed her cheeks.

Oh, God. Brett glanced back down to where his hand massaged her. Now was not the time to have this conversation. Not when he'd finally managed to remove some of her clothes.

Putting his mouth back on her nipple he suckled her, his temperature climbing rapidly. He pressed himself against her hip, wrapped his arms tighter around her as he nursed at her breast. All he needed was another few minutes and he wouldn't be able to stop.

He rested his face against her skin and breathed deeply, taking in her scent and waiting for a little sanity. Finally he pulled her blouse closed to shield his gaze and then watched his hand return to smooth her breast and hold her through the fabric.

Looking into her clear gaze, he said "I want to see you, Katy. But if I ask you out, you've mostly said 'no'"

She blinked and glanced away.

"Haven't you?"

She peeked back at him cautiously.

"I can't get you to agree to make a normal date, so I kind of bully you into going somewhere with me."

Her lips moved in a tiny smile.

"You know it's true."

His finger traced the lines of her mouth. "I want to date you, Katy. I want to make love with you." He watched her gaze go wary again and sighed. "You're afraid of something, afraid of me. I just don't know why."

She couldn't meet his eyes. Looking instead at his shirt, she ran a finger over the pocket stitching. "I think you're too big for me," she whispered.

"What? I'm not too big. Lots of guys are my size."

She coloured darkly. "I think you're too big to come inside me." Her voice was a mere thread of sound, her eyes closing in embarrassment.

"Oh, baby." His throat closed up with emotion and he rocked her in his arms as he tried to sort out his confusion. "Why? Did I hurt you?"

She nodded, staring at his shirt.

"Was that your first time, that time with me?" His voice was strained. "You were on the pill already and I thought..."

She closed her eyes for a moment.

"Had you been with someone else?"

Her head moved in a tiny nod.

His heart quaked in his chest. "So you think... you think I was too big."

She glanced at him sideways. "You're very big."

He stifled a laugh, more like a groan. "Just because I'm tall doesn't mean ..."

"You're not just tall, you're wide and heavy in the arms and legs, too."

"Yeah, but that's muscle from working out, Katy. I'm the same as any other guy down there. I see the guys in the locker room. We're all pretty much the same."

He watched her face, then moved in closer to kiss her tenderly on that lush mouth. "Do you like that, when I kiss you?" She nodded and kissed him back.

He choked. His fingers moved involuntarily on her breast and he slid his hand back inside her blouse to the soft skin and pebbled nipples. "Do you like it when I touch you here? She nodded again.

"So do I", he breathed. "God, do I ever! I don't think I'm too big for you. I haven't been with a lot of women but I've never hurt anyone. Did it hurt with that other guy?"

"Oh," she said and turned her head. "I can't…"

"I know." He hugged her close, tucking her face against his chest.

"We only did it once." Her voice was muffled.

His heart clenched in his chest. She'd only been with one other man, and then only once. He didn't know why but his gut was so damned tight and some emotion pressed heavily behind his eyelids.

She had such a mix in her of magnetic buoyant hope and outgoing optimism, overlaid with a caution and wariness that kept him at arm's length. It tugged him toward her and pushed him away all at the same time. He was caught, captivated.

"There are lots of ways to make love. There are ways to make us both happy without hurting you." He took a breath and eased back to see her fiery blush and smiled slightly, then sobered. "I didn't mean to hurt you, Katy."

Slowly she turned her head, her gaze now clear and open. "I know you didn't," she said. She rubbed his arm with her hand.

He fell like a stone. He could only look at her, wondering why it had taken him so long to find her. He felt himself falling and put his mouth on hers to anchor himself. Her kisses were drugging, she sighed in his arms.

Holding her, his mind was in turmoil. "Did I hurt you the second time? Because I think you came that time."

She blushed.

"That's what I thought," he said with satisfaction and hugged her close again. The sun was on his back, the scent of crushed grass beneath them and with Katy in his arms he wondered what more he could want.

Just then Boots growled, then gave a hoarse bark. Brett's head shot up in time to see a small group of people come through the trees and enter the field at the far end. He pulled Katy's blouse across her breasts and sat up, one hand holding it closed as he stared down the field.

The intruders wandered for a few minutes then settled on the grass and opened a thermos between them. Boots stopped barking, growled a little and lay down at his feet. Glancing down he saw Katy putting the buttons together on her blouse. Damn. He'd finally gotten her top off and hadn't seen nearly enough to slake his thirst.

It was just as well. A glance at his watch showed they were out of time and a survey of the blanket that Boots had eaten the rest of the sandwiches. Leaning down, he pulled her back into his arms and kissed her, a long slow melding of mouths that left him slightly breathless.

He whispered into her hair, "We have to go now or you'll be late and you won't go out with me again." He felt her body shake and prayed it was laughter.

CHAPTER NINETEEN

Brett waited till Frank left for the day. He heard him thunder down the steps as Katy reached for her purse. "Katy, before you go…" He caught her wrist as she walked past. "I just have a few things. Come here for a minute." Tugging her across the room, he sat on the sofa. He thought of pulling her directly onto his lap but she had that wary expression on her face.

"Listen, I'm leaving town tomorrow morning, we're playing in Edmonton and then Lethbridge. I won't be back until Monday. Can I see you tonight?"

"Oh," She frowned up at him. "I can't, Brett. I have to work this evening."

"You're working?" He reared back in disbelief. "I thought you only worked Saturday and Sunday nights."

"Usually. But someone called in sick this morning so they phoned me. I said I'd take the shift. I have to be there by six."

He felt a sudden rush of anger crawling up his gut. He stared at her. "When could we have a date, do you think?" He tried to keep the sarcasm out of his voice but she obviously heard something.

Her expression immediately closed and she glanced away for a second then back at him with narrowed eyes. "Well, I

147

guess it depends on whether your obligations and mine coincide, doesn't it?"

He felt belligerent now and she picked that up right away.

"You're just as busy as I am!" she added. "You don't honestly think I should clear my schedule so that whenever you find you're free, I'll be available!" It wasn't a question.

He stared at her mouth, set in a stubborn line. "Well then, there's nothing else for it," he said and kissed her. Her mouth was tight against his but he just softened the kiss. He felt her fractional easing until she was leaning against him as he ravaged her mouth. He moulded her breast with his hand and his breath came faster. Man, she turned him on so quick he felt his head spin.

"Come here," he pulled her onto his lap after all. "I just need a few kisses because five days is a bloody long time." Her eyes widened at his language but he didn't give her a chance to reply. He fell with her onto the cushions and crushed her under him. "Don't fight me, Katy. I'm getting desperate."

She didn't fight him. She opened her mouth to let him in and wrapped her arms around his neck. He dove in and devoured her. He pushed his hand under her shirt and had her bra unsnapped in seconds. "Oh, look at you." His mouth took her breast and suckled her hard until she was gasping, then softened and soothed against her nipples. His hand moulded her hip and he had a rending, desperate feeling in his chest.

"Sorry baby, sorry." Gentling his actions, he calmed her with his mouth. She was as open to him as she'd ever been, her eyes dreamy and soft.

"Katy, you're driving me crazy. I want to be able to see you. I want to spend some time with you. Not now, I know that." His mouth flattened to a straight line, the dimples deep in his cheeks. "But I don't know when. It's murder on me. I can't..." He thrust a frustrated hand through his hair. "I need to..."

He stared at her. "I want to make a date with you. Can we

do that? Can we make a date?"

"Okay."

His mouth moved over hers, those beautiful lush and now slightly swollen lips. "I'm sorry, I didn't mean to be rough. I just get desperate." He kissed her eyelids, a soft brush of his lips.

"I'm back Monday. Can I see you Monday night?" He grinned. "You mentioned we didn't have dates. Well, this will be a real date, dinner and dancing, or a movie. What do you want?"

"Mmm. Maybe dinner and a movie. We can start with that."

"Great. So it's a promise. I'll call you when I get in on Monday, okay? If your phone isn't on, you have to promise to call me back." The look he gave her was stern.

"I will."

"Okay." His gaze fell to her mouth. "Just another kiss. I'm gone a long time."

He watched the colour rise in her cheeks and then she slowly nodded. "Yes."

Thank God. He crushed her against his chest.

~~~

Katy had just left the yard when Brett heard a loud rap on the open door of the office. Leaning forward from his chair, he couldn't see anyone in the entry. As he was getting up he heard it again. "Hang on," he called and trod across the office floor. There was a young man standing just inside the door, looking around the room. He glanced over as Brett came into view.

"Hi," he said. "My name's Bruno Morelli. I'd like to talk to Mr. Rome, if he's in."

Brett looked him over. So this was Morelli. He saw a man no older than himself, about five foot eight or nine, slim build. He was wearing a suit that had once been a decent piece of apparel but now showed its wear and seemed too large for him. His jet black wavy hair was cut long and styled back from his darker skinned Mediterranean face. He was a handsome man and Brett felt himself bristle.

He put out his hand. "I'm Rome. What can I do for you?"

"Uh." Bruno looked him in the eye. "Sorry, but I've met Mr. Rome. He's an older man. That's who I want to see."

Brett put his hand back on his hip. "That's my father. He's had a heart attack, he doesn't work here anymore. I run the business now."

Morelli glanced around the office again, apparently just to be sure he was in the right place. Then he squared his shoulders. "Okay. Well, do you have a minute? I'd like to bounce a few ideas off you."

Brett swept his hand toward the office. "Be my guest." He pointed to a chair in front of his desk and threw himself into his own chair. He stared at Morelli, waiting, unwilling to make it easy for him.

Morelli cleared his throat. "I've put a group of investors together who are searching for a good place to put their money. Your company was mentioned and we've had a look at what you've got going here."

Brett tried to control his temper. "Had a look at what we have here? How would you do that? This is a private company which means the books are closed. You need my permission to even conduct a credit check."

Morelli held his hands palms out. "No, no, Mr. Rome. I've given you the wrong impression. We certainly haven't had a look at your books or anything like that. We're just aware of the size of the company and the fact that you've undergone an expansion. It caught the attention of one of the investors. So we're interested in putting forward a proposal."

Brett waved his hand. "Propose away."

Morelli became uncomfortable at his apparent lack of interest but struggled on. "We have a couple of hundred thousand dollars put together as an investment pool. And we'd like to discuss investing it in your business."

Brett pursed his lips. "I see. And what do you want in return?"

"To be blunt, we'd need a secure position. We'd take

shares."

Brett shook his head. "This company is simple form and any shareholders would be liable for outstanding debt. So it wouldn't be a secure position. Only preferred shares would give you that and we don't issue those."

He gave Morelli a long look. "However," he continued, "a loan position might be possible. Would your investors be interested in that? We'd have to really examine it, of course. Have a look at the terms you're offering. See who the investors are."

Morelli seemed suddenly eager. "Yes, that's a distinct possibility. What kind of terms would you be looking for?"

Brett leaned forward and began to talk.

~~~

Brett sat in the reclined seat, the seatbelt loosened across his hips. He stared out the plane's tiny window at the field of clouds and didn't notice the stewardess until she'd passed. Reaching, he caught the edge of her uniform. "Excuse me. Can I get a soft drink? Thanks." He stared back out the window.

They'd be landing in about an hour. The gigantic tips of the Rockies poked through the white nebulous layer in a uniform pattern of jagged remote peaks.

"How you doing?" He looked over to see Jerome peering at him.

"Good. You?"

Jerome nodded. "Okay. You seem a bit preoccupied. How are things going with your Dad?"

Brett pressed his lips against his teeth. "Better actually, in some ways. He's willing to talk business. And we've managed to get him to allow home workers to come in twice a week just to do meals and cleaning and shit like that. His medications are complicated.

"But he's drinking pretty heavy right now and of course he's not supposed to drink at all. His girlfriend left him and he's back out in his favourite bar. He's either looking for her, or for companionship. Must get boring as hell sitting at home waiting to get better." He shrugged.

Jerome nodded.

Brett's soft drink came. He snapped the top and took a long swallow.

Jerome leaned across the armrest again. "And how are things going with Katy?"

Brett glanced at him sideways. "What are you talking about?"

Jerome snickered. "You know what I'm talking about. Even your drivers know you're going out with her, or trying to. But she seems a bit wary. Although if being hauled bodily out of a nightclub would make a woman wary, seems odd." He laughed again and Brett writhed in his seat.

"Yeah, that was a bit over the top. I don't know what got into me. I'm surprised she was still speaking to me after that."

Brett knew what had gotten into him. He'd felt such a wave of possessiveness come over him when he saw that guy ask her to dance. And then when he had the nerve to come back and ask her again, after she'd already said 'no'... It didn't bear thinking about. But it had occurred to him to wonder how he would have reacted if she had said 'yes'.

"Well, you sure felt strongly about it." Jerome chuckled. "It's just not your usual style. With Marilyn, you were pretty much easy come, easy go. You're usually a more laid back kind of guy where the ladies are concerned."

"I know. It was a sudden aberration. I'm not sure it impressed her though. Turning into a caveman doesn't really fly these days." Brett stared at the soda in his hand. He was a little disconcerted when his emotions swung him around like that. It had happened that first time on the ice in that fight with the Victoria team and he'd put it down to all the changes he was facing.

But Katy seemed to spark it in him. She pulled back and he bulled ahead chasing after her. He needed to find a way to slow down or he was going to spook her again and who knew if he could recover?

This was all new to him. With Marilyn, she pursued and he

responded. He'd enjoyed their time together, never considered whether he was in love. He got what he needed out of the arrangement and he just assumed Marilyn did too.

With Katy he wanted more, needed more.

He'd given it a lot of thought on this trip and realized he'd been focussed on what he needed, what his body was demanding. But now he figured the way to win her was to focus on what she needed. She was the one holding all the cards, and he just had to encourage her to lay them down.

He'd be content with kisses for now.

~~~

Katy stepped into her black heels, numbers whirling in her head. She'd gone over her money situation and it was very tight. She couldn't bring herself to ask Dad for money. She'd have to admit what a mess she'd made of things, giving her money to Bruno without any assurance of getting it back. Given a little time, she was confident she could dig herself out of this pit. She just needed to hang on.

Inserting a small pearl earring in her lobe she fumbled to attach the back. Sid knocked on the door and poked her head in.

"Almost ready to leave?"

"I've got a few minutes. What's up?"

Sid came in and sat on her bed, a secret little smile on her face. "I've given notice here. I'm moving in with Mike at the end of the month."

Katy's mouth opened in surprise and then she squealed in delight. "You're joking! Just like that? You sneak!"

"I know. He's been asking me and he got rid of his roommate a month ago. So I decided."

"Wow. Are you sure? You must be or you wouldn't have taken that step." She hugged her friend. "I'm so pleased for you, Sid. I hope you two will be really happy."

"Yeah." Sid smiled at her. "It's fun, you know? He's so thoughtful. I love him, I guess. I never thought it would be like this." She giggled and wrapped her arms around herself.

"I'm happy for you. Really, Sid. No one deserves it more

than you. He's a lucky man to get you. You tell him that for me."

Sid laughed. "You tell him. It'll mean more coming from you."

"So, you're gone at the end of the month. That's only a few days. How was Sherry with that? It's kind of short notice."

"She had a friend who wanted to move in, so she was pleased." Sid frowned. "I don't know how it will work out for you here, Katy, when I'm gone. It might be time to find another place. I've met the new girl and she's not a nice specimen. Must be Sherry's clone or something."

"I see." Katy searched the open doorway, then glanced back at her friend. "The thing is, I'm not here a lot. Working seven days a week keeps me busy. So I don't need to get along with her, I just need to stay out of her way, right? And in a few weeks I'll be able to start to find another place. Right now this is what I can manage. Surely, it can work for a couple of weeks."

Sid gave her a curious glance. "Did you go riding today?"

"Yeah. I get fresh air and exercise at the same time. Win-win, as they say."

Sid laughed. "Does Brett Rome ride bikes?"

Katy flushed. "Brett's in Edmonton. I went with Randy."

"And what does Brett think of that?"

"I didn't ask. He's back Monday and we have a date Monday night."

"Aha. A date. Finally. So he *is* your hockey player. At least he seems to think so. The way he hauled you out of Striders…"

Katy put up her hand to stop the flow of words and they both dissolved into giggles. "I've never seen anything like it."

"I think you should make it a little harder for him."

Katy raised her brows. "What do you mean?"

"Well, he's got you right there in his office when he comes to work. You're at his beck and call. I think you need to change up your outfits a little. You know that wine-coloured bustier I bought? With the deep V cardigan over it would certainly get his attention, bring things to a head."

"So to speak," Katy added sardonically. "You're wicked."

Sid laughed. "But in a good way."

Next morning the bustier was sitting on her chair as Sid had promised. Katy considered it for long moments before she decided, why not? It really did match well with the grey sweater and she pulled on a short black skirt and heels.

The comments started the minute she got into the office.

Buster was first. He'd called in that morning to change trucks, No.7 needed maintenance and he was taking No. 3 out to the Sooke project. "Wow, should I look at that? Maybe not," he mumbled and wandered back out the office door. Katy looked down in concern but the outfit seemed modest enough.

Brett was talking with Frank in the inner office and came out to get some papers. He stopped in his tracks, then moved slowly forward. "You sure know how to get a guy's attention," he said.

But when Pete came in she heard him in the inner office saying to Brett, "Should I be able to see that?"

"Apparently so," said Brett dryly.

"Wheew," Pete blew out a breath. "If you say so." But he averted his eyes as he grabbed his keys.

"Frank, we need to decide how we're going to do this billing for Mikkleson. Did Brett say what we're to do?"

Frank just jerked his head toward the inner office as he grabbed his keys. "Check with him."

Katy waited in the doorway while Brett finished a phone call. "The interim billing," she said, holding up an invoice. "How do you want to handle it?"

"Okay." He came out and they worked on it, but his eyes kept straying to her cleavage and he'd forget what he was saying. Katy found herself giggling for no reason, trying to stifle her humour. Finally they sorted it out. "Is there anything else?" She looked up wide eyed.

He slowly peeled his gaze from the tops of her breasts and

shook his head. "No, that's it." He wandered back to his desk.

The phone rang while she was on dispatch. Brett got it.

When his tone changed, became sharp and demanding, her ears perked up. She heard him say goodbye and put the phone carefully back in the cradle. Katy waited, but when the silence continued, she went to his door. Brett sat with one hand still on the phone, staring at the top of his desk.

"Everything okay?"

This time when he glanced up, it was straight into her eyes. He blinked. "Dad's had another heart attack. I have to leave for the hospital." But he just sat, staring at her blankly.

She moved forward. "Don't worry. We'll take care of everything here. You just go."

Nodding, he heaved himself out of the chair. "Yeah. Thanks Katy." He walked past her then turned back.

"Katy," he pulled her against him and gave her a fierce kiss. "Don't wear that thing again. The guys can't think when you dress like that." He stared down at her chest for a few moments then released her and walked out the door.

CHAPTER TWENTY

N ews at the hospital wasn't good. Brett and his sister paced back and forth then sat and drank coffee as time passed. Finally he persuaded her to go home and take care of her family, promising to phone when he had news. At eleven there was still nothing. Arranging for the hospital to call him if anything changed, he went home.

The house was a total disaster. Dirty clothes spilled out of Randy's room and down the hall. Dishes covered with cold food and bits of sandwich were haphazardly discarded. Cups with dried coffee rings sat in clusters on the coffee table.

Brett went into the kitchen, found himself a soda in the fridge and fought his way through the mess to the living room couch. Rummaging around until he found the remote under a cushion, he turned on the television. When the front door opened a couple of hours later, he was dozing in front of a sports channel.

"Randy, is that you?"

"Yeah. Didn't know you were home."

"My car's in the garage."

"Oh." Randy walked into the living room, his eyes focussed on the TV. "What're you watching?"

"Nothing much." Brett snapped it off. "Come and sit down here." He shoved a used towel onto the floor. "We need to talk."

Randy stiffened, standing in the doorway.

"Come on." Brett waved at the couch.

Randy seated himself gingerly on the edge of a cushion. "What's up?"

"I think you know what's up." He just looked at him. The kitchen smells leaking from Randy's sweatshirt, garlic, fat, some buttery smell from marks down the front of his uniform filled the air. It must have been a busy evening at the restaurant.

Randy reddened. "If you mean the mess, I can get this cleaned up. Sorry for leaving it."

Brett grunted. "Paddy just had another heart attack."

Randy looked chagrined. "I'm sorry, Brett. How is he?"

"We don't know yet. Stabilized, it's what they always say. Anyway, I guess our fathers didn't take care of themselves very well, did they? My dad drank too much and yours smoked too much. So here they are in their mid sixties and both in terrible shape. Think we can do any better?"

Randy glared between his knees at the floor. "Hope so."

"Yeah," Brett sighed and leaned back again. "Me too. Listen, Randy. I can't live like this. It doesn't work for me. It's not a matter of cleaning it up. I know you can do that. It just gets to be a mess again. I can't bring a woman back here, I can't even bring the guys, it's such a disaster. Something has to change. I'm finished with this." He waved his arm tiredly toward the hallway and kitchen. "Finished."

Randy didn't say anything.

Brett patted his cousin's knee and heaved off the couch. "I'm off to bed. I'm wiped."

Next morning Brett stared in disbelief at the clock beside his bed. He'd slept for eleven hours. Sitting up he pushed his hands back through his hair. He couldn't remember ever sleeping that long. Staggering to the bathroom, he leaned against the wall with one hand as he gave a jaw-cracking yawn.

Something was different. Blearily he peered around. The

bathroom was clean. The counter was cleared of everything except his shaving kit. He stared. All the dirty towels were gone from the floor, the tub even appeared to have been scrubbed.

What the hell? He yanked the door open and peered down the hall. It was still littered with bits of dirt and stuff stuck to the carpet but the clothes were gone.

He found his toothbrush and slopped some toothpaste on it. As he brushed he made a mental note of what to do first. He called Katy at the office. She answered on the second ring. "Rome Trucking, Katy speaking."

"Katy, it's Brett."

"Hi, Brett." Her voice went soft. "How's Paddy? We've all been waiting to hear. Frank's here and Gert just came in. Gert said we were to pray for him so we have been."

Brett breathed deeply through his nose and his eyes misted. "That's nice, Katy." His voice came out rough. "Thank the guys for me."

"Okay. How is he?"

"He's stable, which they tell me is a good thing."

"Ahh. He's stable, guys. Paddy's stable and they're saying that's good." She talked into the phone again. "And how are you? What's going to happen?"

"I don't know. That's why I called. I don't think I'll be in today."

"No. Everything is fine. Frank has it under control. We sent out our invoice on the Mikkleson job and Claude didn't even question the wait time charges. You don't have to worry. Just take care of your father."

"Claude?" He picked out the one item that caught his attention in all that.

"Claude Mikkleson."

"You call him Claude?"

There was a pause. "He came into the office and introduced himself. He told me to call him Claude. And he said he'll bring the cheque by the office this week."

"I'll just bet he did," Brett muttered. There was silence for a second. Claude Mikkleson didn't strike him as a ladies' man but he was a good-looking guy, quite a bit younger than Paddy and in good shape. Brett knew he had to ignore it, at least for now. "Okay."

"Yes, so don't worry. Frank, do you have any messages for Brett? Here, I'll put Frank on." There was a click as she put him on hold. Damn, he'd lost her again.

When he'd sorted things out with Frank and got Katy back on the line, he said, "Katy, listen. Don't say anything, just listen. I want to see you, and I know something always happens to get in the way but I'll be in touch later today. I want to make a plan, okay? Don't forget."

"I won't," she breathed. "Bye, Brett."

Cripes, even her voice turned him on. He was in a bad way. The hospital call turned up the same information, Paddy was stable. Calling the team office he put his hockey play on hold.

As he turned the phone off, he heard beeping to indicate messages. The first was from Hart, "Where are you buddy, we were going to go out for a beer." Brett realized he'd had his phone off at the hospital all evening. He made a mental note to call Hart and apologize.

Liz had called this morning while he was still sleeping. She was heading to work if he needed her. He made sure he had her work number and deleted the message. Then there was one from Aunt Ray. She was going out of town on a cruise with friends and her cat was too old to go into a kennel. She wanted to keep it at home. Would he be able to stay at the house while she was away? Sorry for the short notice, but maybe it would work out.

Brett paused in the process of shrugging into his shirt. Stay at Aunt Ray's house? That would be perfect. He could get away from Randy's mess. And he'd have somewhere to invite Katy.

Most of his time that day was spent at the hospital. Doc Wilde paused to chat with Brett, assuring him there was very little new damage but Paddy was not in good shape. If they hoped for a better outcome, they needed better input.

Brett nodded. He already knew all of this.

Katy had left by the time he called the office later in the day. The answering service was switched on and her cell phone went straight to voicemail. He left a message.

At Paddy's house he met up with Liz. There wasn't much to do, take the old food out of the fridge, change the bedding.

"What do you think, Brett? Will he just go downhill from here until one of these heart attacks kills him?" Liz's face was so forlorn, Brett wrapped his arms around her.

"I don't know, Sis. It's up to him. We'll just arrange the best care we can and see what he's willing to accept. You know how he is. He was back drinking in the Moonlighter Pub. What can you do?"

She nodded against his shirt. "I know." She sighed. "It's just so depressing. He doesn't have to live this way."

"No, but I don't think he knows any other way. His only friends are from the bar. He stopped doing anything else a long time ago. I wonder why he gave up all his baseball buddies. I mean, I imagine I'll still have hockey friends long after we all stop playing in the leagues. I'll still want to strap on the skates, wouldn't you think?"

"Yeah, I don't know."

Brett dropped his arms and shook himself. "Okay. What has to be done here? You're tired and so am I. Let's hit the road. And I'll do the shift tomorrow at the hospital, okay? Phone me, but don't come in. If it's needed you can do the next day." He pushed her gently toward the door.

As they were leaving the phone rang and Brett grabbed it in the kitchen. "Paddy's house."

"Oh, who's this?" a woman's voice said. "Is that you, Brett?"

"Yeah, this is Brett. Who're you?"

She laughed lightly. "It's Dancy."

Brett stiffened. "Dancy. What can I do for you?"

"Well, I was looking for Paddy but if you're there, do you want to chat?" Her voice dropped low.

"Dancy," Brett gritted, "Paddy's in the hospital. You can visit him there. I'll certainly tell him you called." He laid the receiver back in the cradle.

Liz chuckled. "You could have been friendlier."

"Are you kidding? She's Dad's girlfriend. I'm not going to be anywhere near friendly. I thought she'd dumped him, anyway."

"So what is she calling for?"

"I imagine she's run out of money."

Liz made a face. "I wonder if she has a key to the house."

Brett stopped in his tracks. "A key? Of course she's got a key. What an idiot I am." He pulled his phone out and started texting.

"What are you doing?"

"Making a note to have the locks changed. Dad wouldn't be able to defend himself if she got in here and found his cheque book. Let's go."

~~~

Brett called Aunt Ray the next day. Marie's sister, Aunt Ray was so much like Brett's mother, he had often felt if he wanted to know what Mum would have said, he only had to talk to Aunt Ray to find out. Even the way her dark brown hair lay against her head was reminiscent of Marie.

"Thanks for thinking of me, Aunt Ray. I'll be glad to come over and stay with your cat. He doesn't need me to be home all day, does he?"

"No, Brett. Nothing like that. Cats are easy. He just needs you to be around from time to time and make sure his bowls don't get empty. He's got a cat door. And you can pet him now and then. He likes that."

"When do you leave?"

"Day after tomorrow. Come over and I'll give you the key. How's Paddy?"

"Huh. How'd you know?"

"Liz."

Brett laughed. "You guys must talk every day."

"Just about. So, how's he doing?"

162

"He's coming along. He won't be able to go home for a few days, which is fine with me. It gives us some time before the pressure's back on. You know what I mean. He hates having care people in his house and he kicks up such a racket about it, life is miserable for the rest of us."

"Yes, I know. And Randy and his mess don't help either. At least you can get away from that for a while."

"I guess Liz told you about that, too. Thanks, Aunt Ray. This works for me."

He heard a smile in her voice. "Well, I thought it might."

Brett hung up and called the office. When Katy answered the phone, he said, "Are you there alone or is anyone else in the office?"

"Pardon me?" she sounded startled. There was a pause before she added, "Is this an obscene phone call?"

Brett had to laugh. "Not yet."

She giggled. "No one else is here. Frank's driving a full day. We had to send Wilf out to drive the Mikkleson job. Ken Marshall had a problem with his truck and it's in for repairs. How's your father?"

"He's the same, stable but starting to pull out of it. He's going to be in the hospital for a while. Listen, I wanted to make a date with you." He paused, and heard her breathing into the phone. "Did you hear that, a date."

She laughed. "Yes, I heard. I was waiting to see what you were going to suggest."

"Oh. Okay. My Aunt is going away for a few weeks and I'm house sitting for her. I want to invite you out for lunch there on Sunday. Can you do that? We can eat early. I know you have to leave by about three to get ready for work. So come around eleven."

"Are you going to cook?"

"Yes," he bristled a little. "I can cook. There are a couple of things that I cook."

"Well, I'm impressed."

"You should be."

"Hmm. I'd like that. Where's her house?"

Brett gave her the address. "I know it's only Friday, Katy, and I'd like to see you before then but I'm at the hospital tonight and tomorrow is very busy."

"That's okay, Brett. I'm busy too. Sunday will be fine. I'll see you then."

"Okay." He thought a minute. "What are you doing tonight?"

"Sid and I are going to a movie. Then I'm going to stay the night with Dad so he and I can have a visit tomorrow."

"Sid? Who's Sid? You know more guys!"

She laughed. "Sid's a girl. Her name's Sidney. You met her at Strider's that night."

"Well, okay. Have a good visit with your Dad. Tell him I said 'hi'." Her laugh soothed him and he hated to hang up.

CHAPTER TWENTY ONE

Sunday dawned clear and sunny. Brett did some food shopping the day before between visits to the hospital and meetings with the people who were going to be caring for Paddy. He'd shoehorned in a workout at the hockey gym and rearranged a few things at Aunt Ray's house.

This morning he spent two hours at the hospital getting instructions from the physiotherapy department. Paddy had started to regain some strength and Wilde was talking about sending him home soon.

Brett finished there and made a beeline for Aunt Ray's. The marinade for the halibut was made and the sweet potatoes sliced for the barbecue. He'd bought a salad at the store and found a fancy bowl in the pantry to dump it in. Dragging a little table into the sunroom, he set it with Aunt Ray's good china. He knew she wouldn't mind. One of her favourite sayings was, "What good does it do sitting in the cupboard? Use it." So he did.

He found cloth napkins in her linen cupboard, then went through the side garden cutting roses for a bowl on the table. The doorbell rang just as he tried for the third time to get the flowers to stay in the bowl. Pulling them out, he laid them on the table. Katy would know what to do.

She stood on the front step in the bright sunshine, looking like a flower herself in a gauzy sleeveless cream coloured blouse over a little rose camisole. Her ivory skirt was light and the breeze flirted with the hem.

Brett gave her a slow smile, examining her thoroughly before stepping aside. "Come in," he said and she put her hand in his. He closed the door behind her, his eyes never leaving hers. "You look terrific."

Pulling her into his arms he leaned down to press his lips to hers. The kiss was gentle, a slow meeting of mouths. She blinked. He kissed her again. "Finally," was all he said.

Then he turned and led her to the back of the house. "I'm just finishing some prep work, so sit right here while I get everything done. Would you like something to drink? How about cranberry juice and soda water? I know you like that."

"Thanks, that would be great." Katy glanced around the room. "Oh, this is nice. It goes right out into a kind of sun porch. Is this where we're eating lunch? Wow!" She gestured at the small table set for two with pretty flowered china.

Brett handed her a tall glass. "Do you like it?"

She turned and smiled up at him. "It's really pretty."

"How hungry are you?"

"Um, well…"

"Did you eat breakfast yet?"

She took a sip of juice. "No, not really. I just got up."

"Ah, slept in. Well, I'd better feed you. Come sit out here and I'll get the barbeque going."

He sat her in an old cushioned rattan chair on the porch while he lit the burners. "Do you want to take a tour of the garden while that heats up?"

"Yes, please." She stared eagerly up at him. He felt a little pinch in his chest at her obvious anticipation. Taking her hand, he led her down the steps.

"Aunt Ray's garden is a lot like my mother's was. She has quite a bit of fruit. See, rhubarb there, a big patch of raspberries."

"Oh," Katy moaned. "Can I eat a few?" She immediately disappeared into the tall canes.

"Wait, wait. Your blouse is going to get ruined." Brett stepped in behind her and lifted the filmy material away from the prickles on the raspberries. He slipped his hand to her waist and leaned in to speak in her ear. "Maybe you should take it off." He felt her stiffen under his fingers and suppressed a laugh as she glanced back at him over her shoulder. He couldn't hide his grin. "Well, you don't want to wreck it."

"Very funny," she said crisply and bent toward the berries. "These are so good. Here, try this one." She held a berry on the tips of her fingers and he bent his head to grab it with his lips. "Aren't they good?"

He gave her a searching glance. "We're having some for lunch."

"Oh, great." She gave her sunniest smile. "Can I see the rest of the garden, then?"

"Sure." He managed to get her out of the patch without snagging her blouse or wrestling it off her which he was powerfully tempted to do. The little camisole underneath wouldn't prove much of a barrier and he really wanted to get a better look at it.

"There's a strawberry patch, kind of small. And a couple of fruit trees, apples. One's a crab-apple. And then she has a vegetable garden. A bunch of stuff." He waved in the general direction. "Lettuce, chard and those are carrots. I'm not sure about the rest of it. Oh, those are zucchini."

She laughed and nodded.

"What? You think I don't know my vegetables?"

She giggled again, then gazed around and sighed. "Isn't this lovely? Oh, look at the roses. And smell them," she said, following the path down the far side of the house. She buried her nose in a pale lemon yellow rose that climbed the side of the porch.

Brett stood watching her. "They are nice, aren't they? Come on, I cut some for the table but they wouldn't stay in

167

the bowl. Maybe you can tame them for me while I get started with the cooking."

Katy arranged the roses, clipping their stems, and then settled into the rattan chair with her glass. Sipping, she watched him put the thick slices of yam and a handful of asparagus on the grill, brushing it with sauce. He felt her gaze and knew his tension showed in his face.

"How's your father today?"

"The same." Brett shrugged. "I was up to see him this morning. According to Doc Wilde, he's going to stay the same unless he has a change in attitude. So….." He flipped the vegetables and lifted a heavy piece of halibut out of the marinade onto the grill.

Turning from the burner, he asked, "How are you this morning? How come you slept so late?"

"I usually sleep in on the weekend. But I didn't get to yesterday because I was with Dad."

"What did you do, you and your Dad?"

"Not much. We use the time to catch up and usually get to church, because our church is near his home."

"Maybe it's time to quit the second job. I know you've been there a long time but you must be earning enough at Rome to keep yourself." He was aware his glance was sharp.

"Oh, the wage is more than fair. We talked about that yesterday, actually."

Brett nodded. "And what did your father say?"

"That I had to make up my own mind." She gave him a pointed look.

He nodded slowly and his mouth tightened again until his dimples were deep in his cheeks. "Right."

"Anyway, I miss him if I don't get over there every week or two." She sniffed. "That really smells good. I'm hungrier than I thought."

He smiled. "That's good. Let's get this to the table."

Over lunch she told him about her plan to move. "I mean, my room is pretty small."

"Yeah, I noticed that. How come you get the smallest

room? Is it because you're the smallest girl?" He flipped a curl by her ear.

She laughed. "Well, it was cheaper. And I could manage better while I was going to school. Soon, though, it would be nice to have a little more space."

She took tiny bites of the halibut.

"Don't you like it?"

"Oh, I love it. It's all so good. I didn't know you could cook. Maybe I'll get you an apron for your birthday."

"Very funny," he growled. "Just like I'll get you a hard hat for your birthday for hanging around the dump trucks and drivers." He smiled slowly. "You know, if you need more space you could always move in with me."

Her head spun around, her mouth partly open. Then she snapped it shut. "I don't think so. We just started dating. Didn't we?" She looked uncertain.

He had to laugh. "Hmm, started when, I wonder? Last week, if we believe you. Right from the dinner at Frank's house if we believe me. Maybe the truth is somewhere in the middle." Her face was pink, and he put his hand to her cheek.

"You're cute when you get all flustered." He examined her empty plate. "Have you had enough? Because I have dessert."

"I know. Raspberries." She grinned impishly. "And I was a good girl, I cleaned my plate."

Carrying their plates into the kitchen, Brett thought about what kind of a good girl he'd like her to be. He took a few minutes to load the dishwasher. Better to take time to calm down.

He returned with two bowls of vanilla sherbet and a big bowl of raspberries. "Here you go, you can lay on as many berries as you like." He made short work of his and sat back to watch her eat the berries one at a time. Finally she sighed and pushed her bowl away. "That was so good. Thank you very much."

"What time do you have to leave? Still three o'clock so you can get to work on time?"

"Oh," she said brightly. "I don't work tonight. One of the

girls needed someone to switch with her so I volunteered. I worked last Thursday night instead."

He stilled, then lifted his head as if he caught a different scent on the wind. When he looked back at her he knew there was a new intensity in his gaze. He put out his hand and took hers. "Well, then."

Tugging gently, he shifted back in his chair and pulled her onto his lap. "That's the best news I've had all week."

Carefully he placed his hands at her waist and kissed her. "Mmm, you taste like raspberries." She smiled tentatively. "I better try that again." He put his mouth on hers. As she slowly softened, he felt her tongue reach out for his. Oh, man. Just that tiny step forward, that small giving of herself caused a great leap in his chest. His stomach was taut, his muscles tense.

Tightening his arms until she was laying against him, he felt her breasts press into his shirt. He put his hand there, felt the gauzy material of her blouse and the firmness of her breast beneath. He had to get these clothes off her.

"Katy." Standing, he let her slide to her feet. "Come on, I'll show you the rest of the house." He snicked the lock on the front door as they passed.

"Aunt Ray used to take boarders," he informed her, "so she had her own bedroom back here." They were standing in what was now a study behind the living room. "Then she rented out all the bedrooms upstairs. Come and see." He led her up the stairs, her sandals tapping lightly as they climbed.

"Did she have children?"

"No, I don't think she ever married. There are four bedrooms up here, but three of them have single beds so I've taken Aunt Ray's room. It's the only one with a queen sized bed."

She laughed a little breathlessly. "No, you wouldn't fit those small beds."

"Now, we don't want to go into how big I am," he grinned. "It's because I'm tall that I don't fit."

He backed her up against the mattress. "We have to get

you out of this blouse. It keeps getting caught on everything. See, it even catches on my fingers." He was busy undoing the tiny buttons down the front, the backs of his knuckles brushing against her breasts.

Meeting her watchful eyes he pulled it off her shoulders, gently pushing her down onto the bed and falling with her. "That's better." He looked his fill of the little camisole.

"I thought so," he muttered just before he kissed her. His hands found the strip of skin showing above the waistband of her skirt and slid up under the camisole. When he came up for air, he stripped the camisole and bra off her in one sweep.

"Oh, baby." The sight of her made him breathless. He fell on her, his mouth taking the satin skin, the rosy nipples. "Your nipples taste like raspberries," he whispered. "Just let me get my shirt off." He ripped it over his head and slung it to the floor. "That's better."

His hands travelled knowingly, pushing her skirt up. Her thighs were like velvet and he slid his fingers higher under the thin elastic leg of her panties. Her breath caught.

"It's okay, it's okay. Don't worry. We can do this without anyone getting hurt. I promise, Katy. I won't hurt you."

Her skirt was at her waist and her panties gone. He brushed his chest across her legs and opened his mouth hot at the top of her thigh. She tensed but he rubbed, soothing her. Moulding her buttocks in his palms he lifted her to press his mouth to her core. Her breathing quickened, his was bellowing.

He licked her in that secret place. Just once and he caught her scent, that musky Katy aroma that was burned indelibly into his senses from their first time. It had clung to his shirt, haunting him.

Shucking the rest of his clothes he wrestled her skirt down over her hips and settled in to seduce her, his mouth opened against the thin skin just inside her hip as he urged her legs apart. He moved over her, licked her folds open, stroked with his tongue, suckled lightly until her fingers tangled in his hair and he heard her groan.

Then his tongue travelled over her stomach, tasting her skin. His fingers took over below as his mouth moved up her body. He began to stroke her fast down there, then slower, firm and then light. His mouth began a slow seduction on her breast, tugging a nipple with his tongue as she lifted herself against his hand. She jerked, then groaned and wrapped her arms around his head.

He could feel her tension rising as she moved against him. He caught her anxious panting in his mouth with a deep penetrating kiss that went on and on. When she began to moan, her contractions started around his fingers. He held her, his hand rubbing and sliding until she eased and lay panting.

Carefully he moved over her, levering himself into position and began to press in. She stiffened. "It's okay." He placed his mouth over hers and pushed further. She closed around him.

He was only partway seated when she began to contract again and he pressed, burying himself. His head ground into her hair across the pillow as he gritted his teeth and waited.

Katy panted, her breasts vibrating with the force of her breathing. He moved slightly, pushing further in and she caught her breath again. "Does it hurt? Are you okay?" he gasped.

She gazed at him, her eyes unfocussed.

"Katy, does it hurt?"

Slowly she shook her head. He tried to concentrate, to focus. Her heat, her slide were incredible. He pushed and waited, then pulled himself out almost to her entry before he began his slow thrust again.

She stiffened under him then moved her hips, angled herself and ground upward against him. It was too much and he felt the tide washing over and dragging him under. She contracted around him again as he sank.

~~~

Much later she stirred in his arms, lifting her hand out of the nest of hair on his chest, then dropping it limply. He watched her face, her dark lashes a solid crescent against her pale skin in the softly falling light from the window washing across the sheets. Her hair was dark brown but in the light, reddish tones caught and shone in each curl.

His hand moved against her waist, fingers tightening, gripping her softly and releasing. He brushed the underside of her breast back and forth with the ball of his thumb. Skin like satin gleamed against the darker tone of his hand. She sighed in pleasant exhaustion.

"How do you feel? Are you okay?"

She tried to move her head, her eyes flicked open and then closed.

"Hmmm." Finally she opened her eyes and focussed on his face so close above hers. He smiled, brushing the hair back from her temple.

"You slept for a little while."

She nodded and stretched, rubbing his chest with her fingers. "I was tired."

"Wore you out, huh? Did I hurt you?"

"No," she focussed on his eyes. "You didn't hurt me."

"Good." He measured her gaze. "Did you like it?"

She blushed, he saw the heat rising up her throat. "You know I did."

"Well, I needed to check. Because last time you ran away."

She stilled, her eyes locked with his. "Not this time."

"I was afraid to loosen my grip. Afraid I'd wake up and find you gone."

"Oh," she closed her eyes a minute in distress. "This time was different."

"Yes, different. I was inside you."

She flushed darker. "Yes."

"And you liked it this time."

She dropped her gaze to his chest, where she brushed her fingers lightly in the matt of hair. He gave her a little shake to get her attention. "I think you came three times."

Startled, her gaze flew up to his. He was still smiling, couldn't help himself. "I could tell," he said.

"You were counting?" She looked slightly shocked and embarrassed.

"A guy has to keep tabs on what's going on. It's in his best interest."

She didn't answer.

Gripping her waist, he rotated his palm against her. "I'm teasing, baby. It just blew me away, that's all. You came three times and I had to work like hell to get you into bed."

She laughed a little and leaned her face into his chest. "Well, it was worth the wait then, wasn't it?" she whispered.

Tugging her closer he folded his arms around her. "That's for damned sure."

He rocked her, running a palm down her spine. It was worth the wait alright, even if it had almost killed him. He remembered what the team doctor had told him when he'd asked him about their "problem". He'd been puzzled, but said, "Let me have a look at you. There might be something."

"Yeah, that's what I wondered," Brett had replied, shucking his jeans. "But it's not as if I haven't been with other women. There wasn't a problem before."

The doctor checked him over and shook his head. "No problem that I can see," he said. "On the other hand, you're a big boy, Brett. Maybe she's just built real small. Go slow, is my advice. Take it easy, make sure she's really aroused before you enter her."

And doc had been right. There wasn't a problem. Not this time.

His hand wandered lower, brushing her skin, finally cupping her bottom. She stilled. He pressed further, his fingers reaching between her legs to find her slippery hidden place. She waited and he pressed inward, seeking, finding.

His erection rose against her, probing from the front. She leaned her head back to bring him into focus but he put his mouth down on hers in complete possession. His hands took control again, one cupping and moulding her breast, the other coming around to spread her legs, prepare her.

When he rose up and thrust his length into her this time,

there was no question of his claim. He held her to the sheet as he penetrated, one hand gripping her hip, the other sliding under her lower back to angle her for his entry.

"Don't run away again," he panted, his hand firmly pinning her in place. "Katy, don't run away again. I couldn't bear it."

CHAPTER TWENTY TWO

Just before sunrise when Brett rolled over and turned off his alarm before it rang, the light in the room was dim. Due in the gym in half an hour, he ran a hand over his jaw and looked sideways across the bed. Katy's face was buried in the pillow, her hair tousled around her head, the bump of her bottom rising under the sheet. He cupped her gently, just to feel her shape once more.

What a luxury it had been to finally see her body. He'd relived that night in the office in his mind so many times that as a fantasy it was almost worn out. Smiling to himself, he revised that. It wasn't exactly worn out. He'd relieved his tension more than once in the shower while thinking about that brief frantic encounter on the office couch. But it was just so much better in the flesh.

Watching her back rise and fall, he realized the sight of her naked body had turned him into an idiot. He lost all sense of himself when he saw his fingers disappear between her legs, his hand grip her hip, her breast change shape under his grasp, or her nipple rise up to his mouth.

The third time they'd made love had been so good. She came to him that time, not gazing watchfully as if she couldn't trust him. The fact they'd made love twice and he hadn't hurt her must have been the turning point.

She was open to him. She smiled such an invitation his loins and his heart clenched in unison. He'd wondered for a moment if he'd ever breathe again. Maybe he was having a heart attack, like his old man.

She'd welcomed him in and his mind went blank. It was like being hypnotized, in some kind of trance, one that he didn't want to end. Yet his body had been on fire. Somewhere in his head he'd been aware that he should hold back, not scare her, because this was all new and tenuous still. She was shy like a deer and he needed to go slow.

Now he eased off the mattress and slipped his workout gear on, his bag already packed and waiting downstairs. He reset the alarm and left it on the bedside table.

He'd had to work a little to get her to stay the night. After all, she told him, she hadn't been home the night before either.

"Well," he answered, "I doubt if your girlfriends will miss you as much as I will if you don't stay." She laughed and he'd grinned and pulled her close. "Besides," he added, "I've been a good boy."

She'd blushed but nodded. "Yes, you have."

~~~

Katy checked the lock on the front door. She pulled it closed behind her, listening for the click and testing the handle. Aunt Ray, whoever she was, her house was locked. She ran down the steps to her car.

She'd be on time for work if she hurried and she didn't want to be late. It would be bad enough normally but she'd feel doubly guilty if she was late because she was sleeping with the boss. Not that everyone would know, but *she* would know.

The day was hectic and she didn't lift her head until it had almost ended. The trucks started to pull into the yard, Frank first. He tromped up the steps, sheaf of papers in hand and laid them on her desk. "Whoa," he said, "that was a day and a half. But we got it all done."

Katy picked them up and stacked them neatly. "That's

good. It's been busy alright." They both heard a loud grinding noise and she hurriedly stood to peer out the window. Wilf pulled into the yard as Gert darted out of the mechanic's shop, alerted by the sound. The pup was pulling at an awkward angle, wheels locked on one side.

Gert was already down on one knee, feeling underneath and shaking his head. "Not good, Wilf," he pronounced. "Axle's broken. I'll have to order one." He stood up and dusted his hands. "Well, at least the truck's still good. Help me get off." And he set about loosening the bolts that attached it to the truck hitch.

The phone shrilled in the office and Katy ran back to catch it, a customer who wanted a delivery tomorrow. Stifling a yawn she laid the phone back in its cradle. When she glanced up, Brett was leaning against her desk.

"Hi," he said. His smile was wonderful. His face was different than it had been yesterday morning. The compressed lips, the grimness had disappeared, replaced by a relaxed mouth, the expression in his eyes lazy and satisfied as they rested on her face. She smiled back.

"Hi, yourself."

He laughed and reached for her hand. "Are you coming over to my place after work today?"

"No," she shook her head. "I have to go home."

"Can't you just stop home to get what you need and then come over?" he wheedled.

"No, I can't," she said firmly. "I have to do laundry, a bunch of things. I haven't been home for four days."

"You could do laundry at Aunt Ray's, with me."

"No, I can't. And I'm really tired. I have to sleep."

He frowned. "Sleep is highly overrated." Then his eyes lit up. "You can sleep with me."

"I don't get any sleep with you," she whispered hotly.

He laughed, the colour suddenly high on his strong cheekbones. "Well, tomorrow night won't work. Paddy's coming home and I've drawn the first watch."

She nodded in sympathy.

Wilf and Gert strode through the door followed shortly by Pete, and Brett turned to deal with the broken axle. When Frank came in the conversation moved on to schedule adjustments until the pup was repaired.

Katy gathered her purse and keys and called goodnight to the crew. Brett left them talking in the middle of the office to follow her out onto the steps.

"Hold on, Katy." He put his hand on her arm and drew her away from the open doorway. "What about the next night?" he asked, then slapped himself on the forehead. "I've got a game Wednesday. That won't work. Unless you want to come over after the game, which would be about eleven…" He let the suggestion hang in the air as he looked at her hopefully.

Katy laughed. "No, thank you. I'm going out Wednesday with my friends. We've had it planned for a while now."

His expression darkened. "Going out where?"

"Never mind. You can't come after me and haul me out of every nightclub I go to."

He frowned. "I didn't say I'd do that," but he looked slightly guilty. "Where are you going?"

"I can't tell you. You'll come and spoil it."

His face was flushed. "I promise I won't, okay?"

"Well… We're going to celebrate Sid moving in with her boyfriend, and it's Girl's Night at the Cougar Club. We're going dancing."

"The Cougar Club? Isn't that where all the women go to pick up guys?"

"Brett! Women go to all the clubs to pick up guys. Guys go to the clubs to pick up women." Katy frowned at him, her exasperation rising.

"Sorry." He pressed his lips together, gazing across the yard at the broken pup, then back to her face. "I know that. Listen, if we can get organised I might bring a few of the guys after the game." His eyes were pinned to her face. "I could meet you there. And I promise I'll behave."

She laughed. "Okay, if you promise." She gave him a prim

schoolmarmish look that had him grinning back "That would be fun. Anyway, see you tomorrow at the office, right?"

"Maybe. But I'll call even if I can't get in. What about Thursday? I have to book in advance or I don't get any Katy time. Are you free Thursday after work?"

She smiled up at him. "Yes, I believe I am."

"You believe you are. I will take that as a guarantee. Thursday night is mine." He leaned forward slowly, his eyes boring into hers. "Give me a kiss."

She blushed furiously, glancing at the office doorway behind him. "Brett. The guys are inside there."

"I know. I want a kiss." He leaned further and laid his lips on hers for the briefest touch. It sent a shock through her whole system, making her aware of every nerve ending. From the expression on his face, he felt it too.

His colour high, his eyes piercing hers, he stepped back and said, "Have a good sleep." She knew he watched her all the way to her car.

His intensity delighted her, made her heart beat fast. She didn't know what to think of the night she'd spent with him. Was he her man now, or was this casual? She should ask if he was seeing anyone else, but couldn't bring herself to form the words.

Hockey players had women, didn't they? Just look at Sherry. Katy honestly didn't want to know. This affair, if that's what it was, excited and satisfied her. She was going to enjoy him. She shivered with the memory of how she had enjoyed him. His size no longer frightened her. She wanted more.

~~~

Brett felt like he was always watching her walk away. But now he was getting somewhere with Katy and he wouldn't let anything stop him.

He'd been blown away by the afternoon and night she'd spent with him. Finally, finally she was in his bed and it had been as good as he'd known it would be. Better, in fact. That first encounter of theirs in the office had been so sudden and unexpected that it'd caught him off balance. Not that he hadn't enjoyed it. No way could he say that.

But now was different. She was soft instead of standoffish. She watched for cues and responded, even if a bit hesitantly like now. He'd never had such a night as last night.

She woke in the dark to kiss his neck and chest. By the time he was awake he was already on fire. And when he slid into her, she was ready.

It was slow and lazy, so relaxed he wanted to laugh. He'd felt some kind of joy bubbling up inside. But all she had to do was run her hands down his back and across his buttocks or grip his hips and tug a little and he jerked to life. It morphed into a battle where they fought until they both won.

He turned back into the office to see what decisions had to be made. He was going to be very busy with Paddy and a different battle he was sure would ensue about home care. Then he had two games this week. He'd better organize what he could while he was here.

~~~

Katy dragged her overnight bag out of the back of the car, stuck her purse under her arm and picked up the takeout food on the passenger seat. She had four days of dirty clothes in that bag. Well, tonight was laundry night. There was very little on her shelf of the refrigerator, thus the hot curry takeout clutched in her hand.

She unlocked the door and backed in, dragging the case. Edging down the hall, she dumped everything on the bed. Then she hauled her laundry basket out of the closet.

Frowning, she pawed through the clothes. This wasn't right. Some of these weren't even her clothes. She stepped back and examined the clothing hanging in the closet. Some of those weren't hers either.

A quick scan of the room showed more disturbing evidence. Her laptop and jewellery case were kept in the trunk of her car ever since Sherry started getting so hostile. But some of the items on the top of her dresser were unfamiliar.

Her little desk had been disturbed and the book on the plant stand she used for a night table wasn't one she was reading. She'd never seen it before.

Well, this was going to stop. She pulled out her own clothes and took them down the hall to shove into the washing machine. She added soap and turned it on.

Then she sat down in the kitchen to eat her dinner. She was right, there wasn't much on her refrigerator shelf but the few pieces of fruit and cheese she'd had were gone. She helped herself to a banana from the bowl on the top of the counter, put her clothes in the dryer and went back to her room for car keys. A quick trip to the liquor store and she had a car full of boxes.

Wrestling four of them into her room, she'd just finished packing her college papers into her car when Sherry walked in the door.

"Hi Sherry," she said lugging her basket of clean clothes down the hall.

Sherry paused. "Where have you been?"

"I was visiting friends. Why?

"We thought you'd moved out."

"Really?" Katy gave her a quizzical look.

"Well, you weren't here for days, so we thought..."

"Don't be stupid Sherry. You know I haven't."

Sherry watched Katy for a minute then leaned in the doorway. "But you will."

"Who says?"

"I say. Wednesday is the end of the month and you're gone. Don't come back Thursday."

"Sherry, if you're giving me notice it has to be in writing a clear month in advance. You know that. Don't act dumb.

"Those rules apply to me, because I rent this house from the landlord," Sherry hissed. "They don't apply to you, you're a sub tenant. Look it up." And she walked away.

Katy felt panic rising up her throat and threatening to choke her. Where could she go? She couldn't move in with Dad at his assisted living residence. It was okay to stay there a few days at a time when the common guest room was free. But that was the limit. It was a temporary reprieve but not an answer.

If only she hadn't lost her money to Bruno. Now she was afraid of him. Maybe it hadn't been him driving that car the day she was at the Rockland gates, but he'd known she'd be there. On the other hand, it could have been a simple accident. She couldn't seem to decide.

But the rear end collision when the truck hit her car was no accident. There'd been no one else on the road. The driver couldn't help but see her. She was afraid of Bruno now, yet she needed her money desperately.

Realizing she was so tired her brain wouldn't function, she had a quick shower and crawled into bed, her door securely latched from the inside.

Trying to relax, she thought of Brett and her whole body warmed like melting wax. He made her feel things she'd never felt before. She'd known what he'd want once he found out she didn't have to work Sunday. She'd wanted it too in a way, but she'd also been a little scared. The first time they'd made love, the discomfort had overshadowed her pleasure.

There'd been no pain this time. Just delight. She didn't know it could be like that. He must have felt that way too because he made love to her again right away. It kind of took her out of herself. They'd found some dinner to bring upstairs and eat in bed. Then he'd loved her again before they went to sleep.

When she woke in the night wanting more, it seemed all she had to do was touch him, kiss him and she got more. She settled into the sheets, feeling slightly sore, her body still humming with pleasure. Or maybe it was anticipation. She wasn't sure.

CHAPTER TWENTY THREE

B rett dragged Jerome and Hart with him to the Cougar Club at the end of the night. They'd won the hockey game in a brutal contest, with Hart scoring the winning goal in overtime. He was loud and boisterous.

"Now, guys," Brett said. "We have to behave in there tonight. No repeat of the last time I saw Katy in a nightclub." His friends guffawed loudly.

"Brett, you're talking to yourself, man."

Brett's colour was strong. "Yeah, well, just don't let me get out of hand, that's all. Katy will skin me alive if I do something dumb like that again."

Hart snickered. "I'll bet she will. Hold onto your hats, men. We have arrived." There was a long lineup at the entrance. Brett tried unsuccessfully to harass the doorman into letting them in ahead of the crowd.

It was late and they could barely see across the dimly lit room when they finally entered the club. The place was jammed, music booming from the group performing on the corner bandstand. Jerome went one way and Hart the other, so Brett headed straight through the crowd searching for Katy.

He spotted her on the dance floor at the same time Jerome did. From the corner of his eye he saw Jerome go still, then his head swung to catch Brett's reaction. Why? Because Katy was slow dancing with some big dude who was holding her way too tight. He'd swear her breasts were touching that guy's chest. He felt his hands ball into fists and his breathing constrict. He tried to turn away but his head wouldn't budge. The blood began to roar in his ears.

He felt a touch on his arm and looked down. Katy's friend Sid smiled up at him. "Hi, Brett," she shouted above the din. "Katy said you were coming. We're sitting right over here." She tugged on his arm and he forced himself to follow her between the tables. He waved to Jerome to point the direction but his eyes stayed pinned on Katy.

"Katy's just on the dance floor," Sid shouted.

"So I see," he muttered. The waitress came by and he ordered drinks for the table. There was another girl seated and a guy he didn't know. Hart joined them.

When he glanced up, the song had ended and Katy and her partner were heading through the crowd toward the table. Her face lit up when she saw him and he couldn't help a grin.

She pulled a chair close to his side. "Hi. I thought you'd be here sooner."

"We went into overtime. Who's your dancing friend?" The big guy was still hovering at the table.

"This is Mike, Sid's boyfriend. Mike, this is Brett Rome." The men shook hands and Brett felt a band of tension ease in his chest. Sid's boyfriend. Well, alright. He looked back at Katy, examining her little blouse with the tiny straps and the low cut front. He wanted to take his shirt off and cover her. He wanted to pick her up and carry her home.

What was his problem? He'd never been like this. But with Katy everything was different. He felt so protective. She wasn't helpless but he wanted to make sure she was okay. He was driven to take care of her.

He felt so possessive. He wanted to fend off other men, even when they looked at her it ticked him off. If they talked to her he got even more edgy. If someone laid a hand on her arm, he felt like knocking their block off. He figured he was regressing to a more elemental species.

And the sex, the need for sex was still there like it had been with Marilyn but stronger and more insistent, like a driving force. Not that he'd had lots with Katy but he felt that he needed lots. He didn't know how he was going to get through the rest of the evening without showing his true unwelcome primitive colours.

To his surprise, he had a great time. They danced. Katy obviously loved to dance. They did fast dances, a couple of line dances. She and her girlfriends liked those and everyone got into it, even Hart. They did a few slow dances that warmed him right up and left his arms empty when they were over. Man, he wanted that little girl.

When the band packed it in, Katy reluctantly grabbed her purse. "Come on, everyone. I have to get home, I have work in the morning."

She made a funny face at Brett and he laughed. "You have my permission to sleep in," he said.

"Oh, no you don't." She shook her head. "I'm not going there." Outside, Katy pointed the way to her car. Sid had already gone with Mike and they took the other girl with them. Hart and Jerome stood waiting for Brett. Katy unlocked her car and leaned into Brett's chest. "That was really fun. I'm glad you came."

"Me, too," he said. "I like dancing with you."

"I'll see you tomorrow," she whispered and held her face up to him.

"Can't you come over to my place?" he whispered back. "I'd let you sleep."

"No, not tonight, but I did agree for tomorrow." He gave her a long slow hot kiss and reluctantly let her go.

~~~

Sherry had warned her about Thursday, and Katy was anxious to get home.

As she found a parking spot on the street, she spotted Sherry's car in the drive. Unlocking the front door with her key, she stepped inside. A night light was burning in the hall.

From that light she could see her clothes piled on the couch and spilled onto the floor.

In her room there was the profile of a body under the covers. Her covers, her bed. Someone else's clothes hung in the closet, different things stood on her dresser and small desk.

That's how it was going to be. Ugly. Sid had warned her. She just hadn't been able to find anywhere to go. Dragging her extra blankets out of the closet she went back to the living room. One hand swept her clothes onto the floor as she flung the blankets on the couch, stripped down to her underwear and fell onto the cushions. She'd sort something out tomorrow.

When she arrived at Rome Trucking the next morning, there were more boxes packed into the trunk of her little car. The morning routine took her attention but her mind was working furiously on her predicament. The basement of the office held old junk and a bit of furniture, presumably from when it had been someone's home. She'd already found an empty spot in a dim back corner where her boxes of college course textbooks and papers were neatly stacked. As she worked, she contemplated her next move.

When the calls on dispatch had trickled to a halt, she opened the basement door, turned on the light and went down the stairs. The badly lit concrete space was mostly empty. She'd never seen anyone come down here but she'd have to be careful.

Sweeping an area clean she began bringing in the boxes from her car, placing them near the others. Then she hustled back upstairs. It was almost lunchtime and Gert would be in for coffee soon. Sometimes one of the drivers dropped in as well.

Early afternoon she was back in the basement. Her boxes were piled in two stacks with the broom handle balanced across the top. She stood back and examined her work. Good but unstable. She put a smaller box on top of the broom end. That was better. Then she hung her clothes on the handle like a closet rod. All her underwear in one open box on the floor, shoes in another. This would work, just for now, just for the moment.

Back upstairs she called her father, booking herself into the spare room at his place for the next available night but that turned out to be weeks away.

She examined her calendar on the desk. She could manage. In the meantime, she didn't have any rent to pay. She'd have enough for a damage deposit once she found a place and by month end she'd have enough for rent. She just had to wend her way through the few weeks ahead of her. And if Brett had his way, she'd be with him some of the time.

Could she sleep down here? There was an old, decidedly used couch. She beat on it with a folded bathmat, but very little dust rose. Maybe it was just heavily worn. She dug out some sheets, spread a couple over the cushions and lay down. It would do. She still had to go back to get the rest of her stuff. That other girl wasn't going to have her bedding.

But her furniture would have to stay. Would she ever get it back? She couldn't haul it away in her little car. Brett would probably help her when she had somewhere to move it but for now, this was all she could do.

Brett called at three from Aunt Ray's house to confirm she was coming over. At four he called to ask another question. At four fifteen he called again.

Katy laughed into the phone. "I can't talk now, Brett. The trucks are coming in. Would you like me to call you back?"

"Just get over here," he growled. "I'm pacing the floor."

When she walked in the front door of Aunt Ray's house, Brett hustled her straight upstairs. "You've definitely got too many clothes on," he said, his hands busily undoing buttons and zippers as he backed her up against the bed. "Good Lord, woman. A man has to do so much work just to get you out of all this." He had her stripped and onto the bed in seconds, rolling to pull her on top of him.

"That's better. That's way better." His tight mouth relaxed and a faint smile appeared, growing in warmth as his hands travelled down her spine and pulled her snug against him pressing her breasts into his chest. He lifted his head to kiss her, a slow languorous kiss that turned her insides to jelly.

"Do you like that? Tell me what you like." He kissed her again.

"Katy," he said as he fondled her breasts, "I think you should move in with me. No, don't pull back. Never mind, we'll discuss it later. We have more important things to do just now." He laughed raggedly.

She was alarmed at his suggestion to move in but couldn't help her giggle and his eyes flashed a humorous look at her. "You don't think so?"

"Maybe," and she wriggled against him. His face immediately sobered and his hands jerked down to grab her hips. "None of that," he said. "Things will be over before they've begun. You won't want that to happen." He rolled her to her side.

"There. You have to be a good girl now. You can be bad to me later." He grinned and pulled her knee up over his hip. Focussing his gaze on her mouth, he nudged himself against her.

"Katy, let me inside now, baby. Let me in." There was a desperate note to his voice. He kissed her mouth, stroking with his hands until she was ready for him. So ready.

~ ~ ~

Later Brett lay with her head on his shoulder, his arm securely around her, his chest still heaving. He had the horrified notion that he was crying. Moisture gathered in his eyes and ran down his temples.

Rolling his head to the side, he buried his face in her hair and inhaled. She smelled like woman and Katy. He loved that smell. He missed her desperately when he couldn't see her, couldn't be with her. But from the expression on her face earlier, he'd better not press too hard on the "move in with me" part.

Downstairs he flipped burgers and watched Katy as she played with Boots. She was wearing his tee shirt, her panties and nothing else. He almost burned the buns when she bent over to ruffle the dog's ears and pat his head.

"Aunt Ray is back early next week," he said. She stood and left the dog to walk over to his side. "That means I'm back with the cousin from hell." He stared down at her. "How are we going to have any time together?"

"Time together?" She peered at him thoughtfully. "You mean bed time, don't you?"

He gave her a smouldering look. "Yeah, that's what I mean. And this kind of time." He pulled her flush against him and gave her a long possessive kiss.

"Something's on fire," she said. He whipped around, yanking the burgers off the barbecue onto a plate. "See, we don't have enough time together and I'm already getting sidetracked." He frowned at her darkly.

She gave him a pointed glance and then sighed. "I guess I'll just have to take you back to bed after we eat. You obviously got out on the wrong side last time and we have to put that right." She pursed her lips.

He gave a guffaw. "You sure learn fast. You wouldn't go to bed with me at all and now you know enough to take me back there when I'm getting cranky."

"Well, it's not that difficult to figure out," she said primly.

He reached to fondle her. "Yes, ma'am."

CHAPTER TWENTY FOUR

Brett sat on the couch at Paddy's house, a stack of papers in his hand. "The caregiver is coming for two hours at eight in the morning and again at four in the afternoon. In the morning, they'll do breakfast and leave lunch ready. Then they come back to do dinner and whatever needs doing. I don't know what. Probably medications and stuff."

Paddy was dogmatically shaking his head.

"Forget it, Paddy. You don't have a choice. The whole point is to look after the medication and the nutrition. Don't be so damned stubborn.

"Liz and I will still be around but you need steady care. Then the physio starts. We'll have the Handy-dart van service take you. You have to go to the hospital for that."

"Not the Handy-Dart. I won't go." Paddy's mouth set, his eyes narrowed.

"Doc Wilde said you can either accept help at home or go into care. Your choice. I said you wouldn't want a care home, but maybe I'm mistaken."

"Don't be ridiculous. I don't need a care home."

"That's not what Doc says. And the way you're talking, maybe you'd rather move into assisted living."

"I'm not taking nurses up my ass all day here. Forget it."

191

His protests seemed weaker and Brett seized the advantage.

"You'll go to physio." Brett looked daggers at his father. "You'll go if I have to drag you there. Because you're going to get better and back on your own two feet. So get behind this, instead of bucking it. What a waste of energy that is."

They glared at each other.

Brett glanced at the papers in his hand. "He did say you're probably too weak to do it."

"Who said?" Paddy snarled. "Who said I was too weak?"

"Doc Wilde. He said you're probably too weak to get better. He didn't mean physically. He said you wouldn't have the guts." Brett had a self-satisfied expression on his face.

"That pokey-assed doctor. He doesn't know what he's talking about."

"Well, I think he does. Here you are saying you won't do this, you won't do that. He's probably right."

Paddy pondered that for a few minutes while Brett pretended to read the papers in his hand. Then he straightened in his chair. "Okay. I'll cooperate. Just don't push it too hard, son. And no Handy-dart."

"I'm not backing off on that. You can use Handy-dart until you're strong enough to take a taxi." Brett heaved himself off the couch. "Sounds good. Thanks Dad. What are we going to have for dinner?" He wandered out to the kitchen and opened the fridge to see very little looking back at him. "I'll just go get something."

"Okay. I liked that wor won-ton soup you brought one time," Paddy called from his chair, his voice decidedly weak.

When Brett arrived back at Paddy's house an hour later he had the soup, some other Chinese food and a cheque for twenty thousand dollars in his back pocket made out to "Rome Trucking". He couldn't deposit it in the account until Monday and then he'd have to wait a few days to see if it cleared but he had the cheque.

Stopping at the office, he'd found the foreman just leaving. "Go ahead, Frank. I've got a few things to work on."

Shortly he heard steps at the door of the office. "Frank, I

thought you left," he called from his chair.

"Mr. Rome."

Brett walked around his desk to find Bruno Morelli standing in the entrance. They'd had several meetings here at the office and he thought he was making progress with the little weasel. All he needed was sixteen thousand dollars and Katy would have her money back.

When he'd tried to offer Katy some money because she was obviously short of cash, she'd gotten all stiff and offended. He laughed to himself but was pissed off about it, that she wouldn't let him help.

"Mr. Morelli," he said. "Come on in."

Morelli seated himself in front of the desk and smiled. "I thought we might close our agreement today. I've brought some papers."

Brett took the document and leafed through it. It was about five pages long and it appeared Morelli might have put it together himself. He folded the papers and laid them on the desk in front of him.

He looked Morelli over. He didn't like this man, partly because he suspected he was the man who first slept with Katy. That was enough to make him top Brett's instant dislike list. But he also knew about his swindle with her money.

He tapped the paper. "Interesting. I'd have to read it and digest it. But before that happens, I need a goodwill deposit. Twenty thousand dollars. You deposit twenty thousand with me as goodwill, I'll have the documents vetted and we'll put something together."

Morelli seemed unsure. They talked further and he wasn't persuaded. "What proof do I have that I gave you the money, if we're not signing the document?"

"You'll have a cancelled cheque, Morelli. And I'll write you a receipt."

The discussion went on from there. Twenty minutes later when Brett rose from his chair to say he was out of time, Morelli reluctantly pulled out a cheque book and wrote one out. Brett said, "Thank you", and walked him to the door.

~ ~ ~

Bruno woke with a start. Someone had pulled the blind up and fierce sunlight poured onto his bed. Squinting, he used his forearm to shield his face. "What?" he muttered. "What's going on?"

Tyler leaned over him. "Wake up, Bruno. I've got some questions for you."

He relaxed back against his pillow, little energy left. Last night had been... Well, he couldn't remember last night. It had started out well. Tyler gave him a bag of coke and he'd headed off with Balson to the bar. The rest was a haze in his mind. His head ached, his eye sight was blurry, his hands shook.

"Sorry," he mumbled. He must have dropped off to sleep again, because Tyler was jerking his arm, thumping him in the chest with his fist. "I'm awake now."

"Good." Tyler stood and stretched. "Get up. Meet me in the kitchen."

Bruno rolled to a sitting position and swung his feet to the floor. What he needed was a smoke. He gave a ragged cough and reached for his shirt, fumbling a cigarette out of the pack in his pocket. Lighting it, he inhaled the smoke and held it a moment. Ah, that was better. He dragged on his underwear and pants, shrugging the shirt up his arms. Tyler didn't like to wait. Hopefully there was some coffee on in the kitchen.

Tyler started in on him as soon as he appeared in the doorway. "You've done it wrong, Bruno," he said. "This isn't what we agreed. You were to get the contract signed, then give him the money."

Bruno nodded, looking longingly at the coffee pot steaming on the warmer. "I know, Tyler. I can explain." He grabbed a dirty cup from the counter and filled it with liquid the colour and consistency of used diesel oil, then sat at the table, careful not to spill any.

"Listen. He was backing out. At first he had a little interest, but he was backing out. He told me to leave if I didn't want to give him a goodwill deposit. No one else has shown any interest." He shot a sly glance at his boss.

Tyler had identified four businesses he thought were good targets for investment. They hadn't gotten anywhere with the others. Tyler wouldn't show his face and relied on Bruno to persuade the business owners to let them invest. But they were either suspicious or didn't need the money, because Bruno hadn't gotten past the front door with anyone else.

"So what does a goodwill deposit mean? And how do we get it back?"

Bruno shrugged and took a sip of his coffee. "He wrote me a receipt. I already gave that to you. And the cheque itself is some sort of proof. He said he'd read the contract and sign it. That's what I got out of it."

Tyler glared at him as he huffed out a breath. "He'd fucking better. Because if this goes sideways….."

Bruno took another puff of his cigarette and realized he'd sunk lower than he ever thought he would when he replied, "Think of it as losing Katy's money, not yours.

Tyler laughed, and Bruno quaked at the sight.

~ ~ ~

Katy spent her first night on the basement couch in the office. She worried about her car being seen out front. If any of the drivers were to drive by the yard after work, they'd notice her car there. Then she discovered a spot behind the mechanic's shed that couldn't be seen from the street. It was perfect.

She'd spent hours debating with herself. She could stay in the basement until Frank came in. Once he arrived, she'd leave through the basement door at the back of the old house and pull her car into the yard as if she were just arriving from home. That settled, she told Frank she had an appointment and he covered for her while she made another trip back to the townhouse in the early afternoon.

There was no one home. She went in, combed her room for everything portable and packed it into boxes. Satisfied she had everything she could carry but the few pieces of furniture, she stripped the bedding, stuffing what she could into the trunk and piling the rest in the back seat of her car. She just hoped no one would notice at work.

No such luck. There wasn't anything she did that didn't attract attention. "Looks like you're moving, Katy," said Pete as he stalked through the door that afternoon. "Got a lot of stuff loaded into that little car of yours." She smiled and scrutinized the papers he handed her.

"Yeah, going somewhere?" chipped in Wilf.

"No, just getting rid of a few things," she replied as she pretended great interest in his forms.

"That so? Need any help?" That was Ollie.

Katy had to smile. It wasn't just idle curiosity. They were interested and willing to lend a hand. "No, I've got it under control. Thanks, anyway."

"Well, okay," he said dubiously. "Looks like a lot of stuff to haul out of there."

The others muttered amongst themselves and finally left. Frank was still there, so Katy gathered her keys and purse and waved goodnight. She went to a drive-through restaurant and sat in the parking lot to eat her dinner. As she ate, she considered her precarious situation.

What she really needed was a reprieve, she needed things to slow down. She was bone tired from the long work weeks as well as dealing with all the upheaval, frustrated and a bit scared by the two recent seemingly random attacks on her and flustered by how much she was being forced to handle.

Brett wasn't scary any more. She had to admit she enjoyed his size. When she ran her hands over his heavy shoulders, he shivered in response. The muscle mass was a definite turn-on. He was gentle with her but not hesitant, firm but tender and she liked that. But he was a very demanding complication in an already complicated life. It felt like a juggling act.

It was certainly quiet sleeping in the basement. She could use the shower in the back bathroom, grubby as it was. She'd clean it up but not too much or it would be noticed. And if she showered in the evening, all the signs would be gone by the time the drivers came in the next day.

She could just hear the comments. "Is that powder I can smell? Is that perfume? How come the showers wet? You been cleaning up, Frank?" It would go on and on. No, she definitely had to shower at night.

Then she'd go to bed, read a bit and turn the light out. If she got a few nights like that, it would put a whole new perspective on things.

She slept like a baby. Her alarm went off and she was ready to leave long before Frank pulled into the yard. When she heard his boots on the floor above her head, she opened the back basement door and walked around the building to where her car was hidden. It worked like a charm.

Coming up the office steps she gave Frank a sunny smile.

"You're early," he said.

"Yep, turning over a new leaf."

"The alarm wasn't set last night for some reason." He frowned at the wall panel. "I was pretty sure I set it."

Katy could feel colour climbing her throat. "Oh, dear. That's not good."

"No." He shook his head. "It happens, though. I'll be more careful. Maybe Brett came in last night. He does that sometimes. He might have forgotten to set it."

Katy immediately froze. *He did?* That wouldn't be good. Well, she'd deal with that if it happened. This arrangement wouldn't be for long. It would work, she'd make it work.

~~~

Brett watched Katy's little car disappear down the street. Aunt Ray was back tomorrow, this was their last time together here. He didn't know what he was going to do about that. But he wasn't giving her up. He'd rent a hotel room if he had to, even though he knew she wouldn't like it. He was a desperate man.

They'd had a wonderful time. She took Saturday off work at the restaurant, spending the day with him. She was just leaving now to get ready for her Sunday night shift. He couldn't stop smiling. First of all the sex had been fantastic, second of all the sex had been fantastic. He laughed to himself. Well, there had been other highlights as well.

It was such a luxury to have her in bed beside him, her hair tousled, her face stuck in the pillow. Once he'd woken to find her head on his shoulder, her hand curled into a little fist tucked under his arm.

He remembered she did that sometimes when they were making love. She'd put her hands under his arms and curl into the soft hair there, almost like a bird in the nest. Something unfamiliar clenched in his chest. He couldn't want her again already. They'd made love just before she left.

When he got over to Paddy's yesterday afternoon to check on the Old Man, he'd taken her with him. Spotting the garden in the back yard she went out to explore and came back raving about the rhubarb garden, asking for a bowl to pick raspberries from the straggly patch in the back that no one bothered to water. Then she gave some to Paddy.

He'd gawped at her as if she was from Mars, but she said, "Come on. Eat some. They're really good and they're good for you, too."

"I know that," Paddy snapped and ate a few. Then he ate a few more. First thing Brett noticed he was engaged in conversation with her.

"You don't have to act like I don't know they're there," he remarked. "My wife grew those berries for years. We ate them all the time. She made raspberry pie sometimes or she froze them. We'd have them on ice cream."

"Yes, it's a shame she's gone," said Katy. "But you've still got your children and grandchildren. You're a lucky man."

Brett smiled. He'd heard that line before and so had Dad. Paddy gave him an enigmatic glance over her head, and then peered back when she said, "Who's your doctor?"

"Doc Wilde."

"Oh, he's good. You're lucky to have him."

"How do you know how good he is?" Paddy growled.

"A friend of my Dad's has heart problems and he has Doctor Wilde. He says he's the best in the city."

"Oh." Paddy regarded her thoughtfully. "And how'd he

do? Did he get well?"

"Yes, he did. But it was a lot of work. Not everybody can do it. So maybe you will and maybe you won't."

Paddy gave her a look that could strip paint but she seemed oblivious. "You think I don't have the gumption to stick to the programme?" he demanded.

"Well, I guess that remains to be seen. From what's happened so far, I'd say you don't. But you could surprise me." She smiled sweetly and Brett guffawed. Paddy gave in to a grudging chuckle.

"You've got your nerve, little lady. Watch your step."

"I'm watching it."

Paddy hadn't intimidated her at all. Brett thought she was good for the old man. Maybe he'd bring her back for another visit. It perked Dad up to have her challenge him on his own turf.

Now he just needed to find a way to be with her on a regular basis or at least as regular as his schedule of hockey games and hers of working seven days a week would allow. Get her to move in with him or something. There had to be a way.

He stripped the bed and shoved the sheets into the washer, then gathered his stuff together in his duffel bag. The kitchen was next. It'd all be ready for Aunt Ray by tonight and he'd go back to see Randy the Raider and find out what his own place looked like.

CHAPTER TWENTY FIVE

Brett sat on the bench in the Lethbridge arena at the end of the second period listening to Coach Ruxton ream them out. His chest was still heaving from his last stint on the ice. It had been a very physical game, full of body checking and aggressive slams.

Hart had taken a header into the boards and wouldn't be returning, although he'd managed to skate off the ice under his own steam. One of the forwards had a broken left thumb and was sidelined.

Coach wanted the Victoria players to start slamming back, make their opponents retreat into their own end instead of all the play being down the Victoria end around their beleaguered goalie.

They'd been outshot and outplayed all game. The score stood at 2 -1 against and it had been a hard fought single goal.

As the players trooped back onto the ice, things heated up. Brett was getting a lot of ice time and he felt it in his legs.

They managed a second goal at twelve minutes and that buoyed the team. The play got even more vicious. Another player was hurt. Then at nineteen minutes their opponents scored again. The game ended 3 – 2 against Victoria with three men down. It had been a gruelling, disappointing game.

Back in Victoria next morning, Brett arrived home to the sound of Randy banging pots and pans in the kitchen. The living room was empty of junk, the hallway was vacuumed. "Hey, Randy," he called and walked into the kitchen.

His cousin was in the process of sliding a grilled cheese sandwich onto his plate. A bowl of soup sat on the counter.

"Whatcha got there?"

"Lunch. Want some?" Randy grinned.

"No thanks. I need a sleep more than anything."

"How'd the game go?"

"We lost." Brett shrugged. "Won the first one, lost the second."

"Too bad."

"Yeah. Hey, the house looks great. What's the catch?"

Randy laughed. "No catch. I decided it wasn't that much work to keep it tidy. I'll wash these pans when I'm finished eating." He moved his food over to the table.

"Okay." Brett watched him for a minute, realizing he hadn't made any real effort to get to know his younger cousin. "How's work going?"

"Good." Randy appeared surprised at his interest. "Good," he repeated. "First cook is a little difficult but I can get along with just about anyone."

Brett laughed, acknowledging the dig. He sat down across from him. "Just about anyone, eh? So what's first cook like?"

"Well, her name is Juno so that's your first clue. Katy, one of the waitresses, said she's easy but you have to work at it."

"Katy?" Brett stilled, his smile disappearing. "Katy who?"

"Uh, I'm not sure what her last name is. Why?"

"What restaurant do you work at?"

"Perry's. That's its new name, anyway. It's in the Regent Hotel."

"Right. Dark curly hair, about five foot four?"

"Yeah….." Randy answered slowly, eyeing him.

"So how well do you know Katy?"

"Huh?" Randy looked confused. "Fairly well," he said

slowly. "She's nice, we go for bike rides on the weekend sometimes."

"Do you?" Brett felt his whole body stiffen. "Where to?"

"What is your problem? You don't think I can behave myself with a girl?"

"Bike rides where?" Bret's face was flushed. "What kind of bike rides?"

"Brett, you're a jerk. What is it to you where I go or who I see? Back off!"

Brett breathed heavily through his nose. "Okay. Sorry." He glanced away and then back. "Katy's my girlfriend. She's dating me."

Randy gaped at him. "You're joking. She's dating you?"

Immediately, Brett bristled. "What's so hard to believe about that?"

"Nothing. Everything. How would you even meet her? You've only been in town for what, two months?"

"So?" Brett gritted his teeth. "You just took me by surprise, that's all. I'm a little protective of her. She's kind of vulnerable."

Randy studied him for a minute. "Yeah, she is. I mean, she has a full time job somewhere….."

"At Rome Trucking," Brett interrupted.

Randy's mouth hung open. "You're joking."

Brett laughed and felt some tension ease inside him. His cousin was a good guy. He wouldn't hurt Katy.

"How did that happen?"

"Well, see, it's a little complicated."

Randy motioned to him to keep talking.

"We had a driver who broke his leg and couldn't drive and we had those big new trucks that I must have told you about. Paddy bought them when he was in a lustful state and the company really couldn't afford them."

Randy laughed and Brett had to grin.

"He thought it would impress his girlfriend. So Frank at the office had to go back to driving just to keep the trucks busy and try to make the payments, and that same day Katy walked in asking for a job. So we hired her to run the office."

"Whoa." Randy pondered that. "Does Uncle Paddy know you've got a woman working in the office? No, seriously. I can't see it, myself."

"You're right. It isn't something Paddy would do. But he's met her and he was rude, of course. That's Paddy."

Randy nodded.

"But I think he actually likes her."

"She's pretty likeable."

Brett gave him a sharp look.

"Well, she is. Everyone at the restaurant likes her. Juno, the first cook, is always singing her praises. I just don't know why she has to work two jobs. She hardly has any time to do other things."

"Tell me about it," Brett shook his head. "I think she got into a tight jam financially. Her father lives in an assisted living place. He's got a back injury so Katy has to fend for herself."

The two men eyed each other for a minute. Then Randy finally admitted, "I knew she was dating someone. I asked her out, but she said she was already seeing someone."

Brett nodded, a gratified feeling washing over him, the muscles in his chest relaxing. He didn't know why he bristled so quickly over her, he should trust her more.

"How long have you been dating her?"

Brett recognized the protective tone of voice. "Not too long, maybe a month after I got here."

"I thought you had a girlfriend in Vancouver. You lived with her." Randy's tone was faintly accusatory.

"Yeah, she found another hockey player."

"Oh, sorry."

Brett shrugged. "Where do you guys ride?"

"Just along the Trails. It's kind of fun, we get some fresh air. It's not much of a challenge but Katy likes it." He flushed.

"Does she? I didn't know she rode a bike."

"Well, her bike's pretty old."

"Yeah?" They pondered that for a minute. "I wonder when her birthday is."

Randy nodded. "Good idea. I'll chip in. We don't have to wait for the actual day."

The cousins eyed each other.

"How would you feel if she moved in here?"

Randy blanched. "Uh, it's your place."

"Yeah. We'll see." It might not be a good idea, not if Randy had a crush on her. That would be awkward for everyone.

~~~

Later that day Brett arrived at the office to a pile of work waiting on his desk. The quotes were the first priority and he was slowly getting better at them. Frank was a big help but it still took time.

"Where's Katy?" he asked as he gathered his papers.

"She's at the bank," barked Frank around the dispatch speaker.

As he worked on the numbers for a large gravel job, his mind flipped back to the conversation he'd just had with Paddy. When he'd called in there on his way to the office, Paddy had been amazingly chipper. He'd introduced him to the caregiver, asked him how the games had gone.

Brett was surprised. It was a while since Dad had asked anything about his playing. Then Paddy said, "How's that little girl doing at the office?"

Brett bristled. "She does a good job."

"Yeah? Well, she's smart enough."

"Oh, you think so?"

"Mmm." Paddy glanced away. "It was cute when she found the raspberries."

Brett grinned. He didn't mention the raspberry picking at Aunt Ray's. What Paddy didn't know, he couldn't use against him. "Yeah," he said. "She likes raspberries."

Paddy seemed to ruminate on that. "You know, you don't get raspberries without a woman around."

"What do you mean? I can pick raspberries as well as the

next guy."

"Yeah, but you don't. Men don't." Paddy looked wistful.

This was the first time in a long while that he'd heard anything from Paddy that indicated he missed Mum. But he shouldn't be surprised. Paddy had probably been doing a lot of drinking over a lot of years to try not to notice how much he missed Marie. It was strange to see that now after so much time.

His attention was distracted by Frank's voice in the outer office, then Bruno Morelli poked his head in the door.

"Uh, Mr. Rome. I'm wondering how you're doing on the agreement I gave you."

"I haven't gotten anywhere with it, Morelli. I'm waiting for your cheque to clear the bank."

Morelli reddened. "I'm not sure this is the best way to go about it. Maybe if you were to just give me back the money we can work on it from there."

"I don't think I can do that. Your cheque's been deposited in the bank and we can't do anything one way or the other until it clears, can we? Why don't you come back and see me next week."

Morelli was sweating. "Next week?"

"Yeah. Sorry, but I'm busy right now." He escorted him through the office to the door, hoping to get him out of there before Katy returned. As he sat down at his desk he heard the sound of a car enter the yard. He darted over to his window. Damn. Katy was already back from the bank.

Through the window he watched Morelli about to climb into his vehicle when he stopped and glanced at Katy who was calling and waving to him. Morelli looked around as if seeking a way to avoid her, and then back as she trotted over to his car.

Brett dashed for the office door. He could see them talking, and Katy was gesticulating excitedly. Morelli glowered and shook his head. Then he seemed to relent. He examined his watch and said something. She considered him for a moment, nodded and turned to the steps just as Brett started down toward her.

Her face was pale but she smiled. "Hi, Brett." They both turned at the sound of Morelli's car leaving the yard. "What was he doing here?" Her clear eyed gaze pinned him where he stood.

Out of the corner of his eye, he saw Frank look out the doorway. He took Katy's arm and turned her away. "He called around, wanted to invest in the business."

"Yes, I told you he'd done that. I thought you said you didn't know him." She narrowed her eyes.

Brett met her gaze with difficulty. "I didn't until a week ago. He caught me at my desk a couple of times after everyone else had left. He introduced himself and made a pitch to invest."

He stared at her. He knew she needed the money but he didn't have it yet, not officially. And if it didn't clear the bank he'd be sorry he'd held out the hope of getting it back for her. On the other hand, what if it did clear the bank? Then if he gave it to her, would she stay?

He was pretty sure she'd come to Rome Trucking because she'd lost that money and was trying to get it returned to her. What happened when she got it back? Where would she go, and where would that leave him? It could backfire either way.

"What were you talking to him about?"

"I just asked if I could get my money back." She tried to appear nonchalant.

"And?"

She gave him an unreadable look. "He said, he'd see."

Brett turned to go back inside. "Come see me in my office when you're free."

When Katy came in a few minutes later, Brett rose and closed the door. "Come here."

Taking her hand he pulled her round the desk. "Sit here," he said and hauled her onto his lap. "That's better. Did you miss me while I was gone?"

She laughed. "Yes, actually."

"Oh, you did, actually? Well, that's something. Do you

want to go to an early dinner tonight? I have a game later. Are you coming to see it?"

She shook her head. "You didn't get me those tickets you promised."

"I know. I've been busy. I'll get some tonight and then you can bring a friend. We can get together after the game."

"Not tonight, though. Next time. I'm busy tonight."

"Huh." He kissed her, laying his mouth gently against hers. He didn't want to get too fired up before the game. But there was no halfway with Miss Katherine. She fired him faster than his Corvette when he turned the key. Whoa.

He lifted his head and held her tight against him. "You're a mad woman. You get me all worked up and there's nothing I can do about it. Very frustrating." He felt her laugh and smiled into her hair.

"What are you up to tonight?"

"Not much."

"But you said you were busy."

"Oh. I promised to meet Bruno to see what he can do for me about my money, and then I'm having a quiet night. I've been really tired."

Brett stiffened. "Meeting Bruno? I don't like the idea of that."

She batted him on the shoulder. "Brett, stop it. You can't tell me what to do."

"No, I know that," he said doggedly. "I've learned that." His smile was rueful. "But I don't like that guy. He's not honest. There's just something about him. Where are you meeting him?"

"At the Skyway Restaurant. It'll be perfectly safe."

He brooded on that for a minute. "What time?"

"Eight o'clock."

"Huh." He couldn't make eight o'clock. The game would be starting.

"How about a different time so I can be there?" She wriggled in his arms and he held her tighter. "No, just listen. I've been working on him. I thought if I could get him to give me some money on the pretext of investing in the company, I'd give it to you and he would effectively be paying you back."

She was listening now, her gaze pinned to his face.

"So," he continued, "I got him to give me a cheque for twenty thousand dollars." He couldn't decide if this was a mistake, but he didn't want her meeting that asshole. She'd discover the twenty thousand in the bank anyway, the next time she examined the account.

"I've put it in the bank. We just have to wait until it clears."

She thought for a minute. "So there's twenty thousand already deposited?"

He nodded.

"And he thinks he's investing in the company."

Brett nodded again.

She stared at him. "I don't know what to think. It's kind of pulling a fast one on someone who pulls fast ones."

He smiled. "So you don't need to meet with him. I'd rather you didn't," he said with forced restraint. "I don't trust him."

"No, neither do I. Not anymore."

He relaxed and feathered more kisses down her throat. "Do you think you could come over to visit me tomorrow? My cousin works evenings, so he's gone about five."

She pursed her lips and seemed to consider. "Possibly."

He laughed. "Possibly or not, you'd better be there. Why don't I pick you up, then I can take you home afterward."

She shook her head. "No, I have some things to do after work so I'll come in my car."

He wanted to argue but thought better of it. He didn't win many of these arguments with her and he didn't want her to back out now. "Okay. Just don't be late. You know how I hate to wait."

"Poor baby." She ran her hand across his chest and he had to grab her fingers and pin them to his shirt in self defence.

"Don't play with me, Katy." He tried to make it sound like

a joke, but he was pretty sure he failed.

~~~

Katy got to the Skyway Restaurant just before eight but Bruno was nowhere to be seen. She waited for a half hour, nursing a coffee. The scum, he couldn't even keep an appointment, too chicken to face her. She rummaged in her purse for her phone and called the number she'd found on Brett's blotter. He answered on the third ring.

"Bruno, it's Katy. I'm waiting for you."

There was a long pause. "How'd you get this number?"

"How do you think? I work at Rome Trucking. Now I want to know where my money is. I want it back."

"But I deposited it with Rome Trucking. You'll see it in the account."

"Bruno, you have to meet with me."

"I can't, Katy, and I warned you not to phone me." His voice sounded strained. "I'm busy now. Something's come up." The line went dead. She dialed again but it went straight to voicemail.

She wasn't as disappointed as she might have been. Now that she knew about the money in the Rome Trucking account, it sounded like she'd have her money soon and she'd be able to pay some rent. If the cheque cleared.

By the time she got back to the office and hid her car behind the mechanic's shop, she was exhausted. It was like a seesaw, this life she was living. She barely managed to set the alarm and have a shower before she collapsed on the couch in the basement and fell asleep.

CHAPTER TWENTY SIX

What do you mean, Randy the cook is your cousin? Randy who?" Katy surveyed Brett's kitchen from her chair at the table.

"Randy Rome, the cook who works at the Regent Hotel. You know him."

Her mouth dropped open. "Really?" She stared. "Well, I do know him. I just never asked his last name and he did mention he was staying with his cousin. I didn't know you were the cousin."

She eyed the place critically. "It's not such a mess. You said you couldn't bear it."

Brett looked smug. "He's turned over a new leaf. Pretty good, eh?" He put more salad on her plate. "I actually took advice from my sister, Liz. When I was complaining about the mess, she said tell him he's got a week to move out. I thought that was pretty mean."

She laughed. "So what did you tell him?"

He ate a piece of salmon. "I warned him, waited for a while, and it got worse. So finally I said I couldn't live with the mess. I didn't actually say he had to move. But it had the desired effect. He cleaned it up."

"Hmm. I guess that means we can't leave any dirty dishes after dinner."

Brett leered at her. "Don't worry about it. I have better things for you to do with your time. I'll take care of the dishes later."

She laughed. "Now, now. We don't want him telling you he can't live with the mess, that you'll have to move out."

Brett shook his head. "Ain't gonna happen. Listen, there's a party coming up with the Victoria hockey team and I was hoping you'd come with me. It's a week Saturday at the Strider's Club. They're closing the club for us. Can you come?" He raised his eyebrows. "You'd have fun. All those big guys to talk to, and I know how you like big guys."

She snickered.

"What do you think?" While he waited for her answer, he forked a slice of grilled zucchini onto her plate."

She glanced down. There was so much food in front of her, she knew she'd never be able to eat it. She put her fork down. "Would you like me to?"

"Yes. I figured you need a bit of time to organize your weekend job."

"Thank you. I'll ask around for someone to fill in for me."

"Good." His dimples deepened and she realized it wasn't just anger that caused them to appear like that. This event obviously meant a lot to him.

"Have you had enough?" He was examining her plate.

"Yes, thank you."

"You didn't eat much."

"I ate quite a bit." He looked a question at her. "You kept putting more food on my plate."

He flushed lightly. "I'm trying to take care of you."

"Oh."

He stood and pulled her up. "Time for dessert," he said, walking her down the hall.

"Brett."

"Mm." He was busy finding the zipper on her pants. "What?"

"Am I dessert or are you?"

Laughing, he pulled her flush against him. She could feel

his erection pressing into her stomach and she felt the heat rise, her excitement mounting.

"We both are."

~~~

Brett sat on the bench and frowned down at the floorboards between his skates. They were wet, slightly slimy from all the water and juice that got spilled and spit during a game.

He stamped his skates as he pondered. He wasn't going back out on the ice tonight, they had it sown up five goals to two anyway.

He couldn't get his mind off Bruno Morelli. He'd been by the office twice since he'd run into Katy in the yard. Both times he'd come in right after Katy left, which led him to think Morelli was watching the office.

Bruno wanted his money back. Brett had explained the first time that he was still waiting for it to clear the bank, so Morelli would have to be patient. The second time, the money had actually cleared and he didn't have that excuse.

He sat Morelli down and explained the situation. Morelli had taken sixteen thousand dollars from Katherine Dalton. He hadn't paid it back. Where was the money?

Morelli raised his hands palms up but stayed silent, his face set and pale.

Brett now had his money and he was going to pay Katy the money Morelli owed her. His debt would be cleared. Then he'd give Morelli whatever was left.

Morelli turned white. His hand shook as he wiped his mouth. "You can't do that. I loaned you that money."

"No, actually you gave it to me as a goodwill gesture. So as a goodwill gesture, I'm going to pay your debt and refund the balance. Come back next week. I should be ready to pay you out."

"Please don't do this. I'm not the only one involved in this investment and it's not a good idea to play it this way."

Brett narrowed his eyes. "Are you threatening me?

Because if you are I'll call the police right now. You're the only person I've been talking to, and you're the only person named on the document you gave me."

Morelli's eyes darted around the room as if he'd forgotten the document. "Listen, if I could just get ten thousand back. That would be good enough. Just ten thousand."

"No. Now get out and talk to me next week." Morelli left, but Brett had the uncomfortable feeling that he wasn't giving up. It worried away at the back of his mind.

Now he shook his head and looked up quickly at the sound of a roar from the crowd. They'd made another shot on goal but no score. The game was over. Trooping back into the dressing room, he heard calls from the other players for who was going out and where to meet. Brett was going home.

Things were on an even keel for once. Paddy was doing better and actually cooperating with the caregivers. He'd committed to start physio. There was hope there.

The company was in the black this week. Not next week, Katy had pointed out. Everyone was cheered by that.

Katy herself, well, things were getting better all the time. And she was coming to the team party. It was too late to call her tonight, so he'd go home and sleep.

~~~

Bruno sat in his van and waited for Tyler. The house was dark and no one was home. Tyler's grey car, fender repaired and painted sat at the curb so Tyler must be driving something else.

Bruno pondered his future as he waited. Right at the beginning he'd made a mistake with Katy. He knew that but she'd disarmed him with her enthusiasm and excitement. He'd told her about the investment scheme to impress her, not encourage her to invest. This was Tyler's investment strategy and he had no business sharing it. He'd already gotten shit about that.

Tyler's little story about Katy being in an accident and not bothering them again hadn't proved true either. Katy called him within a couple of days, wanting to know where her money was. So Tyler either didn't know what he was talking about or he made it up as he went along. He strongly suspected the latter.

Now he waited to take it in the ear again. Tyler was expecting a signed loan agreement, and if not that, then his money returned. Bruno didn't have anything to give him. He was worried. He thought about the hammer in the trunk of Tyler's car and felt his guts clench.

Just then a black pickup with one working headlight pulled up and parked behind the grey BMW. Balson was driving. Tyler climbed out of the passenger seat, glanced over at Bruno's car and waved him in, then headed for the front walk.

Bruno climbed reluctantly out of his old van. He kept an eye on Balson, but he seemed to be stationed in the truck and occupied on the phone. He walked through the door and Tyler hit him on the side of the head as he entered. He staggered a few steps and felt another blow to the back of his neck. It didn't feel like a hammer. Maybe he was lucky it was only fists.

He turned around, his head swimming. Tyler stood in place, breathing hard. "Where's the money, Bruno?"

Bruno shook his head to clear it, dodged another blow. "I don't have it yet, Tyler. But I can get it." Maybe he could sell the van. It might bring a few thousand.

Tyler advanced. "What do you mean, you don't have it?"

"The guy kept it. Rome said we owe the girl and he's going to pay that debt for us."

Tyler stopped as if to think about that then took a giant step and sucker punched him. Bruno went down. Then he used his feet, aiming for the kidneys.

"That's not good enough, Bruno," he heard just before he passed out.

~~~

Brett was in a deep sleep when the cell phone on his nightstand vibrated and then rang shrilly. Rolling over, he fumbled in the dark, finally snagging it and knocking over his water glass. He pressed the button as he struggled with the lamp switch. "Yeah?"

"Mr. Rome?"

"That's me." He managed to turn the lamp on and attempted to brush the water off the sheet.

"There's been an alarm at Rome Trucking. First the intrusion alarm sounded then the fire alarm. We've already sent out the call to the police and emergency services."

Brett was now fully awake. "Say all that again."

"Yes sir. The intrusion alarm signal came in from your office building at Rome Trucking about fifteen minutes ago. We were just verifying it when the fire alarm went. It's actually a heat alarm but we treat it as a fire. We've called the police and emergency services and they're on their way. I'm not sure if the yard is secured but perhaps if you got out there, they wouldn't have to break down any fences, or anything."

"Yeah, yeah. Thanks." He hung up and slung on some clothes. The Corvette roared down the road and by the time he was within a half mile of the place, he could see flashing lights at the entrance to the truck yard. They'd obviously crashed the gate.

Flames leaped from the roof of the office. The car skidded to a stop outside the mechanic's shop and he ran the rest of the way.

The police tried to stop him but he identified himself and ran on. Several hazy figures were on the roof attempting to chop a hole to get at the flames. It was such an old house, Brett didn't expect anything to be saved. Surely it would be quickly engulfed. But with hoses pouring in from various angles the flames appeared to be subsiding somewhat at the front.

All the records were in there. It would be a hell of a mess trying to rebuild that information from scratch. Brett stood in his unlaced boots, squinting in the smoke and watching the action, when from the corner of his eye he caught some motion at the back of the building. The exterior door leading to the basement of the old office slowly opened.

He didn't trust his eyes and blinked to clear his vision of smoke. What was going on? What was that? He started to move toward the door, and watched with horror as a small figure stumbled out the doorway into the weeds at the back of the yard.

She was dressed in what seemed to be baby doll pyjamas, her hair tousled around her head, clutching a square black object to her chest. She staggered, struggling for breath.

He started to run but felt like he was plowing through wet cement, his boots dragging and sucking through the muck. He could see sparks pouring down off the roof onto her head. The roar of the fire dimmed in his ears as if he'd gone deaf.

Brett reached Katy after what felt like months of running, wrapping his arms around her, staggering backward from the flames and dragging her with him. He could hear himself roaring with rage, bellowing in fear. He wasn't sure what he was saying as he dragged her bodily back from the house. The laptop in her arms fell to the ground and he stumbled on it with his boots as he staggered toward the fence.

A fire fighter saw her at the same time Brett did and came running, calling into his radio. He and an ambulance attendant converged, picking Katy up and carrying her to a waiting stretcher.

Brett yelled at them but no one paid any attention. An oxygen mask was strapped over her face. Attendants felt her arms and legs, checking for injuries or burns.

Breathless, Brett stood panting, his head hanging like a gutted steer. There was so much compression in his chest he thought he might be having a heart attack. He clutched at the front of his shirt, holding both hands over his chest, and they came to take him to the other ambulance.

"No, no, I'm fine," he panted.

"Right over here, sir. Just lay down for a few minutes." He collapsed on the stretcher. Maybe he did need help. He couldn't breathe, it felt as if there was a metal band strapped around his chest. When the oxygen mask was taped on he went limp.

He began to feel better almost instantly.

"Okay, I'm okay now. How's the girl?"

"She's fine, just lay here a few minutes." They couldn't hold him down long. Prying himself away from the attendants he staggered over to the other stretcher and peered down at Katy.

She was covered in soot, her face smeared with it. The whites of her eyes showed clearly as she looked up at him, tear tracks running down her cheeks.

"Are you crying?" he said, his voice hoarse.

She shook her head, the mask making it hard to read her expression.

"Are you hurt?"

She shook her head again.

The ambulance attendant whispered, "Just some smoke inhalation, not severe." A police officer tried to find out if she'd been alone in the building. Katy stared at him and nodded uncertainly.

Brett stood his ground, his gaze focussed on her, roving over her body. "No burns?"

"A few, yes. Minor ones," said the attendant. "Falling debris mostly from inside the building."

He took a deep breath and gripped his hands together. His shoulders shook.

The emergency personnel finally determined Katy could go home, releasing her into Brett's care.

~~~

Dawn was just showing on the horizon as he spooned her into the Corvette, backing carefully out of the yard. He'd make some calls when he got home. Frank would get there before they were finished fighting the fire and see to security.

Luckily the flames hadn't spread to the trucks, although Wilf had left his pickup parked overnight near the office and the paint had blistered all down one side from the sheer force of the heat.

It was quiet in the car. Katy was breathing slowly, Brett was speechless. He parked in front of his place, opened Katy's door, leaned in and lifted her out. "I can walk," she whispered. He growled something and kicked the door shut.

Inside the house, he sat her on a kitchen chair. "Katy, can you manage a shower? You're covered in soot. It'll itch like crazy and stain your skin."

She nodded.

"I'll help you," he said. Picking her up again he carried her into the bathroom, placing her on the closed toilet seat. "Wait here a minute." He came back with one of his clean tee shirts and laid it on the counter, pulled a fresh towel from the small cupboard.

Starting the shower, he found soap and shampoo, then began undoing the tiny buttons on her pyjama top. She covered his hands with hers. "I'll do it."

"Let me help," he growled.

She shook her head. "I'm fine. I'll do it. You wait outside."

He stood indecisively.

She gave him a stubborn look.

"Don't lock the door," he barked.

He stood outside the door for long minutes before he heard the shower door slide and the sound of splashing. Then he walked down the hallway to find the phone and call Frank.

When the bathroom door finally opened again he was waiting. He followed her into the living room, watched her seat herself gingerly on the edge of the couch. There were numerous small red marks on her arms, a larger one on her hand and a few on the side of her face. He stood for a moment then sat down across from her.

She gazed back at him warily. "You're exactly like you were the first time I met you," she croaked.

He gave her a blank look.

"You were wearing those boots with the laces undone. And you had a tee shirt on with the neck ripped out and those old cargo shorts. You had the same black expression on your face. The only thing different is you don't have a black eye this time." Her voice wobbled on the last words and her body began to tremble.

Brett heaved off the sofa, gently grabbing her up in his arms and seated himself again with her on his lap. His arms wrapped firmly around her. "Katy," he whispered and she began to cry, great heaving sobs she tried to muffle in his shirt. She cried till she couldn't catch her breath and started choking.

"Katy, stop it. Please. Please, baby. You'll make yourself sick." He kissed her head and wherever he could reach. "Katy, sweetheart. Calm down." Her sobs eventually slowed and she lay limply against him.

He tried hard to forget she was sitting on his lap with her naked bottom across his legs, his tee shirt her only cover. But what he couldn't forget was his rage at seeing her emerge from the basement door of the office, soot all over her face, smoke pouring out around her, flames leaping down from the roof above.

He could only speculate that she'd been sleeping in there. But why? Why would she be sleeping in the office basement? Was she meeting someone that she couldn't meet at her house? He didn't even want to think about that.

Had she been kicked out of her house? If so, why wouldn't she have told him? She was exhausted, in shock, with smoke in her lungs and small nasty burns all over her tender skin. He was furious. His rage was hot, seething under his skin. And he couldn't let it out.

Randy's bedroom door opened and he staggered out, yawning loudly. "What's going on, guy? It's pretty early for visitors." His jaw dropped as he took in the sight of Katy curled up on Brett's lap, still heaving with slow sobs.

"What the fuck?" His gaze shot to Brett's face. "What's going on?" The second question was much more demanding.

"I'll tell you, just wait a minute."

Katy was almost asleep. Standing, Brett carried her toward his bedroom door. As he bent over to deposit her on the

219

mattress, she opened her eyes. "Brett," she whispered, "I've got my period. I need some supplies." She gazed up at him, desperation on her face.

"Okay." He pulled the sheet up around her. "Do you need them right now?"

She nodded. "I can't go to sleep without something."

"Do you mean painkillers or other supplies?"

She blushed. "Both, but especially the other supplies."

"Okay. I'll get you some. I've got pain killers here." He found a bottle in the bathroom and came back with a glass of water. She carefully selected two from his palm and drank them down.

"Now, lay down. I won't be long. And if you go to sleep I'll wake you so you can take care of yourself."

She lay back and heaved a sigh. "Thank you," she said faintly.

Brett silently closed his bedroom door and stood in the hallway, his hands covering his face. He could barely control himself. His emotions were all over the map, swinging him around like the tail of a cat.

Then he looked up to see Randy glaring at him from the living room doorway. He sighed and headed in that direction.

"What's wrong with her?" Randy demanded in a low voice as soon as he was within spitting distance. "Were you too rough with her?"

Brett stopped and held up his hands, but Randy bulled ahead. "I could see she was naked, she just had your tee shirt on. It pulled up when you carried her in there. And she's crying." He face flushed as he pointed forcefully at Brett's door.

"Randy. Calm down. There was a fire at the office."

"So?" His expression became quizzical. "I thought I smelled smoke. What does that have to do with her?"

"That's what I'd like to know. When I got there they were starting to fight the fire, and in the middle of it all the basement door opened and she walked out surrounded by smoke."

Randy gaped at him. "She was in the office, at night?"

"Yeah, she was wearing pyjamas."

"She was sleeping there!" He said it as a statement. Brett knew it must be true, he just couldn't believe it.

"That's what it looks like."

"What did she say?"

"I haven't asked her yet. You saw her. She's in shock. They had to give her oxygen and treat some burns before they let her go."

He thought about needing oxygen himself and knew he hadn't inhaled much smoke. It was something else entirely that he'd been suffering from.

"Whoa. She's lucky she woke up and came out."

Brett backed up like he'd been hit. "That's for damned sure!" His face was tight with rage, his voice low and vicious. "Lucky?! No one knew there was anyone in there. They weren't searching for anyone. They were just trying to stop an old building from burning down and taking all the trucks with it. I could break something! What a fucking stupid thing to do! *She could have been killed! We wouldn't have known until they found a body!*"

He saw the alarm on Randy's face and realized how loud he'd gotten. "Yeah. I need to dial it down. I can't… I'm trying to…" He swung his head from side to side. "I don't know what she was doing in there, but I mean to find out." He breathed in deeply through his nose.

"I have to go get some stuff for her. Are you up for a while? Just listen for her, would you? She might get upset while I'm gone."

Randy nodded, hesitated, then said, "Sorry for the accusations, Brett. I just couldn't figure out what was wrong."

"Yeah." Brett left the house.

CHAPTER TWENTY SEVEN

When Katy woke it was early afternoon and she was alone in Brett's bed. The sun was high in the sky and creeping insistently round the blind. She was sore and hungry and needed the bathroom. She listened. It sounded like there was noise coming from the kitchen.

She wasn't in any rush to confront Brett. He'd been angry last night. She'd been frightened, frightened and mortified.

Still, she couldn't stay in bed all day, especially as it was his bed. She searched around for something to put on. She had his tee shirt and it came to mid-thigh on her, but didn't give much comfort.

She spied a housecoat hanging on the back of the door. It wrapped around her twice and came to her ankles. Perfect. She grabbed the big bag of supplies Brett had bought her and smiled faintly. She should have been more specific, there was everything in that bag.

When she emerged from the bathroom the sounds from the kitchen were louder and a wonderful smell of fresh food wafted down the hall. She followed her nose. Randy worked at the stove, stirring a pot. He saw her come in and examined her gravely. "Hi, Katy. How are you? How are the burns?"

"A little bit sore." She shrugged and pushed up the sleeves of the housecoat. "There aren't that many."

Randy looked at the freshly scabbing patches carefully. "I think you were really lucky."

She nodded. "I guess so."

"I know so. Are you hungry? I have crab chowder here."

"Oh, it smells heavenly."

"Good." A timer went off and he pulled scones out of the oven. "I figured you'd be hungry, and Brett said he'd be back soon. He's just gone over to the office to see what has to be done."

She went slightly pale. "Oh," was all she said.

"Well, you have to talk to him sometime."

He placed a bowl of soup in front of her and one for himself. Then the scones on a plate with butter, cheese slices and jam. "There you go, eat up."

She smiled back at him and dipped her spoon in the bowl. "Oh, it's terrific Randy. Really good."

They ate in silence for a few minutes. The front door opened and they both stilled. Heavy footsteps proceeded down the hall and stopped at Brett's open bedroom door. Randy called, "We're in the kitchen, Brett."

He got another bowl of chowder for Brett and set it on the table. "There you go, I'm finished. I've got to get in to work early today. There's a big party in the restaurant tonight." He cleared his place at the table and left them alone.

Brett sat down and let his gaze rove over her face. She knew she looked bad with dark shadows under her eyes and fresh scabs on her cheekbone. Her hand was sore and bright red marks showed on one arm where the sleeve of the housecoat had fallen back.

He stared at her with a kind of horror in his eyes and she couldn't think of anything to say. Her spoon hung suspended from her fingers.

"How's the soup?" His voice was amazingly calm.

She nodded, momentarily relieved. "Good."

"Yeah, he'd started making it before I left." He took a scone and split it, laid it on his plate, let his hands fall. "How are you feeling?"

"Tired. But basically okay."

Brett put his elbows on the table, folding his hands, resting his forehead on them for a moment. When he looked back at her his face was set. "Can you please tell me what you were doing in the office last night?"

She tried to hold his gaze but couldn't, looking into her bowl instead. "I was sleeping there."

"Yes, I figured that out for myself. What I can't figure out is *why?*"

Anger rolled off him in waves and she found it hard to form an answer. "Because they kicked me out of my room at the townhouse. I didn't have anywhere to go. I booked into the spare room with Dad but couldn't get in there right away, so I needed somewhere short term."

He just looked at her. She felt the colour climb her cheeks. She bit her lip but couldn't think of anything to add.

"Why didn't you tell me you needed a place to stay?"

Tears started in her eyes. She opened her mouth, then closed it. She glanced down but no words came.

"Katy." His voice gritted out. "Why didn't you tell me?"

"I thought I could handle it. I wanted to manage on my own." She was whispering and tried to clear her throat. Why was this so hard? Her decisions seemed to make sense at the time and he was throwing her mind into turmoil with his questions.

"You didn't want my help? You didn't think I had a *right* to help?"

She glanced up at his tone. She'd always managed on her own. That was her job. "I don't... I thought I could handle it for a few weeks, and I'd be able to put it all back together."

"You nearly got yourself killed!" His voice shook, she saw his eyes get moist. Her gaze nervously followed him as he stood, walked to the counter and back. They heard the front door shut behind Randy.

Brett peered down at her. "Katy, you could have died in there. No one was searching for you. We had no idea there was anyone in the building." He glared till she had to drop

224

her head to avoid his gaze. "They were just trying to stop the fire from spreading to the trucks. That's all."

She nodded.

He sighed and sat down. "I don't know what to do with you."

She felt resentment rise in her breast, underneath the overload of shame and fear. "I'm not a child. You don't have to talk as if I am."

"I know you're not a child. You're all woman. That's mostly what has me so tied up in knots." He took a deep breath, slowly let it out. He seemed to concentrate on a spot on the wall in front of him.

"I think I had the right to know that you needed help. I had the right to offer you some help. You took that away from me."

She gazed up at him, startled. It had always seemed to be her job to take care of herself. It hadn't occurred to her that their relationship would change that. How was it different now, that he demanded to share the responsibility?

His face was grim, the dimples deep in his cheeks. "Don't you think so? Don't we have a relationship here? I'm not some gigolo. I don't just fuck you and leave it at that!" His voice cracked.

She reddened. "I'm sorry." Maybe he did have the right to know what was happening, the right to share the decision. It had never occurred to her. Tears started again and dripped into her soup. "I'm sorry."

"Oh, Katy." He groaned and grabbed her. "You scared the living hell out of me. I thought I was having a heart attack. I've never been so terrified in my life." His arms felt like steel bands wrapped around her.

"You can't run your life as if I don't matter. It's not right!" His face flushed. She could feel the heat pouring off him.

She choked back a sob. "I'm sorry."

~~~

In the end Brett tucked her back in bed and went out to the office again. She needed some clothing and he was determined to find a way into the building to get it. After some negotiation, the Fire Marshall let him into the basement to retrieve a few things.

He found her purse. He and the attendant went through it together while he picked out the items he knew she'd need. There were her driver's licence, credit cards, a package of birth control pills that he kept a firm grip on. It was all examined and documented. Everything else would have to wait until the investigation was finished.

Frank had already organized the delivery of a trailer to house the office. The phone would be installed tomorrow, a plumber arrived to hook up temporary water and sewer service. Frank had a fair idea of what jobs were lined up for the rest of the week.

The laptop that Katy had been clutching when she emerged from the building turned out to be from the office. Brett brought it home with him in the hope it was still working. Katy could search through it when she felt better, fill Frank in on whatever information she had stored in there regarding ongoing work.

He arrived back at the house just as the police drew up outside. Two officers emerged from the marked car and walked toward the door.

"Mr. Rome?" one of them called.

Brett nodded and waited for them to catch up. "That's right."

"We're here about the fire. I'm Constable Breck, this is Constable Peters. Can we come in? We were hoping to talk to the young lady who was found in the building as well. We understand she's here."

Brett showed them into the living room and went to see if Katy was awake. She was just sitting up, her hair tumbled around her head in dark curls, her cheek creased from the pillow. He sat on the side of the bed. "Katy, the police are here. They want to talk to you."

"The police?" She gave him a confused look.

"Yeah, about the fire. They're investigating it."

"Oh. Of course. Did you….. Did you get any of my clothes?"

"Yes, but they're wet and smell strongly of smoke. We can wash them but there's nothing for you to put on right now." He checked the bedroom.

"Use the housecoat. It covers everything, right?" He pulled it from the hook and held it out for her. He watched as she scooted to the edge of the bed, his gaze more intent as the tee shirt pulled up and he caught a glimpse of the tops of her thighs, the triangle of dark curls.

He didn't know when she'd be well enough to make love and he felt like a hound for even wondering about it. His needs swung wildly between yelling his anger at her, and throwing her onto the bed while he screwed her brains out. He didn't know which he wanted to do more, neither was right.

She went down the hall to the bathroom and Brett walked back to talk to the officers. "Can I get you a coffee or a soda? Katy was sleeping, she had burns and suffered some smoke inhalation. She'll just be a minute."

Brett poured four coffees and set them on the coffee table in the living room, then went back to see if Katy needed anything. There was no sound in the bathroom. He stood in the hallway, head down, waiting. Finally the door opened. He looked at her pale face. "You okay? Maybe they can come back later."

"No, I'm fine. It's just embarrassing not having any clothes to wear." She gestured at the housecoat wrapped around her slim body.

"I should have bought you something. It's just been…"

"No, I'll get the other things washed up and then it won't be a problem."

Following her unsteady progress out to the living room he sat down protectively by her side. The younger fellow, Constable Peters began with Katy, asking about what she'd done the day before and what time she'd returned to the office. Where was her car?

It was behind the mechanic's shop.

Brett gritted his teeth. He hadn't seen her car there last night, he'd only noticed it this morning after combing the whole yard trolling for anything unusual. How had she known to hide it there? *Why* did she hide it there? He would have answers if it killed him.

When did she go back to the office?

She went back about nine o'clock. She went for a bite of dinner and stopped in to see her friend, Sid. She left there at about quarter to nine. She set the alarm on the office exterior doors, then had a shower and went downstairs to bed.

Did she go to sleep right away?

No, she read for a few minutes. But she was really tired and turned the light out just after nine thirty.

The police officer gave her a steady gaze. "That's pretty early," was his comment.

"Yes, it was. I was tired. It's been quite a stressful time."

He just nodded and Brett clenched his fists. That was the understatement of the century.

"Did you go to sleep right away?"

"Yes, I think so. The next thing I heard was the sound of a crash. You know, like glass breaking. It sounded like it came from upstairs. Then there was another bang or crash like wood splintering. My first thought was that a tree had fallen on the office. There's an old tree in the yard and I've often thought it might come down in a windstorm or something. So that's what I thought had happened at first."

"At first?"

"Yes, but then I heard more noise, the sound of footsteps going across the floor above me. I turned on the light and went around to the stairs and up them. Then I turned the light off, just in case, because I didn't know what I was going to find…"

Brett was holding his breath, his jaw clamped shut, afraid of what was going to come out of his own mouth. Of all the stupid, pig headed, idiotic, moronic, imbecilic… He noticed the other cop watching him as his fists opened and closed, so he stood to pace across the room and back. Then he remained motionless, hands on hips, as he listened to what Katy said.

"I carefully opened the door at the top of the stairs and I saw someone in Brett's office. They were rummaging around in the papers on his desk and then in the drawers. They were searching for something."

"Could you see what the person looked like?"

"No, not then, it was dark. But then there was a different noise and the smell of fuel. Not gas, but something, maybe diesel. I'm not sure but I think it was diesel, and then a flare of flame. I shut the door right away, and I could hear them running out of the office."

"Them? There was more than one person?"

"Yes, there were at least two. So I opened the door and came out because I needed to get the laptop. All the records are on there, and I didn't know what would happen if I couldn't get it…"

She glanced up quickly at a smothered exclamation from Brett. He glared at her with a white hot heat that must have scorched her already tender skin.

"Brett," she said softly, "I thought I should rescue the laptop."

"You thought you should? You weren't thinking at all!" he roared. "You should have run for your life! Don't you know you're worth more than some damn laptop?"

Constable Breck slowly rose to his feet. "Calm down, Mr. Rome. We're just trying to find out what happened, aren't we?"

"It's what almost happened that I can't get out of my head." His voice sank to a quiet mutter and he breathed heavily through his nose. "Just give me a minute." He stalked to the kitchen, ran the water. When he came back he had a glass in his hand.

He sat down again, drank some and offered it to Katy. She took it and drank the rest. When she leaned against him, he wrapped his arm around her, pulling her tightly against his ribs.

"Okay, okay," he muttered. "Let's get this over with."

Breck's eyes seemed less stern as he took over the questions. "What happened next?"

"I thought if it was diesel it wouldn't flare as fast as gas, it'd give me time, so I ran and grabbed the laptop and just yanked it off the desk, the cords all dangling.

"The first guy was gone. The second guy was running out the door and onto the steps. He looked back, I think to see how the fire was going. I don't know if he saw me but I saw him in the light from the fire coming from Brett's office.

"I just ran as fast as I could down into the basement, shut the door and locked it. I didn't want him to be able to come after me." She took a breath and sagged heavily against Brett's side.

"It was pitch black down there. I tried the light but it wasn't working any more. I had to feel my way down the stairs and around to the back through the boxes. It took me a few minutes to find the door, and then I had to get the bolts undone so I could open it."

Brett's face must have been as pale as Katy's, and was covered with a sheen of sweat. She continued, "Then I came out. That's all." She sagged further against him and his arms tightened possessively around her.

"Anything else?" He glared a challenge at the two officers. "Are we finished?"

"Not quite. What did the man look like?"

"Oh, yes." Katherine lifted her head and stared into Constable Breck's eyes. "He looked like Bruno Morelli."

CHAPTER TWENTY EIGHT

Brett closed and locked the door behind the officers as they filed out. He peeked into his bedroom, Katy was sleeping. She hadn't moved since he carried her in from the police interview.

She'd explained to the officers how she knew Bruno Morelli and talked about the money she'd given him. When she admitted the last time she talked to him had been on the phone when he didn't show up for their meeting at the Skywalk Restaurant, Brett had nearly hit something. He'd thought she agreed not to see him that night. Little did he know, apparently.

But she'd collapsed after that. He carried her into the bedroom and lay her down on the bed, peeling his housecoat away. Lifting the covers carefully over her, he wanted to lay down beside her, hold her tight against him, just hold her. He wanted to cry.

Instead he went back into the living room and told the police what he knew about Morelli. He told them about his plan to get her money back. He didn't know how legal it was, what he'd done, but he'd do it again in a heartbeat. She wouldn't take any help from him, no matter how he presented it.

At least now the police were paying attention to the incident where Katy had been rear ended by that truck. It had just been a phone in claim before, but with the fire added to the picture, they were going to be investigating it closely.

He sighed and hefted the garbage bag from his car, dumping all her clothes that he'd salvaged into the washer. The smoke smell was overpowering. He quickly dumped extra soap in and turned it on. Then he opened a few windows and stepped into the shower.

As he soaped up, he went over the list in his head of things he had to do tomorrow. No game or practice but Paddy needed some time, he knew Katy needed to talk to her father about the fire, and he and Frank would try to pull things together at the office.

There was the insurance company to deal with and he had to find a restoration company to restore whatever they could from the mess of the records. Katy wasn't up to going back to work yet, even though she'd been making noises about that very thing. His plate was full.

He towelled off and fell into bed, carefully drawing the warm bundle of woman back against him before he tumbled into a deep sleep.

~~~

"No, you shower first. I'll take care of these dishes. I have some calls to make." Brett turned with purpose toward the sink, splashing water in the pots and clattering the plates together in the dishwasher.

As he heard the shower go on, he stilled at the sink, hands resting on the counter. How was he going to get through the night? She seemed so fragile, the burn on her face was scabbed over but the bright red marks on her hands and arms glared at him as if in accusation. There were dark shadows under her eyes.

Those shadows kept him from even trying to make love to her. They hadn't made love since before the fire and these last nights had been murder, lying beside a small curvy body that was seemingly unconscious while he wrestled with his baser urges.

His workout today had been heavy, four hours of labour that should have left him burned out. Instead, he just burned. He finished the dishes and wandered into the living room to turn on the television. Maybe he could distract himself.

It had been Liz's day with Paddy, he called her to check. The news was the usual. One step forward, several steps back. Paddy was grumpy, cantankerous and just barely willing to continue his physio. The first session had tired him out too much.

Brett's next call to Frank caught him up on the office situation. A restoration company had been over, removing everything that hadn't burned. Most of the damage was from the water from the fire hoses. They'd do an assessment, give them a timeline for returning the records. The insurance company had sent an inspector around to view the mess.

His call to the police was even more disturbing. So far they hadn't found Bruno Morelli. He'd gone underground, wasn't at any of his usual haunts. They advised caution about leaving Ms Dalton alone. Morelli might have seen her or even recognized her in the house. Although their original contact had been brief, he might be aware that she could identify him.

Brett pondered that. His problem was he didn't know exactly how brief her original contact with Morelli had been. She'd known him long enough to trust him with her money. And Brett strongly suspected the bastard had been involved in some heavy duty sexual activity. If so, he sure as hell would remember what she looked like.

But more important, the police had taken a closer look at the shattered window removed from Katy's car. Gert had shown it to them, still lying in the truck garage. They were pretty sure it had been broken by a bullet from a small calibre pistol. When they searched under the dashboard of her car they found the bullet embedded in the carpet.

Brett was determined she wasn't going to leave his sight until the police caught these guys.

Katy must be asleep by now. He had a quick shower and quietly opened the bedroom door. To his surprise the lamp was on low. Turning her head, Katy smiled at him. "I wondered where you were."

"How come you're still awake? I thought you'd be sleeping by now," he said, lifting the covers and sliding under.

She shifted over and rolled on her side to face him. "No, I've been waiting for you."

He stilled. "You have?" Her hand pressed against his chest, rubbing the rough hair under her palm.

"Yes, I wondered if you … That is, I wanted…" She stalled. There was a pink tint on her cheeks.

"What are you worried about?" He covered her hand with his and rubbed her fingers.

"Well, just that..." She finally rolled away and lay back on her pillow.

He followed her over. "Katy?"

She took his hand, placed it on her breast and just watched him. His fingers flexed automatically, squeezing the sweet flesh. He could feel her nipple digging into his palm. His breath left his lungs.

"Oh, baby. Aren't you still sore? What about your burns?" He searched his mind frantically for all the reasons they couldn't make love. They'd left his suddenly feeble brain.

"I'm not sore," she whispered. "Not much. We can just be careful." She seemed uncertain.

The urges he thought he'd tamed with phone calls and diversions surged back with a vengeance. "You want to make love?" He gazed intently at her, the dimples deep in his cheeks.

Her cheeks went brighter. "I've missed you."

Oh, God. He caught her mouth with his as his hands took possession. He tried to be gentle, tried to take care with all the red marks on her skin, tried to keep his emotions in check, those hot feelings of burning anger that erupted whenever he thought about her even being in that building, sleeping there, let alone that she'd gone upstairs into the office and exposed herself to both the fire and Morelli.

Then there was the fierce hurt that she hadn't turned to him for help. She was without a place to live and she didn't even mention it. Underneath it all was a layer of fear, fear for her safety, and fear that she would turn away from him.

By the time he entered her, the sweat was running off him. He swiped at his forehead with the sheet, pushing himself in to the hilt. She gazed up at him with glowing eyes. Something long held tight began to ease in his chest, an unbearable tension began to loosen. He felt the anger leaving him, slowly ebbing away.

"Katy," he said hoarsely, but no more words came. The feeling of rightness, of connection was so powerful he couldn't speak. Her eyes darkened. As he lowered his lips to her already swollen mouth, he froze.

They both heard the lock click in the front door at the same time, then the door opened. Her suddenly sharp gaze snapped back to his and she pushed against his chest. His arm tightened around her hips to hold her steady, to hold himself seated inside her.

His mouth lowered to her ear. "Don't move," he whispered. "It'll be okay. Just hold on a minute."

"He'll hear us," she hissed. "Randy will hear us."

"No, just wait." He reached desperately, snapping off the lamp. They heard footsteps wander down the hall, then into the living room. The television sprang to life.

Brett began to move inside her in the darkness. She was unyielding in his arms. His mouth travelled over her face, gently kissing her burned cheek, her soft lips. Now she was firm against him, not yielding yet not pushing him away. Slowly he felt her soften.

He pressed himself in, gradually withdrew, and pressed again. He held himself there, lightly grinding into her most secret place. She laid her mouth to his shoulder to muffle her whimpers, those soft feminine sounds, as her hands gripped his lower back. Even then, small desperate moans escaped.

He kept up a steady slow ruthless pace, unrelenting as he

felt her stiffen, gripping him, her nails digging into his skin. His breath came fast, but he held himself in check waiting for her, waiting. She came in a rush and he felt her teeth sink into him as he climaxed.

~~~

Brett watched Katy flit about the small office trailer as she organized her new desk. Frank was doing his best to help, pointing out the piles of records he'd recovered and organized during her absence, the small replacement file cabinet he'd brought in.

"And this chair is yours until we have time to do something about office furniture. We just brought in what we could find," he apologized.

"This is fine, Frank. Works for me. Where should we put the laptop?"

"You keep it. You're the one who knows how to work that gadget. Listen, if you're here for the morning, I'll take off to the bank with the deposit."

"Oh, of course. Thanks, Frank.

"Don't thank me, Katy," Frank offered gruffly. "We're just mighty glad you escaped the fire. That was a close thing, a damned close thing." He shook his head, glanced at Brett and grabbed the deposit book.

"Someone has to pick her up for work each morning and take her home at the end of the day."

Frank nodded. "I know."

"Brett!" Katy frowned at him.

"That's how it's going to be. I can take you home today. We'll work out who will do it tomorrow. And Katy's only working a part day," he reminded Frank as he hurried out the door.

"I got it." Frank waved his arm and broke into a jog toward his truck. "I'll be back, don't worry."

"Brett, I'm fine. I can stay here until later this afternoon." She gave him an exasperated look.

Brett stared back at her moodily. "Not if I have anything to say about it."

Dropping what she was doing, she lowered her hands into her lap and gazed at him.

"What?" he barked. "The doctor said come back slowly, that means no more than half a day."

"Okay. But I'm fine. Now what do we have here?" She began to sort the papers in piles as Brett watched her. "I wonder….." she mused. "Maybe it would be best to start from where I left off just before the fire. I can sort of piece it together…" Her head was buried in a stack of invoices.

Brett straddled the chair across from her and laid his arms along the back. "Katy, you don't have to move out of my place."

Her head popped up in surprise. "Uh…"

"You can stay there, with me."

She glanced at his mouth set in a stubborn line. "We already talked about this, Brett."

He nodded with dogged determination. "I know, but we need to talk about it again, because…"

She put up her hand to halt the words. "It's not just Randy. I was embarrassed last night, I know. When he came home it was bad timing…"

He smiled slowly. "Yeah, bad timing. But it ended up alright."

She flushed to her hairline and her gaze skittered to the window and back. "It's not just Randy."

"What then?"

"It's me. I don't do that. You have to understand, Brett. I know other people date and then move in together, but that's just not me. I don't know, I have certain... well, certain principles you might call it. I don't move in."

He'd known that somewhere at a gut level. His gaze roved over her face, wondering where he was going with her. Or more to the point, where was she going with him?

At his workout at the hockey gym this morning, Hart had given him a look and clapped him on the back. "Had a good night last night, I gather, my man," he joshed and gave a pointed glance at his shoulder.

Brett gazed down in surprise and saw the deep crescent-shaped bite mark on his bicep left by the pressure from her perfect little teeth. He knew he flushed. Damn, he threw his towel over the mark and stepped into his clothes. He'd forgotten that bite, how she sank her teeth into him trying to keep silent. And she'd made little sounds anyway, little breathless moans that had him reacting right there in the gym at the memory.

"What do you plan to do?"

She watched as he schooled his expression. "I don't mean to hurt you, Brett."

His nod was short, his lids lowered. "Do you have a plan?"

"Well, I go to Dad's tonight, I have about four days there. That will give me some time. I'll start searching for a place."

"What if I know a place?"

"You do?" Her eyes sharpened. "What kind of place? Is it expensive?"

"I'm not sure. I'll check it out and let you know, okay? So don't commit to anything until I have a chance to do some research."

She studied him. "Okay."

"Good." He slapped the top of her desk. "I'll get to work on the next set of estimates. You sort the books as best you can. But no more than four hours max."

He followed her to her car when she was leaving. Frank was back and Gert was in the office having lunch and emptying the coffee pot. Brett's keys were in his hand, he would tail her to her father's building.

He backed her up against the side of her car door. "Give me a kiss, Katy."

"Brett, anyone can see us!"

"But they're not watching. Come on, just a kiss. You see, I've gotten used to having you beside me at night and it's going to be damned lonely."

She put her soft mouth up to his.

~~~

Brett slowly walked the upper deck of the Vancouver Island ferry as it wended its way between the Gulf Islands heading south. They'd had two games away, winning both, which greatly boosted both their meagre standings in the league and the spirit of the whole team.

Jerome's cigarette flared and then faded in the lee of the bulkhead. But he sought the wind tonight. It helped blow the cobwebs out of his head.

He was ready. He'd suggest the idea tonight to Katy, gauge her reaction. She was still staying at her father's but they were expecting him to drop by when he got back to town. He shook his head in frustration, turning to walk back the way he'd come. Katherine Dalton was not a typical girlfriend, their history not a typical history.

He scrubbed his face with his hands. Right from the start, she'd been so wary she went backwards as often as forwards and bristled at the slightest thing. He should have known it wouldn't be easy. Well, he *had* known. And he was okay with that. Because he wasn't after easy, he was after Katy.

He rotated his bruised shoulder a few times then thrust his hands into his pockets. If she'd agree to this, prickly little thing that she was, it'd give him some breathing room. That's all he needed, a little time. Time to gather himself, time to sort everything out, time to pin her down.

Katy opened the door of her father's apartment when he knocked. She smiled and he took her in, head to toe. How could he not love this perfect compact package of woman, from the curls sprung loose around her head to the bare feet with pale pink toenails? He leaned in to kiss her as she rose on her tiptoes to meet him. His heart did an irregular beat in his chest. First things first, get her to agree.

"Who's winning?" He eyed the fan of cards in her hand.

"Come in, we're just about finished."

"Is that you, Brett?" Les called from the other room.

"Hi, Les. Yeah, it's me." Katy led him into the kitchen and he took a seat at the table.

Her father swept the cards aside. "We're done here. How

are you doing? We watched your game this afternoon. Pretty good hockey."

"Thanks. It's about time we started winning some of these games."

Les laughed. "That bad, huh? Well, it brought you up in the standings, and it's early in the season so there's lots of time to turn it around."

"True. Listen, Katy, did you get any further in finding a place to live?"

She looked doubtful. "Well, not yet. You asked me to wait, so I thought…"

He nodded. "Yes, I did. I don't know how you'll feel about this but I have a proposal for you. Paddy has space in his house."

Katy opened her mouth to comment, then closed it as Brett held up his hand. "I know, he hasn't been very polite to you. So it's probably a long shot that you'd even consider it. But here's what I've been thinking. Dad needs help. We have people coming in, enough to take care of the basics, so you wouldn't need to do meals and stuff like that. The medical part is taken care of."

He took a deep breath, gauged her reaction and ploughed on. "But he's alone at night, so if there's a problem, there isn't anyone there except him. That's one thing. In that way it would be a help to us all if you were there. But the other side is your own safety. And given that Morelli hasn't been found yet," here he gave her a dark look, "then it's not okay for you to be alone either. You need to live with someone."

"Now, Brett, that's not fair…"

"You know it's true. I told you what the police said."

Les sat back. "What did they say?"

"The police informed me before I left on the road trip. Katy, I told you to tell your father."

"I don't like this, Katy." Les appeared as stubborn as his daughter. "It wasn't a good idea to sleep there in the first place." She glared at him and he ignored that. "But what's done is done."

"Thank you very kindly," she muttered.

"And if Bruno Morelli recognized you in the office… Les let the observation hang. Katy had obviously been quite open with him about the events that had taken place.

"The thing about Paddy's house," Brett interjected, "is there are people coming and going. There are caregivers twice a day. My sister Liz and I take turns calling in to see him and it just makes for a busy place where it would be hard to catch you alone." From the corner of his eye he saw Les nod in agreement.

"I know he's been snarky, Katy. I don't know if you can get past that." He watched her face soften. That was the thing about her, if he appealed to her good nature she always forgave. He could see it happening now.

"Maybe the question is, how does your father feel about me being there?"

Brett grinned. "See, that's the thing. He likes the idea. Surprised the hell out of me because he hasn't cooperated with anything else that I've suggested so far. But he was very enthusiastic."

CHAPTER TWENTY NINE

Striders nightclub was packed with hockey players and
their partners. When the music ended, Brett led Katy to
the side of the dance floor. She was a little out of
breath. "I'm so relieved the police caught that bastard," he
said. "I hope he pays big time. You could have died in that
fire."

Acting on a tip and information gleaned from their
investigation, the police had found Tyler, Bruno and an
accomplice by the name of Balson hiding in the back room of
a rundown auto body repair shop just on the outskirts of the
city. Bruno had confessed to being at Rome Trucking when
the fire was set, saying he needed to find the contract he'd
signed with Mr. Rome and get rid of it. He'd made a mistake
with that contract, and his "partners" were upset about it. He
denied setting the fire though. It was his boss, Tyler, who
would go down for that.

"I'm sure he wouldn't have done it if he'd known
someone was is the building, Brett."

Brett gazed sadly at her. "Don't defend him, Katy. He
didn't care if there was someone in there or not. And he
probably did know. He must have seen you when you came
up to get the laptop."

She bit her lip. "I didn't think he was like that."

"No. But when they found the two guys he was in business with, they found two drug dealers trying to funnel their spare cash into some kind of legitimate business. He was doing deals with bottom feeders."

She looked away for a second. "Yes, I can see that."

He tugged her up against him and held her gently. "He targeted you, because you're an innocent. Even worse were the attacks with those vehicles, especially the truck. The fact that Tyler shot at you….." He shuddered. "I can't think about it."

Katy's face paled. "No, I can't either. I just didn't want to believe it."

Brett rocked her in his arms. "I'm sorry it happened, sweetheart. I'm sorry you were hurt."

Her clear grey gaze turned back to him. "It wasn't your fault, Brett."

He glared helplessly around the room. "Do you want a drink? I'll get you one." He threaded his way through the crowd, heading toward the bar, fending off efforts to draw him into conversation. He didn't want to leave her alone too long. She was still on the mend from the fire and its aftermath, and didn't know many people here tonight.

By the time he pushed his way up to the counter and placed the order, he could see over the heads of those around him that she was back on the dance floor waltzing with Jerome. He smiled. Good old Jerome. He'd come with Katy's friend Ericka from Vancouver, hooking up with them earlier in the evening.

Brett was grateful. Katy was more comfortable with one of her friends here, and she already knew Jerome. Hart was here as well with a woman he said he'd picked up in a bar the previous night. Hart was always picking up women, they just didn't stick. He claimed it was their high expectations. Brett figured it was Hart's low expectations but he kept that opinion mostly to himself.

He was having a fantastic time. Being new to this team, he already felt like he belonged. His fixation on Vancouver had ebbed, leaving contentment behind, not just contentment but satisfaction. It felt like he was making positive decisions with positive effect.

He thought back on the night he'd received Dancy's phone call about his father's heart attack as the Great Divide, the watershed. That phone call had changed his life, as if a door had been slammed in his face but another one quietly opened.

He couldn't go back, he could only go forward. His duty lay here yet it hadn't given him any joy. He'd sustained a series of such profound losses. Loss of his position on the Vancouver team, of his teammates, loss of the job offer as assistant coach, loss of his girlfriend. When he looked around, he'd lost pretty well anything that meant something to him. He'd been resentful and hostile, dutiful but angry.

Dragging himself to Victoria, he'd faced an angry sick parent and a job at a family business for which he had neither training nor authority. It hadn't worked well. It was like being brought to a full stop and then chained there.

Suspended animation, his university prof used to call it. He wasn't making any progress but rather stood in suspension. What a frustration, pushing to get the company working and being undermined, dragging Paddy to doctor appointments and discovering he was back drinking. It had been insufferable.

Katy changed all that. Even now he didn't know how, but she'd changed it. Here he was moving forward as fast as his legs would carry him. He had a position on a new hockey team, one that challenged him, excited him, and gave him great satisfaction.

At the same time, he was building a business, taking a failing enterprise and making it not just work but thrive. And in the process he'd found Katy. Katy of the direct grey gaze, the wary trust, the beautiful smiling soft mouth, the body that made him hyperventilate. The whole package enthralled him, excited and soothed him at the same time.

He watched one of the guys tap Jerome on the shoulder,

taking Katy off his hands, leading her into a new dance. He motioned to the bartender to hurry it up, keeping an eye on her as she moved around the room.

She looked fantastic. Her hair was swept up at the back but the curls still pulled free and sprang up on her nape and her temples. Her dress was great, moulded to her shape, making her seem taller, or maybe it was the heels. The number of other team players around the room who were keeping an eye on her didn't bear counting. He needed to get back to her fast.

Drinks in hand he shouldered his way through the crowd, reaching the edge of the dance floor as still another guy butted in to dance with her. This wasn't good news, this was Johnnie from the team support staff and he had a trigger temper. The dance was a fast one but he wanted to slow dance. He and Katy were having trouble negotiating what they were going to do.

Brett set the drinks down on the nearest ledge, waiting at the side of the throng. He'd be patient if it killed him. His days of dragging Katy away from other men, starting disturbances in the middle of the dance floor were over. He'd learned his lesson, he couldn't act like a caveman around her and get away with it. He didn't need to be told again.

He saw Katy pull back and question her partner but he just tugged her in tight against him, trying to snuggle her close and waltz. Brett glared around.

Was this really all right? He couldn't let it go, especially when she was forced up against him like that. Brett forged his way through the crowd, his good resolutions forgotten.

"My turn," he said, placing one heavy hand on Johnnie's shoulder and putting his other arm around Katy's waist. When he saw the amazed and then belligerent expression on Johnnie's face, Brett wondered if he shouldn't have taken a more diplomatic approach.

Johnnie made a grab for Katy, snagging the shawl collar of her dress and stretching it as he tugged, giving everyone a glimpse of the tops of her breasts and her lacy bra with the little bow on it. Brett's temperature levered up another couple of notches.

"Hey, hey, come on now. Let her go. I brought her and I'm going to dance with her. Get your own woman."

Hart appeared on the other side and just stepped in between them. Johnnie jerked back in surprise, the collar of the dress snapped out of his lax grasp and Brett pulled Katy across the floor, swinging her into his arms.

"That's better. See, I didn't even start a fight. I'm learning."

She grinned up at him mischievously. "We can probably thank Hart for that."

"True." Brett smiled slightly and looked over her shoulder to see that the ruckus had died down and Johnnie was asking someone else to dance.

~ ~ ~

Later, Brett carefully tugged the zipper down her back, letting her pretty dress slide to the floor. He turned her in his arms and pressed a desperate kiss to the side of her neck. "Katy, lay down with me." He threw the covers back on the narrow bed in the back bedroom of Paddy's house, the one he'd slept on that first night back in town.

He pulled her over him. She giggled into his chest. "Shhh, Katy. Dad's sleeping and we don't want to wake him up."

Her beaming face rose over him. "Is this what you did with your girlfriends when you lived at home?" She laughed softly.

"What? Lord, no. I didn't have girlfriends when I lived at home. There was never anyone like you, anyway." He massaged her breasts, gave her a searing kiss, tugged her gently against him. "Get on top of me, baby. It'll be more comfortable in this small bed. Just spread your legs, let me in. That's right."

He guided her, his hands tight on her hips as she lowered herself slowly onto him. He groaned, a sound centred deep in his chest. He levered himself upward, seating himself firmly as she gasped and braced her hands on his ribcage.

"That's it. Oh, baby. That's so good. I've been waiting all night for this." He reached up to kiss her until he had no breath left and fell back panting against the pillow.

"Katy, you take my breath away. I can skate all day and not get winded, but when I finally get inside you, I can hardly breathe." He gazed up into her beautiful grey eyes.

"Katy, will you marry me? No, listen," he said hurriedly, his voice hoarse, when she started to say something that looked like a protest. "I know this isn't the best time to ask. It just came out." He stopped her mouth with another kiss.

"It's been there in the back of my head, waiting for me to blurt it out. Don't say "no", don't say anything."

She rubbed her hands across his chest as she began to move over him, on him. His gaze was fiercely pinned to her face. She rocked against him, then folded her fingers into her palms and slid her hands into the soft hair under his arms. His chest clogged and he stopped breathing altogether. It was such a trusting gesture, so innocent.

Locking his gaze with hers, he rolled them both carefully to the side, beginning to thrust into her, moving slowly so the bed didn't squeak, moving steadily as he watched her face take on that faraway look even as she gazed at him, that expression that told him she was getting closer, moving into herself to that altered state where the feelings took over, the rush of power and heat, the flying apart and coming slowly back together, back to herself.

Brett buried himself with force, moved again, ground into her and came in a rush of liquid and fire.

Sometime later she stirred under his hand, stretching as he massaged her breast, tenderly squeezing the nipple. "What did you ask me?" she whispered.

His mouth opened, then closed. "I….. Well, I just said….." He stopped and gazed at her for a second. "You heard me, didn't you?"

She gave a sleepy, cat-like smile.

His laugh was low, rusty. "Will you marry me, Katy?" he said. "I love you. You make my world spin. My head too, for that matter. Will you?" He held his breath.

She smiled again. "I love you, too."

"Do you? Oh, Katy… I was afraid…" He buried his face in her hair and breathed her in, the perfume, the scent of her. When he lifted his head, he was flushed and triumphant.

"We could get a decent bed and have our own bedroom. Wouldn't that be novel?" His hands travelled tenderly over her body.

"We could buy your old home back if you want. Do you want to live there again?"

She gazed at him in the dim light, her eyes soft. "No, not that house. But maybe one nearby, where we could be a family."

He hugged her against his chest. "Yes, a real family."

Note to Reader -

I would really like your help. Book reviews are the lifeblood of what I do and your review of my book would mean a lot to me. If you would take a moment or two and leave your review on Amazon.com or wherever you bought the book, that would be wonderful. If you want to send it to me, my contact information is at the bottom. I honestly thank you.

Last but not least, if you find an error in this book, please email me. This will help me fix things that my editors and I might have overlooked and make for a better read for others. In return, by way of showing my gratitude, I will send you a free copy of the next book with my sincere thanks.

Sylvie Grayson

You can learn more or contact Sylvie Grayson at her website- www.sylviegrayson.com or contact her at sylviegraysonauthor@gmail.com

Sylvie Grayson has done it again. Here's an excerpt from

LEGAL OBSTRUCTION

The dog barked sharply, then once more and Joe put down his coffee cup. "That must be them now," he said, heading for the door, his long legs covering the carpet in swift strides. Geoff came more slowly, setting his cup on the fireplace mantle and pausing to adjust his shirt collar and check his image in the mirror on the hallstand before following his older brother down the granite steps to the front drive.

Joe was already at the car, hand on the door, the sheepdog bustling about his legs and whining anxiously. He joshed through the window with Dubuy about being late, getting lost the minute he left the city, too much of a tenderfoot to follow perfectly straightforward directions. The older man levered himself out of the driver's seat and turned to grasp Joe's hand in a firm shake, a wide grin on his face.

Geoff watched with undisguised interest as the passenger door opened and a young blonde woman stepped onto the pavement of the drive, adjusting the jacket of her suit and leaning back to take a briefcase from behind the seat. As she straightened, the sunlight glowed on her hair. Not blonde really, more honey brown, pinned up in a roll on the nape of her neck. Geoff grinned, watching the look on Joe's face as he caught sight of her. Stunned, that's how he looked, momentarily lost for words. His jaw went slack and eyes widened as he stood holding Andre Dubuy's hand forgotten in his own big fist.

To his credit he recovered quickly enough. His mouth snapped shut in a grim line, his eyelids drooped to that guarded look that Geoff had seen so often in the last couple of years.

The young woman walked around the back of the car. She wore a well-cut light grey suit, the short skirt showing off fantastic legs, the fitted jacket very conservative. Medium heeled shoes, black. Briefcase held with confidence. Under her jacket she wore a charcoal grey sweater with a cowl neck, just enough to soften the businesslike effect of the suit, frame her face and hide her chest. Good move. She obviously meant business, in a well-bred and competent way.

"Joe," said Dubuy, taking the young woman by the elbow and bringing her forward, "I'd like you to meet Emily Drury. Emily, this is Joe Tanner, president of Tanner Enterprises. And this is Geoffrey Tanner, his brother. Geoffrey, Emily Drury."

Joe had taken her hand and held it for the required moment, giving her a hard level look that would have had Geoff running for cover if he'd been this woman looking for a position. He sometimes wondered if his brother knew what effect he could have on people with his tough aggressive stance.

Geoff elbowed his brother out of the way and stepped between them, extending his hand. "Welcome, Miss Drury, come on in and let's get comfortable. I know this is your first time here, but Andre's visited before. He knows we don't stand on ceremony." He tucked her hand in the crook of his arm, pushed past a frowning Joe and led her into the house.

"This house was built by our grandfather, another Joe Tanner, when he first came to Vancouver Island and began to farm here. I guess they thought they'd have a lot of kids, because he went crazy on size, but in the end they only had two children. The main floor is made entirely from fieldstone taken right off the farm from a quarry at the other end of the land. It's quite unique. When they added the second story, they went to the post and beam style."

Geoff was rambling but he was comfortable with the topic and he felt obliged to fill in the gap and to ease this woman's situation. If he left it to Joe she'd be running for the hills after the first few minutes of interrogation.

She smiled gratefully at him and it transformed her face. She was quite a heart stopper, younger than he'd first thought. Too bad he was already engaged. No, not too bad, he loved Vanessa with all his heart. But she sure was easy to look at. Joe was going to have a hard time with this if she agreed to come on board.

"It's a lovely house, Mr. Tanner. You must be very proud to live in a home your grandfather built."

He shrugged good-naturedly. "Oh, I don't live here, Joe does. I live in town, much more civilized. Now, the offices of Tanner Enterprises are in the left wing, down that hall. Joe likes to keep things close to home." Geoff gave a warm chuckle and shot a glance over his shoulder at his older brother.

"I'm not the one you need to be talking to; I only hold a small interest in Tanner Enterprises. It's primarily Joe's baby, but he felt there might be things you could do for me as well, if we decide to go ahead with this idea of hiring in-house legal counsel. I have a couple of hardware stores in town, with Dad as a minority shareholder. We like to work together, Joe, Dad and I, keep it in the family. It saves resources."

He led her to the family room and gazed happily around.

The room was spacious and comfortable, big old sofas ranged around the perimeter with side and end tables standing in a haphazard but charming fashion within arm's reach. He seated her in the big firm overstuffed chair that was customarily Joe's domain. That should put a burr in his shorts if there wasn't one there already. He smiled to himself.

"Sit here," he said with a welcoming grin, "you should be comfortable here. I'll get you some coffee. Do you take anything in it?"

"Just black, thanks." Emily smiled at him and settled herself, briefcase at her side. As she looked around the room Andree Dubuy and Joe came down the hall. Geoff took coffee orders as they arrived.

A huge fieldstone fireplace big enough to roast an ox took up most of one wall. Double glass doors led through the back to a red brick patio where they often relaxed in summer. Planters were grouped at one end, empty this time of year, some dead dried plants still hanging over the sides and blowing stiffly in the intermittent breeze. Mum usually came out to plant them in the spring. Aspens formed a type of windbreak down one side of the field behind the house, waving leafless branches in the chill winter wind.

Andre took a seat near Emily and he saw him reach to give her hand a reassuring squeeze before he settled back to adjust his jacket. Then he turned to address the others. "You've discussed several times hiring legal counsel in house, especially given your present rate of expansion and plans for the future, Joe. And since I'll be retiring shortly and not able to take care of business for you much longer, time seems to be of the essence. Did you know I've sold the law firm?" His bushy brows waggled with the excitement of his announcement.

"Did you now, you old fox?" Joe replied. "I knew you were planning on making a move. I didn't think it would be this quick."

"Well, I'll be seventy in the spring, so it seemed to be time. That's one advantage to being self-employed, eh, boy? You can work as long as you like. Of course, the opposite isn't always true. No early retirement package, is there? Not unless the bottom line is damn good and healthy!" They all laughed.

"Yes, so," Andre continued, his voice smooth and flowing like aged brandy. It was one of the keys to his success in the courtroom, Geoff thought. What jury could resist that full-bodied voice with its reassuring, confident flow of words.

"I sold the firm, amalgamated really but I'll get paid out, nice lump sum up front along with continuing payments over a ten year period. All confidential, of course." Emily snickered and Andre grinned at her. With lawyers, Geoff thought, everything was confidential.

"My partner Sam is going to head up the new firm and Emily has the option of staying on with them. They want her very badly for her courtroom experience as they're rather lean in that department. But you and I had talked and Emily has some interest in pursuing this matter. So, here we are." He sat back and beamed like a fond father on his beloved children. Geoff wasn't fooled for a minute. He detected the familiar sharp glint in his eye even if the others didn't.

Joe took the proffered coffee from his brother's hand as his piercing hooded gaze swung to Emily. What an impact that gaze had. Did he understand how unfriendly he looked? "You have some interest in this idea. How much?" he asked.

The colour in her cheeks climbed and faded but she held her gaze steady. "Some, Mr. Tanner, as Andre said. The amount of interest I have depends on what kind of position we're talking about, what kind of working conditions, your expectations, the remuneration package.

"Andre mentioned accommodations being part of the package. I'd need to see them, decide whether it would be better for me to stay onsite or live in town and drive out. I have a household of three, so these are all things to consider. Perhaps you could begin by telling me what you had in mind and what your own expectations are."

Geoff mentally clapped his hands. He'd seen Joe make grown men squirm with that flat look and abrupt manner.

Emily hadn't blinked an eye. He snuck a look at Dubuy and saw the small smile of satisfaction as he leaned back against the cushions and sipped his coffee. Dubuy was no fool, he knew what he was doing.

Joe's face relaxed a little as it always did when he talked about the business, and he began to discuss his plans for expansion. He talked about the goals of the company, the recent growth of the import part of the import/export business, his hopes for expanding the export side.

As he continued he spoke more and more to Emily. She met him head on, questioning him where he was vague, asking for details, explanations, until it seemed they were unaware of the other two people in the room.

Finally she reached for her briefcase and extracted a folder, opening it on her knee. "It's getting late and we don't want to take up more of your time than is necessary. Here's a copy of my curriculum vitae. I'm sorry, Geoff, I only brought one copy. I hadn't realized two would be more appropriate. I hope you have an opportunity to read it."

She flashed him a brief look and he felt the warmth of that impact. She knew enough to take her allies where she could find them, she seemed to be saying.

"This is a breakdown of the type of work I've concentrated on, files I've handled since beginning practice with Dubuy, Jefferson three years ago. You'll note, Joe, that over the last year I've done ninety percent of Tanner Enterprises work, under Andre's supervision of course."

She slanted a smile at Andre that transformed her face and captured Joe's attention, but she reverted to her more sober expression as she swung back to continue addressing them. "I conducted most of the Chambers work for the firm. Sam Jefferson is a solicitor and prefers not to go to court. Any actual Supreme Court trials were conducted by Andre and me, with Andre as lead counsel."

She handed the papers over and rose. "I'd like to see the offices before we go, if you don't mind. And the accommodation. Would we be staying in the house?"

Geoff leaped to his feet when she stood. He felt like cheering. She'd essentially run the meeting once Andre sat back and relinquished the reins to her. And now she was gracefully bringing it to a close. Instead, he took her hand and held it, smiling into her face and ignoring Joe as he rose to his feet. "There's a second house on the property not far from here. I'll show you," he said.

~~~

Joe stalked back into the living room and glared down at his brother. Geoff had cracked himself a beer and sat in Joe's chair, feet propped up on a nearby stool. He frowned. "That's my chair, you hound. First you put Emily in it, then take it for yourself."

Geoff barked a laugh and his brother had to smile. He went to the kitchen to get his own beer and cuffed him on the back of the head as he went by. "Well, what do you think?"

Throwing himself down onto the nearest sofa, he propped his shoes on the armrest. "Does she know what she's doing? Will she do a good job for us? Will she *stay?* I don't want to get her all moved out here just to have her change her mind." He sounded decidedly disgruntled at the thought.

Geoff was amused. "Who is in her 'three person family', may I ask?" he countered. "Could it be a loving husband and maybe a child?"

"I asked her that already." Joe waved his beer airily. "I didn't want a commune out here. I asked if her husband is coming out. She said no, her son and his nanny."

Geoff's jaw dropped. "You're joking. So it's not *Miss* Drury, it's *Mrs.* Drury."

"Nope, I asked that too. She prefers Ms. Drury, thank you very much."

"Whew, she doesn't look like she has a kid. Too young looking. I don't know." He shrugged at Joe's acerbic expression. "I couldn't tell if she liked the house, or not."

Joe lifted his brows. "Nor could I. She plays it pretty close to the chest, doesn't let her expression give her away."

"Speaking of her chest. When she took her jacket off, I couldn't help but notice…"

Joe froze him with a look. "You're an engaged man, you ass! What do you think Vanessa would make of that comment?"

"What? I can't look? I was just admiring the scenery. I noticed your eyes were riveted somewhere in that area, big brother."

Joe dismissed him with a glance. "Well, we'll hear from her Tuesday, so we need to make up our minds before then. She seemed competent. She asked all the right questions. She even had me questioning my decisions a few times."

"Face it, Joe, old man Dubuy's a pretty sharp cookie. If she was his right hand man, so to speak, it's because she knows her stuff not because she's got a great pair of legs. Although that doesn't hurt, from my point of view."

Joe sat up irritably on the couch and glared at his brother. "God, you never quit, do you? Vanessa better get you to the altar before you change your mind."

Sighing he sank back against the cushions. "I think you're right though. She's sharp as a tack. So why is she interested in moving out of the city to this backwater town of Bonnie and working exclusively for us? Something's not right."

Geoff felt himself bristle. His big hardware stores were thriving in this *backwater town* as his brother so inelegantly put it. "Maybe she's had enough of the big city hustle. She's got a child. Her husband's dead or they've divorced and she's on her own. Maybe she hopes for a better quality of life in Bonnie for her little family. Who knows? It's a sure bet that she isn't going to make her decision lightly. And if she does decide to take the job, she won't be quitting in a hurry to move her child again. So from that point of view, she's probably a good bet."

"On the other hand," he added, "good thing you changed your mind about her office."

Joe looked startled, then their eyes met and they burst into bellows of laughter. When Joe finally caught his breath, he gave in to a final chuckle. "That's for sure. I honestly never gave it any thought, but when she said she wanted to see the offices, I started to panic."

Geoff rolled his eyes. "No kidding. I was thinking, where's Joe going to put her? The only vacant room is that little cramped space at the back."

Joe snickered and shook his head. "The deal would have been finished before it got started if I'd shown that to her. Well, Dad can just take what he wants out of that office and we'll clear the rest. He hasn't used it for years, anyway."

"No," said Geoff, "but I can hear the howls of protest already." They both chuckled again then lapsed into silence.

Geoff roused himself. "What are you going to do about Shirley?"

Joe looked blank. "Shirley? What about her?"

"She's an old battle-ax, that's what. She's been working for you for years and thinks she owns you, lock, stock and barrel. She worked for Dad and you just took the easy road and kept her on. Half the time even *I* can't get to speak to you because you're *busy, in a meeting.*"

Joe frowned. "She does the job. What more can you ask?"

"She gets in the way, and doesn't add a whole lot. Her computer skills are next to nil. And she's going to resent the hell out of any newcomer. You know how she is every time you get a new girlfriend. What are you going to do about her?"

Joe moved his shoulders in a disgruntled twitch. "Hell, I don't know." He thrust his hand through his thick dark hair and it fell forward again, hanging over his forehead. "I know she's a bit protective but sometimes that's a blessing. I don't get a whole lot of work done if I have to answer every phone call that comes in. And she doesn't seem to mind the long hours. All I really need her to do is answer the phone, type a few letters and keep the office open. Surely to God they can work together!"

"Joe, you're a wonder." There was amazement in Geoff's voice. How could his brother be so obtuse? "You know damn well Shirley will try to eat that girl for breakfast, first of all because she's young and good-looking, second because she'll have access to you and your office without having to get her permission and third because she'll have to share you. It's a recipe for disaster."

Joe rose to his feet and moved restlessly around the living room, finally stopping at the glass doors to stare moodily out at the bleak landscape. The evergreens at the end of the lower field were black conical shapes in the gloom of oncoming evening. The arbutus grove down by the ocean's edge glowed a lighter green with their shiny leaves reflecting the late sun. Their peeling red trunks were the only spot of colour down there, picked up and reflected back by the red of the old bricks in the patio.

Geoff watched his tense shoulders and wondered what it would take to pry Shirley out of the Tanner Enterprises office. Joe just didn't like to deal with change. He'd had enough of it with his marriage and then divorce, his battles with their father. He never took on a new battle now unless he had absolutely no alternative. His money was on Shirley staying.

"Well," Joe said, turning back to the room, "we don't even know if Emily's going to accept yet. One thing at a time, here. We'll have to deal with that when we get there."

Geoff snorted.

… also from Sylvie Grayson…

Contemporary suspense, romance and attempted murder!

…when a police detective falls for his main suspect, life gets complicated…

When Chloe Bowman wakes to find her husband gone, never does she imagine it will take so long to find him, or that in the midst of the search she'll discover she doesn't really know this man at all. She soon realizes she has been left alone with her young son and a time bomb on her hands. Then the earthquake throws everything into question. Lurking in the shadows is the mysterious Rainman who travels under an unknown name.

Police Detective Ross Cullen is already investigating

Chloe's husband when he disappears. Although he's powerfully drawn to Chloe, Ross also knows that when one member of a family disappears, the first place to look for the suspect is among those closest to him. No one is closer than Chloe.

But the deeper Ross digs the less he knows, and the more he's attracted to the young wife as she struggles to put her life back together. Can Ross break through the Rainman's disguises to solve the case so he can be with Chloe?

SYLVIE GRAYSON

Sometimes you
get a second chance...

MY BEST
MISTAKE

Jordie let her get away the first time, that was his mistake.
He's determined it won't happen again.

Jenny fell for her cousin once before and got burned. Can
she recover, or is this just another big mistake?

Jordie was heartbroken as a young man when he
returned to town to find Jenny had married another man.
Now she lives beside him, and he'll either go crazy or do
what he should have done in the first place - claim her for
his own.

Jenny is back and she's angry. Her husband cheated
and she can't let it go, her kids won't answer her phone calls
and her boss's wife hates her.

But whiles she's off travelling something happens to
her boss that threatens them all, and then someone comes
after her.

Who can she turn to? With her cousin living right beside her it's becoming harder to ignore the chemistry they have always shared. Can Jordie help put her life back together?

Sci-fi/ fantasy from Sylvie Grayson

The Last War series is a stunning portrayal of a new world created from fire and consumed at the edges ...- sci fi and fantasy at its best...

The Emperor has been defeated. New countries have arisen from the ashes of the old Empire. The citizens swear they will never need to fight again after that long and painful war.

Bethlehem Farmer is helping her brother Abram run Farmer Holdings in south Khandarken after their father died in the final battles. She is looking after the dispossessed, keeping the farm productive and the talc mine working in the hills behind their land.

But when Abram takes a trip with Uncle Jade into the northern territory and disappears without a trace, she's left on her own. Suddenly things are not what they seem and no one can be trusted.

Major Dante Regiment is sent by his father, the General of Khandarken, to find out what the situation is at Farmer Holdings. What he sees shakes him to the core and fuels his grim determination to protect Bethlehem at all cost, even with his life.

Ms Grayson has created a fascinating new world with a lot of the same old problems. Sci fi and fantasy rolled into one with a sure hand and enormous imagination

Abe Farmer may survive the Sanctuary, but he won't escape the Emperor

THE LAST WAR
BOOK TWO

SYLVIE GRAYSON

From the mud and danger of the open road to the welcoming arms of the Sanctuary, from attacks by the dispossessed army to the storms of the open sea, Son of the Emperor takes us on a wild ride into danger and on to the dream of freedom.

The Emperor is defeated yet already unrest is growing in the north of Khandarken. After Julianne Adjudicator's father disappears, she seeks to escape the clutches of her vicious stepmother Zanata, and flees to the Sanctuary. This is the safest place for a woman in a hostile world of unrest and roving dispossessed. But when Julianne seeks asylum, it soon becomes clear all is not as it first appeared.

Then Abe Farmer arrives at the Sanctuary seeking medical

help. Abe isn't interested in taking a young woman with them, as he and his injured bodyguard struggle to return to the Southern Territory. Yet when he discovers her fate if she stays, he finds he has no choice.

But the journey becomes more dangerous as they encounter the army of the New Emperor and are caught in the middle of a firefight as they flee toward the Catastrophic Ocean. Can Abe keep her safe till they reach home?

...a whole new world with the same old problems - fantasy at its best...

When Emperor Carlton makes an offer to Cownden Lanser, can he refuse? Lanser has his own ambitions and Carlton may be offering everything he's dreamed of.

The Young Emperor has been backed into a corner. He holds a bit of land in Legitamia where he marshals his troops, but the skirmishes they've launched to expand his empire have had limited success. Now, his ambitions are aimed at overthrowing everything Khandarken has cobbled together since the Last War.

Cownden Lanser, Chief Constable of Khandarken, is a private man with a close connection to the Old Empire that he doesn't divulge to anyone. Although he's dedicated to his position, things are not what they seem in the rank and file of the police.

Selanna Nettles is a sookie, trained in Legitamia but working near her family in the Western Territory of Khandarken, healing the injured mine workers and the dispossessed. But her life takes a startling turn when Chief Cownden Lanser hires her to attend a set of high-level meetings in Gilsigg.

When these three meet up in Legitamia, the result is explosive. Not just for them but for the future of Khandarken. The Emperor makes Cownden an offer that might be everything he's secretly dreamed of. How can he refuse?

The Last War series is a stunning portrayal of a new world created from fire and consumed at the edges... sci fi/fantasy at its best...

ABOUT THE AUTHOR

Sylvie Grayson has published romantic suspense novels, *Suspended Animation*, *Legal Obstruction*, and *The Lies He Told Me*, all about strong women who meet with dangerous odds, stories of tension and attraction.

She has also written *The Last War* series, a romantic sci/fi - fantasy set in a new world she has created. She has been an English language instructor, a nightclub manager, an auto shop bookkeeper and a lawyer. She is a wife and mother, and lives in southern British Columbia with her husband on a small piece of land near the Pacific Ocean that they call home, when she's not travelling the world looking for adventure.